Before Rebecca, his life had been less conflicted. Utterly lonely, but peaceful nevertheless.

Through her he had glimpsed a sliver of potential happiness, and had rushed toward it like a blind old fool. And what had he gotten for his imprudent act? A deep chasm with his beloved daughter and a wife who thought to boss him as if he were a misguided child.

Aynsley tried to tell himself this marriage was not bad. Rebecca did have a way with lads. Against his will, he pictured her in the coach that morning after church, holding his youngest son on her lap. No one could have seen her and not believed she was Chuckie's natural mother.

It was still hard to credit that he'd married Rebecca. What had possessed him?

Long after he entered the house, long after he climbed the stairs and long after he lay in his bed unable to sleep, he asked himself the same question. Why had he married the bossy Miss Peabody?

CHERYL BOLEN

is the acclaimed author of more than a dozen Regency-set historical romance novels. Her books have placed in several writing contests, including the Daphne du Maurier, and have been translated into eleven languages. She was named Notable New Author in 1999, and in 2006 she won the Holt Medallion (Honoring Outstanding Literary Talent) for Best Short Historical Novel. Her books have become Barnes & Noble and Amazon bestsellers.

A former journalist who admits to a fascination with dead Englishwomen, Cheryl is a regular contributor to *The Regency Plume, The Regency Reader* and *The Quizzing Glass.* Many of her articles can be found on her website, www.CherylBolen.com, and more recent ones on her blog, www.CherylsRegencyRamblings.wordpress.com. Readers are welcomed at both places.

Cheryl holds a dual degree in English and journalism from the University of Texas, and she earned a master's degree from the University of Houston. She and her professor husband are the parents of two sons, one an attorney and the other a journalist. Her favorite things to do are watching the Longhorns, reading letters and diaries of Georgian Englishmen and traveling to England.

CHERYL BOLEN

Marriage of Inconvenience

Love Inspired™

Recycling programs for this product may not exist in your area.

ISBN-13: 978-0-373-82938-5

MARRIAGE OF INCONVENIENCE

This edition published by arrangement with Love Inspired Books.

www.LoveInspiredBooks.com

Printed in U.S.A.

And the Lord God said,
"It is not good for the man to be alone;
I will make him a helper suitable for him."
—*Genesis* 2:18

To my sisters, Suzi Meeker and Colleen Sutherland,
who have enriched my life immeasurably.

Chapter One

London, England
1813

The hackney coach slowed in front of Lord Aynsley's townhouse. With her heart pounding prodigiously, Miss Rebecca Peabody pushed her spectacles up the bridge of her nose and drew a deep breath as the driver assisted her from the carriage. She paid him, glanced up at the impressive four-story townhouse, then climbed its steps and rapped at the door's shiny brass plate. Almost as an afterthought, she pulled off her spectacles and jammed them into her reticule. Though she abhorred going without them due to her inability to see, she had decided just this once it was necessary. One who wished to persuade a virtual stranger to marry her must, after all, make every effort to look one's best.

She felt rather like a convict standing before King's Bench as she waited for someone to respond to her knock. Soon, a gaunt butler with a raised brow opened the door and gave her a haughty stare.

"Is Lord Aynsley in?" she asked in a shaky voice.

She had particularly selected this time of day because she knew it was too early for Parliament.

The servant's glance raked over her. Though her dress was considerably more respectable than a doxy's, he must still believe her a loose woman because no proper lady would come to his lordship's unescorted. But, of course, she could hardly have brought Pru with her today. One simply did not bring one's maid when one wished to propose marriage.

"I regret to say he's out," the butler said. There was not a shred of remorse on the man's face or in his voice.

She had not reckoned on Lord Aynsley being away from home. Now everything was spoiled. Such an opportunity might never again be possible once it was discovered she'd sneaked out the back of her dressmaker's, stranding her poor maid there. All likelihood of ever again disengaging herself from either her sister, Maggie, or Pru would be nonexistent. And to make matters even more regrettable, the hackney driver had left! She fought against tears of utter frustration. Perhaps the butler was merely protecting his master from tarts. She drilled him with her most haughty stare (though he was nothing more than a blur, due to her deficient vision) and said, "You must inform his lordship that I come from the foreign secretary, Lord Warwick." Which was true, but misleading, given that her sister was married to Lord Warwick, and Rebecca made her home with them.

"I would convey that to Lord Aynsley were he here, but he is not. Would you care to sign his book?"

Owing to the fact she had not anticipated his lordship's absence, she hadn't given a thought as to how she should proceed were he not at home. Should she sign his book with a cryptic message? Should she merely leave her card? Should she ask him to call on her? No, not that. Maggie would never allow her to be alone with the earl, and in order to propose marriage, Rebecca must have privacy.

She decided to sign his book.

The unsympathetic butler allowed her to step into the checkerboard entry hall and over to a Sheraton sideboard beneath a huge Renaissance painting. Lord Aynsley's book—its pages open—reposed on the sideboard.

Though it was undignified to remove a glove, she did so before picking up the quill. This was her last pair of gloves that was free from ink stains, and Maggie had persistently chastised her about her endless destruction of fine, handmade gloves.

As soon as she divested herself of her right glove, she heard the front door swing open and a second later heard his voice.

"Lady Warwick!" Lord Aynsley said, addressing Rebecca's back. "How may I be of service to you?"

Oh, dear. Because he saw her from the back, he *would* think she was her beautiful sister, whom he had once wished to marry. Drawing in a deep breath, Rebecca whirled around to face him, a wide smile on her face.

His face fell. "Miss Peabody?"

"Yes, my lord. I beg a private word with you." How she longed to jam on those spectacles and give the peer a good look over. It had been so long since she last saw him, she couldn't quite remember what he looked like. Truth be told, she had never paid much attention to him. At the present moment she wished to assure herself that his appearance was not offensive. But the only thing she could assure herself of was his blurriness—and that he was considerably taller than she and still rather lean.

A hot flush rose into her cheeks as she perceived that he gawked at her single naked arm, then he recovered and said, "You've come alone?"

She duplicated her haughty stare once again. "I have." She gulped. "A rather important matter has brought me here today."

"Then come to my library where we can discuss it."

She followed him along the broad hallway past a half dozen doorways until they came to a cozy room lit by a blazing fire and wrapped with tall walnut cases lined with fine leather books. A much finer library than Lord Warwick's, she decided. Another recommendation for plighting her life with Lord Aynsley.

"Oblige me by closing the door," she challenged as he strode toward his Jacobean desk.

He stopped, turned to gaze at her and hitched his brow in query. "I'm cognizant of your unblemished reputation, Miss Peabody, and I don't wish to tarnish it."

"My unblemished reputation is exactly why I'm here today, my lord."

"I'm sorry. I don't follow you."

"Please close the door and I shall explain."

His gaze bounced from her to the door. He did not move.

Was he afraid she would damage his sterling reputation by intimating that he behaved in an ungentlemanly manner? "I assure you, Lord Aynsley, I have no aspirations to make false accusations against you."

"You have roused my curiosity, Miss Peabody." He crossed the room and closed the door. "Please sit on the sofa nearest the fire."

She did as instructed, then wadded the missing glove into a ball concealed in her fist and hoped he would not notice her breach in decorum.

He came to face her on a silken plum-colored sofa that matched the one she sat on. "It's quite remarkable how much you look like your sister."

"That, my lord, is another reason why I'm here today."

"I'm afraid I don't comprehend, Miss Peabody."

"Allow me to explain. You were once so attracted to my sister, you asked her to marry you."

He nodded. "Your sister is a most beautiful woman."

She drew a long breath, counting to five, then plunged in. "Then you must be satisfied with my appearance, my lord, for we look vastly similar—except for my deficient vision which necessitates my spectacles." If only she could believe that. She was no beauty like Maggie.

Because his lordship was nothing more than a blur, she was unable to observe his reaction to the illogical trajectory of her conversation. The man was apt to think the most deficient thing about her was not her vision, but her mental capacity.

After a mortifying lull, Lord Aynsley recovered and answered as would any well-mannered gentleman. "You're a most lovely girl."

She glared at him. "I am not a *girl.* I'm a woman of eight and twenty. I came out of the schoolroom more than a decade ago, and in most quarters I'm considered past marrying age. That is why I've selected you."

He did not say anything for a moment. "Pray, Miss Peabody, I'm still not following you. For what purpose have you *selected* me?"

"Before I get to that," she said, opening her reticule, stuffing in the glove and pulling out a folded piece of parchment, "I should like to mention the points on my list here."

While she unfolded the list she could see that he crossed his arms and settled back to listen.

Her glance fell to the list, but she was unable to read the now-fuzzy letters. She would have to recite from memory. "Not only do I greatly resemble my countess sister, but I'm a reputed scholar. I read and write Latin and Greek and am fluent in French, German and Italian. I'm exceedingly well organized and capable of overseeing a large household." She paused to sit on her naked hand, hoping the earl had not noticed it. Lord Aynsley was a most proper peer, and she was most decidedly improper to be sitting here not only without a chaperone but also with a naked arm.

"The most important thing on my list," she continued, "is that I absolutely adore children. I dislike the city and would love to live in the country—surrounded by said children. I have decided to marry a man a bit older, a man whose children need a capable mother. I shouldn't mind at all if it wasn't a *real* marriage. I suppose an older man would not still fancy the *romantic* aspects of marriage."

No man who'd ever loved Maggie could be attracted to Rebecca. She understood that. She would never be able to experience a marital bond like Maggie shared with Warwick. Men just didn't feel that way toward her.

"Dear heavens! How old do you think I am?"

She gazed up at him, but of course could not really see him without her much-needed spectacles. "Five and forty?"

"I am three and forty, Miss Peabody, and have no desire for a wife." He stood abruptly.

"I beg that you sit down and hear me out. I'm not finished." It was really the oddest thing how this idea of marrying Lord Aynsley had taken ahold of her. Her desire to wed the earl had nothing to do with his desirability and everything to do with her need to leave Lord Warwick's house before she destroyed his heretofore loving marriage to her sister.

Another strong impetus to marry was the prospect of liberating herself from the strictures of society that rather imprisoned an unmarried lady.

And she was devilishly tired of people pitying her as the old maid aunt to Maggie's darling boys.

Though Miss Rebecca Peabody was void of passionate feelings toward any man, she was possessed of a great deal of passion, all of it channeled into the radical political essays she wrote under the pen name P. Corpus. Ever since the day she'd read Thomas Paine's *Rights of Man* she had felt that expansion of civil liberties was her life's calling. She'd even come to understand—against her initial resistance—that she was meant to leave America and come to England. It was only right that an American like she should show these snooty British just how antiquated—and oppressive—their government was.

It was her forward thinking that continually pitted her against Lord Warwick and the Tory government he served. Last night's argument over his government's resistance to labor unions had been the final straw.

She could not coexist with a man who upheld the wretched Tories' elitist principles—or, in her opinion, lack of principles. How could a man like Lord Warwick—who was so good to his wife, his children and his servants, who read his Bible every day and went to church every Sunday—not follow his Savior's command to treat *the least of his brethren* as he would treat Jesus?

The government should serve all its people—not just the wealthy landowners. How could the Tories think it right to repress men who needed to earn enough to feed their families? It wasn't as if the wealthy, landed Tories would be destitute if they allowed modest increases in their workers' wages.

She was certain the Heavenly Father had guided her to P. Corpus; therefore, He must be guiding her to this proposed marriage. It had become increasingly difficult to post her essays to her publisher without being discovered. A married woman would not have to be constantly watched by her well-meaning sister or her ever-present maid, neither of whom could be allowed to learn of her P. Corpus identity.

As a married lady, she could pursue her writings—and even be at liberty to write that full-length book on a perfect society, the book that was her life's goal.

A pity she could not own the authorship of her essays, but doing so would jeopardize Lord Warwick's career. Were it to be discovered that a woman living under his roof—a woman who had been an American colonist, no less!—so opposed the Tory government he represented, his distinguished career could be destroyed.

Lord Aynsley eased back into his chair without breaking eye contact with her.

"I know eight and twenty may seem young to you, my lord, but I assure you I'm very mature. Your seven children need a mother, and such a charge would be very agreeable to me. I also possess the capabilities to smoothly run a large household. You could attend to your important work in Parliament, secure in the knowledge that your competent wife was promoting domestic harmony in your house."

He began to laugh a raucous, hardy laugh.

Even if the spectacles would obscure her resemblance to her beautiful sister, she must put them back on. It was imperative that she be able to see the expression on his lordship's face. She opened her reticule and whipped out the two spheres of glass fastened together by a gold wire and slammed them on the bridge of her nose.

That was better! She could see quite clearly that Lord Aynsley was indeed laughing at her. It was also evident that he wasn't so very old after all. Granted, a bit of gray threaded through his bark-colored hair, but the man was possessed of a rather youthful countenance. The man also had a propensity to always smile. "How dare you laugh at me, my lord!"

He sombered. "Forgive me. I mean no offense." He cocked his head and regarded her. "Do I understand you correctly, Miss Peabody? You believe I might wish to make you my wife?"

Her dark eyes wide, she nodded.

"Pray, what makes you think I even desire a wife?"

She squared her shoulders and glared. "You asked my sister to wed you."

"That was two years ago when I was freshly widowed and rather at my wit's end as to how to run a household of seven children, a ward and an eccentric uncle."

"You're no longer at your wit's end? Your children no longer run off governesses?"

He sighed. "I didn't say that. It is still difficult to

manage my household, but the task is less onerous now that my next-to-eldest—my only daughter—is a bit older."

"How old is she?"

"Almost eighteen."

Rebecca could see she would have to convince him that his *womanly* daughter was due to take flight at any moment. "Is that not the age when most young ladies choose to take husbands? Do you aim to keep her always with you?"

He did not respond for a moment. For once, the smile vanished from his face. "As a matter of fact, it's my hope that my daughter will come out this year."

"And if she chooses to marry? Who, then, will manage your household?"

"I shall cross that bridge when I come to it." He peered at her with flashing moss-colored eyes. "One thing is certain, Miss Peabody. If I do remarry, I shall choose the wife myself."

"But, my lord, you chose my sister, and that did not work out."

"I have explained why I felt obliged to offer for your sister." He stared at her, no mirth on his face.

"Does it bother you that I'm not yet thirty, and you are over forty?"

His smile returned. "My dear Miss Peabody, my father married my mother when he was six and thirty and she was eighteen, and theirs was a deliriously happy marriage."

"As was my parents'. Papa married Mama—his second wife—when he was forty, and she was but twenty. And Mama was an excellent mother to my half brother."

"As I'm sure you will be a fine stepmother to some man's children, but I am *not* that man."

How could she have thought a man with all of Lord Aynsley's attributes could ever be attracted to an awkward spinster like she? Now that she had thoroughly humiliated herself, she must leave. "I'm sorry I've wasted your time, my lord."

As she strode to the door, he intercepted her, placing his hand on her bare arm.

"Forgive me, Miss Peabody," he said in a gentle voice. "I'm greatly flattered by your generous offer, but I must decline."

"You're making a grave mistake, my lord." Then she yanked open the door and left, determined to walk all the way back to Curzon Street. Unchaperoned.

But how would she explain her brash behavior to Maggie? Sneaking out the back door of Mrs. Chassay's establishment was bad enough, but it would be far worse if Maggie learned of her brazen, unchaperoned visit to Lord Aynsley's.

Though he had planned to finish reading the articulate plea for penal reform penned by P. Corpus in the *Edinburgh Review,* John Compton, the fifth Earl Aynsley, could not rid his thoughts of the peculiar Miss Rebecca Peabody. Until today he had scarcely noticed the chit. In fact, he doubted he'd even laid eyes on her since the disastrous lapse in judgment that had caused him to offer for her sister some two years previously.

He raked his mind for memories of the bespectacled girl, but the only thing he could remember about her was that she perpetually had her nose in a book.

No doubt such incessant reading had ruined the poor girl's vision.

Normally he did not find females who wore spectacles attractive, but Miss Peabody was actually...well, she was actually...cute. There was something rather endearing about the sight of her spectacles slipping down her perfect little nose.

Of course he was *not* in the least attracted to her.

And he did not for a moment believe she was attracted to him.

After pondering her offer for a considerable period of time, he thought he understood why she wished to marry him. The chit seemed intent on removing herself from the marriage mart. She was not the kind of girl who held vast appeal to the young fellows there. By the same token, the young bucks there were not likely to appeal to a bookworm such as she. He believed she just might be more suited for a man who'd lived a few more years, a man who was a comforting presence like an old pair of boots. It took no great imagination to picture the bespectacled young woman with the flashing eyes merrymaking with children. But, of course, not *his* children.

It was while he was sitting at his desk thinking of the dark-haired Miss Peabody—and admittedly confusing her with her stunning sister—that Hensley rapped at his library door. "I've brought you the post, my lord."

Aynsley was thankful for a diversion. The diversion, however, proved to be a single letter. From his daughter. A smile sprang to his lips as he contemplated his golden-haired Emily and broke the seal to read.

But as he read, the smile disappeared.

My Dearest Papa,

It grieves me to inform you that we've once again lost a governess. This time it was worms in her garment drawer that prompted Miss Russell's departure. And if this news isn't grievous enough for you, my dear father, I must inform you that the housekeeper has also tendered her resignation—owing to Uncle Ethelbert's peculiar habit.

I shan't wish for you to hurry back to Dunton Hall when you've so many more important matters that require your attention in our kingdom's government. Please know that I shall endeavor to keep things running as smoothly as possible here until such time as you are able to secure new staff.

I remain affectionately yours,

Emily

He wadded up the paper and hurled it into the fire.

Now he was faced with the distasteful task of trolling for and interviewing a packet of females to replace the latest in a long line of governesses and housekeepers. If only he *did* have a wife to share some of his burden.

But he wanted much more than a well-organized scholar for a wife. He thought of his parents' marriage, remembering when his mother would read over the text of his father's speeches to Parliament, offering suggestions. They read Rousseau and Voltaire together, and shared everything from their political philosophy to their deep affection for their children. It was almost as if their two hearts beat within the same breast.

He had never had any of that deep bond with Dorothy—except for their love of the children—and he'd always lamented the void in their marriage. As he lamented other things void in their marriage.

He wanted more than a mother for his children and a competent woman to run his household. He craved a life partner. He'd been lonely for as long as he could remember—not that he would ever admit it. With none of his closest friends was he at liberty to discuss his forward-thinking views. If he ever did remarry, it must be to a woman whose interests mirrored his own, a woman who cared deeply for him and his children, a woman whom he could love and cherish.

Such a woman probably did not exist. He took up his pen to dash off a note to his solicitor. Mannington would have to start the process of gathering applicants for the now-open positions on his household staff. But as Aynsley tried to write, he kept picturing Miss Peabody, kept imagining her with little Chuckie on her lap, kept remembering that sparkle that flared in her dark eyes when she challenged him. Most resonating of all, he kept hearing her words: *you are making a grave mistake.*

Unexplainably, those words seemed prophetic, like a critical fork in the roadway of his life. As he wrote his few sentences to Mannington, he kept hearing those parting words of hers.

Could it be that he ought to take heed? What harm could there be in trying to learn more about the unconventional Miss Peabody?

Chapter Two

For the past two weeks—since his bizarre visit from Miss Peabody—Aynsley had come to the conclusion he did, indeed, need a wife, a woman possessed of Miss Peabody's pedigree and scholarship, along with a capacity for affection, which Miss Peabody undoubtedly lacked. Miss Peabody herself was completely out of the question. A more mature woman would be far more satisfactory.

He entered his house, anxious to read the newest copy of the *Edinburgh Review,* which had come out that day. On the sideboard in his entry hall—the same sideboard where he'd mistaken Miss Peabody for her lovely sister—he was pleased to find his copy.

Going straight to his library, he settled before the fire and began to scan the pages in the hopes of finding another excellent essay by P. Corpus. A soft smile lifted the corners of his mouth as he saw Mr. Corpus's byline.

This time the learned gentleman wrote a well-thought-out piece favoring the formation of labor unions. *"Were the workers better compensated for their labor, this would result in a more equitable soci-*

ety, a society in which crime and other depravities of desperate people would be eradicated." An excellent conclusion to the thought-provoking piece, he thought, his eyes running over the essay and coming to stop at the author's name: P. Corpus. He wondered if there was some clue in that pseudonym as to the writer's true identity. *Corpus* was Latin for body. P. Body. Peabody!

How coincidental that Miss Peabody should be on his mind! He found himself wondering if the lady had a brother here in England, but the only brother he knew of still resided in Virginia. Miss Peabody had lived there her whole life before sailing to England a few years ago with her sister, who came to claim the property of her late husband, an Englishman.

Being raised in the colonies would make one rather more democratic than those raised in England. He wondered if Miss Peabody even concerned herself with English politics. With her nose perpetually buried in a book, she certainly was not like any young woman he'd ever known. It was entirely possible that a woman as intellectually curious as Miss Peabody could conceivably be interested in matters of government.

Of course she could *not* possibly have written those political pieces.

Could she?

Women—even unconventional ones—had little interest in government. He went to the shelf where the yellowed back editions of the *Edinburgh Review* were stored, grabbed a stack and strode to his desk where he proceeded to read them. Not all of them. Only the essays written by P. Corpus. There was one on compulsory education, another opposing slavery and one lambasting rotten boroughs.

Surely she could not have written the essay opposing slavery. He knew for a fact her father's Virginia plantation had used slaves. Would she dare to criticize her departed parent?

He spent the rest of the afternoon rereading P. Corpus's essays, which dated back some two years. If his memory served him correctly, Miss Peabody and her beautiful sister had arrived in England two or three years previously. Could it be mere coincidence that P. Corpus's essays did not commence until Miss Peabody arrived in England?

For the next several days he could not dispel thoughts of Miss Peabody from his mind. After much thought—and hours studying P. Corpus's essays—he convinced himself that Miss Peabody and P. Corpus were the same person.

Through her writings, Miss Peabody's true character, her considerable intellect and her unexpected maturity were revealed to him. The more he reread the essays, the more connected he felt to her. It was the deucest thing, but he had never before felt so close to a woman, not even to Dorothy. Of course, he wasn't really close to Miss Peabody, but the discovery that there existed a person whose thoughts so closely paralleled his own had taken hold of him like tentacles that could not be dislodged.

Whatever he did, wherever he went, he thought about Miss Peabody. For months now he'd been fired by a thirst to meet Mr. Corpus and engage the man in a conversation where two like minds could have free rein. Now that he knew P. Corpus's identity, Aynsley's desire to converse with Miss Peabody consumed him even more greedily.

So many social reformers were one-trick ponies. One

would criticize slavery, while another objected to the lack of parliamentary representation for the large industrialized cities. Only P. Corpus understood that to achieve a perfect society there must be a successive eradication of each and every social ill.

His country, with its workhouses and factories and bulging prisons, was much like a sofa with torn coverings, sagging cushions and protruding springs. One did not fix the sofa by throwing a length of silk upon it. It could only be repaired by attacking and correcting each underlying problem. Miss Peabody—or P. Corpus—understood that.

The more he thought of her, the more he wanted to speak with her. He found himself wondering what it would be like to have a conversation with a woman possessed of Miss Peabody's uncommon intelligence.

He needed to talk with Warwick. He wasn't sure why he sought to speak to Warwick. He certainly had no intention of asking for Miss Peabody's hand. Even if she was the brilliant, articulate, passionate P. Corpus. While Aynsley did not want her for a wife, he did want her for a friend. That is, *if* she were the brilliant essayist.

He decided to go to Warwick House early in the day, before Warwick went to Whitehall to perform his important duties. By coming early, he would avoid coming face-to-face with Miss Peabody. Women were sure to be still abed in the morning and certainly not be primped to be presentable. He'd rather not see her just yet, not after he had treated the poor woman so shabbily.

At Warwick House, the butler showed him into the light-flooded, emerald-green morning room, then took himself off to announce the caller to Lord Warwick. As soon as the servant turned to leave the morning room, Aynsley saw her.

She had been sitting at a game table perusing the *Morning Chronicle,* a mobcap smashed upon her uncombed tresses, her spectacles propped on her perfect nose. At the sound of disturbance, she looked up. And saw him.

Her face transformed. Had a snake charmer summoned a viper into the chamber, her expression could not have held more alarm.

That he evoked such an emotion distressed him profoundly. It was all he could do not to race to her and draw her into his arms and murmur assurances. Instead, he smiled. What could he possibly say to put her at ease? Obviously she was embarrassed in his presence. His glance darted to the newspaper. The liberal Whigs' vehicle. "I see you're reading about Manchester's lack of representation in the House of Commons. A most enlightening article."

Any embarrassment Miss Peabody may have experienced was completely wiped out by his simple comment. Her eyes rounded, her brows lowered. "You read it?"

Good heavens, did she think him incapable of reading the written word? He nodded. "Just before I came here, actually. It's a distressing occurrence, to be sure."

A fiery spark leaped to her dark eyes. "Distressing! It's an unconscionable injustice."

I am right about her alter ego. "Our government is vastly different than yours, Miss Peabody."

"Mine?" Anger scorched her voice. "I will have you know England is now my home, my country. As long as I can draw breath, I shall endeavor to see this country rectify its ills. Of course, I wouldn't expect an aristocrat such as you could possibly understand that."

"You do me a great disservice."

Just then the butler reentered the room. "Lord Warwick wishes to know if your lordship would object to waiting while he finishes dressing." The butler's gaze alighted on the lady in the mobcap. "Forgive me, Miss Peabody. I did not know you were here, or I would never have brought Lord Aynsley to this chamber."

"You have no need to apologize," she said. "Unlike my lovely sister, I do not care if I'm seen before Pru dresses my hair. And, as you can see, my dress is perfectly respectable."

"Since I have the lovely Miss Peabody with whom to converse," Aynsley said, "I shall be delighted to wait for Lord Warwick."

The lovely Miss Peabody, indeed! Rebecca knew very well how decidedly dowdy she looked this morning. Maggie would be livid if she knew her sister was greeting an eligible caller dressed in such a fashion. "I daresay, my lord, you must need to borrow my spectacles."

He gave her a quizzing look. "Pray, why do you say that?"

"You know very well I do *not* look lovely this morning!"

"I assure you I know no such thing. Just because your hair has not been dressed does not mean you don't look pretty."

No man—not even her dear Papa—had ever said she was pretty. Maggie was the beauty of the family. Her face suddenly felt as if she were leaning into an intense fire. She spun around to glance at the window. Was the sunshine uncommonly bright this morning? But, alas, it was actually a dreary, gray day. Why, in heaven's name, was her face burning? Then it dawned on her. She was blushing! Miss Rebecca Peabody had *never* blushed in her entire eight and twenty years! "Then, my lord, you've been too long away from Society."

He had the audacity to come and sit beside her. "At the mature age of eight and twenty, you should have learned by now how a lady responds to compliments."

She started to tell him she had never received compliments on her appearance, but oddly, she preferred that he not know that. Instead, she decided to be gracious. Even though she knew he was lying. "Then I thank you, my lord."

His glance fell again to the *Morning Chronicle.* "I'm surprised Lord Warwick reads that newspaper."

"Oh, he doesn't. I'm the one who subscribes. It's how I choose to spend my pin money. That and books." Oh, dear. Why had she gone babbling about herself?

"Yes, I seem to recall that you were always reading."

For some unaccountable reason, all she could think of was how matronly she must look in the cap. Why couldn't she be more like Maggie, who never left her bedchamber without her hair being dressed, without looking perfect?

Her gaze ran over the perfection of his dress, his neatly styled, toasty-colored hair, his fine face with clear green eyes, and she felt utterly inadequate. How could she have been so foolish as to think he would give the slightest consideration to marrying her?

It now seemed to her that a man like him would be able to marry any woman he wished. Attractive women.

Women from fine old English families. Women who cared about fashion—and titles—which Rebecca certainly did not.

She could not even think of a single clever thing to say to him. "Are your children in London?"

"No. They're at Dunton Hall."

"In Shropshire?"

"Yes."

The butler reentered the room and spoke to Aynsley. "Lord Warwick will see you now."

Lord Aynsley stood and peered down at her. "May I say with deep sincerity that seeing you this morning has been a pleasure?"

Her quizzing look followed him from the chamber. What an astonishing change in his behavior toward her! At their last meeting, he'd been glacial; today he had been full of warmth. Could it be that after considering her proposal, he was not repelled by her? Sweet heavens! Could he actually be considering her bold suggestion?

In Warwick's library, Aynsley was met by the smiling foreign secretary, who stood and greeted him with affection. "Lord Aynsley, how good it is to see you again. I'm most indebted to you for your support in the House of Lords."

"As it happens, I'm not here today on matters of government."

Warwick's brows lowered a smidgeon and his gaze flicked to the chair before his desk. "Won't you have a seat?"

Though Warwick was a decade his junior, the two men had once been on friendly terms. Until Aynsley became interested in the lovely woman who would become Warwick's countess. Once Aynsley expressed a romantic interest in the current Lady Warwick, Warwick began to needle him—and his sons—unmercifully.

Since Warwick had disparaged Aynsley's sons—who, admittedly, were a bit of a handful—Aynsley had been out of charity with the man. He did not like anyone to speak ill of his children. Of course his two eldest boys—the Viscount Fordyce at Oxford and the soldier in the Peninsula—were well able to defend themselves. It was the lads ranging in ages from three to twelve who elicited their father's protective instincts.

But Warwick's former antagonism was water under the bridge now that Aynsley had long since forgotten his infatuation with Warwick's countess.

Aynsley sank into a chair in front of Warwick's huge desk.

Neither man spoke for a moment. Aynsley wondered if Warwick knew of his wife's sister's radical opinions, ideas Aynsley would give a fortune to be able to freely discuss with her.

He decided to get straight to the point of the morning's visit. "Are you aware that your wife's sister asked me to marry her?"

The foreign secretary's brows formed a deep V. "You cannot be serious!"

"I'll own that it does seem unlikely, but it's the truth."

"Then that's the deucest thing I've ever heard."

"I agree."

"I didn't know you two had even been seeing one another."

"We haven't."

"Yet...*she* asked *you* to marry her? I've never heard of a lady doing the asking."

"Miss Peabody, you must admit, is not like other ladies."

"Daresay you're right."

"Though she does have many other fine attributes," Aynsley added.

"Yes, she does," Warwick agreed.

"I understand she reads and writes Latin and Greek."

"And she's fluent in French, German and Italian."

"Her body of knowledge is quite impressive, I'd say." Aynsley had debated whether he should mention Miss Peabody's essays, but decided against it. As a representative of the Tory government, Warwick would be bound to hold opposing views, and, in her wisdom, Miss Peabody would not wish to bite the hand that fed her. At least not directly.

"She's terribly clever about managing things. Did you know she cataloged the entire Agar library at Windmere Abbey?" Warwick asked.

"But that's the largest private library in Great Britain!"

"Indeed it is. Her organizational skills are just what are needed to run an estate like Dunton Hall." Warwick's brows lowered. "Are you still having difficulty keeping governesses and housekeepers?"

Aynsley nodded solemnly. He had spent the past two weeks interviewing prospective employees with no success. Domestic matters demanded entirely too much of his time.

"I think you should marry Rebecca—not that I wish to be rid of her. My wife would be lost without her efficient sister—whom she dearly loves."

"I must explain that I'm really *not* looking for a wife."

Warwick gave him a suspicious look. "Then why are you here?"

"I wish to ask you a question."

"Yes?"

"I know your wife's father was a slave owner. Are you acquainted with Miss Peabody's opinions on slavery?"

A puzzled look on his face, Warwick said, "I am. Miss Peabody opposes slavery."

Just as he thought. This was as good as confirmation that Miss Peabody was indeed P. Corpus. He could barely tamp down his excitement.

Warwick stood. "Why do you not come to our house tomorrow night? We're giving a ball. If you come, I'll ensure that you be afforded a private tête-à-tête with Miss Peabody in my library."

Aynsley sighed. "Perhaps a tête-à-tête might be agreeable, but I'm not about to offer for her." He stood.

"That, my lord, I am not so sure about."

"I shall see you tomorrow." Good heavens, could Warwick be right? Was he taking leave of his senses?

Chapter Three

Though Maggie had repeatedly instructed her on how to gracefully descend the stairs, Rebecca knew that no amount of coaching could render her as elegant as her sister now gliding down the stairs two steps ahead of her. For one reason, Rebecca kept forgetting she was to pretend a book was balancing on her head. It would have been an altogether different thing were she permitted to descend the stairs actually *reading* a book. That was an art she had positively mastered. Until Maggie forbade it, that is.

As she followed Maggie and Warwick down the stairs, she made her prosaic announcement. "This will be my last ball."

Maggie sputtered to a stop, turned and leveled her sternest glare at her sister. "Pray, why do you say that?"

"Since we've been in England I've given far too much of my life to the Great Husband Hunt—save for the six months I spent cataloging the library at Windmere Abbey—and I've decided I'm of the age to know my own mind." She stopped for a moment. "That mind assures me that of all the things on earth, I detest balls most."

"Since you've decided you actually *do* wish to marry, you must attend balls in order to find a mate."

Rebecca shrugged. Why had she confessed to Maggie about her ill-fated visit to Lord Aynsley's? Now, she would never hear the end of it. "I daresay my desire to wed must not be acute."

Before taking their place in the receiving line at the foot of the stairs, Lord and Lady Warwick exchanged amused glances. Rebecca was growing tired of being the butt of those escalating amused glances.

She joined her friend Trevor Simpson to chat with Lord and Lady Agar for a few moments, then mounted the stairs with him to the third-floor ballroom where the orchestra had begun to play.

Though she found dancing as tediously irksome as getting her hair dressed, she rather enjoyed standing up with Mr. Simpson. He was so fluid a dancer he made her feel as if she tiptoed across clouds.

It was while she was performing a quadrille with Mr. Simpson that she caught sight of Lord Aynsley staring at her. Because he stood a bit taller than the average man, she could see him even though he was on the opposite side of the room.

Despite her annoyance with the earl, her gaze kept flitting back to him as she and Mr. Simpson glided around the dance floor. His lordship looked rather handsome in his black coat, gray silk waistcoat and black breeches. Though he was not a particularly large man and his leanness lacked ruggedness, she thought he emanated more power than any man she had ever seen as he stood alone watching her. *Supreme confidence.* That was what Lord Aynsley emanated. In great quantity.

When his gaze met hers and held, she quickly looked away. Her heartbeat began to drum madly, and she could feel the heat staining her cheeks. Twice now, the odious man was responsible for making her blush. A most distressing occurrence, to be sure! Then she recalled his tender farewell in the morning room the previous day. Perhaps he wasn't *that* odious.

What in the world was he doing here? His previous reclusiveness had assured her she would not have to suffer the man's company ever again.

As soon as the dance was finished, she begged Mr. Simpson to whisk her away for refreshments. From the corner of her eye, she could see that the earl continued to watch her, and she wanted nothing so keenly as to be invisible. But she would settle for finding a chamber where she could seek refuge from his lordship's prying eyes. She reversed positions with Trevor Simpson to shield herself from Lord Aynsley's view. A pity her companion was not possessed of broader shoulders.

"You really wish for refreshments so soon?" a puzzled Mr. Simpson asked.

"I assure you I am positively dying of thirst."

As she and Mr. Simpson reached the west doorway to the ballroom, Lord Aynsley greeted her. "Good evening, Miss Peabody. How good it is to see you again."

A surprised look on his face, Trevor looked from her to Lord Aynsley.

Merely nodding, her eyes fixed on Trevor's diamond studs, her limbs trembling, she refused to meet his lordship's gaze.

The orchestra began to play a waltz.

"I beg that you do me the goodness to stand up with me, Miss Peabody," Lord Aynsley said. "I came here expressly to see you."

She was still hiding behind Trevor, who had the audacity to smirk, then beg to take his leave.

With no Trevor to shield her, she could not have felt more vulnerable had she stood barefoot in her shift in front of Lord Aynsley. She wished to decline. She wished to run to her bedchamber. She wished to never see Lord Aynsley again for as long as she lived. But the good manners Maggie had instilled in her prevailed. Lifting her gaze to his, she nodded and placed her hand in his.

When they reached the crowded dance floor and his hand fitted to her waist, she sincerely hoped he did not detect the tremor that rumbled through her body.

That his dance movements were flawless surprised her. How could he be so fine a dancer when the man never attended balls? Obviously she was not the only person surprised that Lord Aynsley knew how to dance. If she was not mistaken, every eye in the ballroom was on him.

So much for her plan to be uncivil to him. Maggie would most definitely hear of it and become livid. "You, my lord, are the last person I would have expected to see here tonight," she finally said. At least Maggie could not accuse her of being rude to his lordship. Against her own better judgment, Rebecca was actually speaking to the odious man.

"Why do you say that, Miss Peabody?"

"Your distaste for social gatherings is rather well known." Is that one of the reasons she had selected him for her potential husband?

"It wasn't always that way, you know."

"Yes, I have surmised as much, owing to your competence at dancing."

"I thank you for the compliment."

"I did not compliment you."

"But you said my dancing was competent. Is that not a compliment?"

"I do not wish to compliment you. I do not understand why you've come tonight. I do not even want to be dancing with you! Is it your desire to humiliate me that's brought you here?"

His dance step slowed, and he looked down at her, his jaw clenched with concern. He squeezed her hand. "Never that. How could I when you've so singularly honored me?"

Odious man! "If you were possessed of decent manners, you would not mention so embarrassing a topic."

He chuckled. And held her a bit tighter as swirling couples in rustling silks waltzed around them.

She looked up into his amused face. He was tall enough to have rested his chin on the top of her head. "You have not answered me, my lord. Why have you come tonight?"

"To tell you the truth, I'm here because I wish to know you better, Miss Peabody."

"You, my lord, know all you need to know—and obviously dislike what you know."

"Forgive me if I've given that impression." He paused, a contrite expression on his serious face. "Perhaps I wish to know if you are, indeed, as mature as you assure me you are."

Good heavens! Was he actually contemplating the offer she had made him more than two weeks previously? In that instant, an odd sense of well-being exploded inside her. She was suddenly incapable of responding. If ever she needed to converse in a mature, intelligent manner, it was at this moment. And for the first time in her life, Miss Rebecca Peabody was speechless.

Also for the first time in her life, Rebecca Peabody wished she had no need for her spectacles. She wondered if Lord Aynsley would find her becoming in the peach-colored dress. Had Pru arranged her hair in a flattering fashion?

When the orchestra stopped playing and she found herself being escorted from the dance floor by Lord Aynsley, she was still moritfyingly mute. Even when he failed to relinquish her arm and led her down two flights of stairs and along the marble entry hall to Lord Warwick's library, she could not find her tongue.

Lord Aynsley led her into the library, a room that was lit only by a single taper in a wall sconce and the fire blazing in the hearth. He closed the door behind him and solemnly gazed into her eyes. "I wish to take this opportunity to get to know you better, Miss Peabody." Then he walked to the hearth. "Do you not find the room cold? I beg that you join me."

It was a moment before she joined him, and in that moment he took the opportunity to study her. She looked far too fetching in that gown that duplicated the color in her cheeks. The girl was possessed of the creamiest complexion, which was a perfect setting for those deep brown eyes of hers. She was really quite lovely—even in her spectacles.

"So you wish to determine if I'm truly mature?" she asked.

He peered down at her. "I do."

"The only way to do that is to converse."

"I agree."

"Then, my lord, I would like you to explain something to me. I've a keen interest in politics and I keep up with Parliament the best I can, but I've been unable to determine if you align yourself with the Tories or the Whigs. You must own, you seem to embrace both factions."

Could there be another young lady in the kingdom who had such knowledge of Parliament's activities? He would vow many of his colleagues in the House of Lords had been unaware that he played one side against the other in order to achieve his goals. A smile broke across his face. "You're very astute, Miss Peabody. I've found that to accomplish what I wish to accomplish I must not alienate either faction. It's my intent to make both sides think I'm with them."

"Pray, my lord," she asked, gazing up at him with those mesmerizing eyes, "what is it you wish to accomplish?"

"Reform." He had never told this to another person before. "I must ask that you tell no one I'm a reformer. Such knowledge would dilute my effectiveness in Parliament."

Her eyes began to dance. "Yes, I can see that it would."

Not many young women, he would vow, understood so well the compromises that were the backbone of politics.

"I suppose that's one of the reasons I wished to marry," she said.

"You've lost me. What was one of the reasons you wished to marry me?"

She scowled at him. "Really, my lord, must you allude to the humiliating act that reacquainted us?"

How ungallant of him to refer to the offer she had so brazenly made. "Forgive me, but please do explain *one of those reasons* for wishing to be wed."

"The reforms," she said.

Excitement began to course through him, but he could not allow her to know he had unmasked her pseudonym. "Yes? What reforms would that be?" He tried to sound casual.

"All the reforms, actually. As long as I live in Lord Warwick's house, I can't very well promulgate reforms against the very government he serves, but that is exactly what I wish to do. Unfortunately, I'm totally dependent on Lord Warwick, owing to the fact I've no money of my own." She stopped abruptly and peered up at him. "So I must marry in order to gain my independence. The pity of it is, I have no dowry."

There was not a morsel of doubt in his mind that Rebecca Peabody was indeed P. Corpus. A smile tweaked at the corners of his mouth. "Your lack of a dowry shouldn't matter to a man of means."

"Do you mean a man of means like you?" she asked, her voice squeaking, her lashes lifting as she innocently gazed into his eyes.

She reminded him of a frightened puppy as she looked up at him with those big eyes of hers.

He patted her hand. "I am a man of means, though I'm not in the market for a wife."

As they stood in front of the fire, her gaze fanned across the chamber, stopping at a large bookcase some ten feet away, its gilded leather volumes bathed in the fire's buttery glow. "Are you aware that I cataloged Lord Agar's entire library at Windmere Abbey?"

Miss Peabody obviously wished to acquaint him with her organizational skills. "Actually I am. Warwick told me."

Her mouth dropped open. "Please say that you did *not* reveal to Warwick that I asked you to… I won't discuss what I asked you to do."

He could not help himself. He laughed. "I beg your forgiveness if I've upset you by telling Warwick, but is the man not as a guardian to you?"

Her eyes grew even larger. "Pray, my lord, what did you discuss with Warwick?"

"I asked him if you could possibly be possessed of more maturity than you have heretofore demonstrated to me."

"And how did his lordship answer?"

"He assured me you were most mature as well as wonderful with children." He must not give her false hope. "Were I interested in marriage, I should desire a wife who was attracted to me, and I know you are not."

That curtain that concealed her emotions dropped over her delicate face.

Neither of them spoke for a moment. The only sounds merging into the deep silence were the muffled laughter in the hallways beyond the library door and the sputtering fire before them.

"I cannot lie," she finally said, "and say I have romantic designs on you."

"Since you've never had romantic designs on any man?"

The firelight reflected off her spectacles as she nodded.

"It won't always be that way, you know," he said. "As a man and woman—or husband and wife—grow close to one another, intimacy is as natural as breathing."

"I do understand that," she said, her voice soft and devoid of embarrassment. "I read my Bible. *A man shall leave his father and mother and cleave unto his wife: and they shall be one flesh.*" She peered into his eyes. "I've seen it with my sister and Warwick and with Lord and Lady Agar. Both couples are deeply in love."

The curtain went back up over the softened features of her face, and she changed the subject. Without looking at him, she spoke. "Will you answer a question, my lord?"

"Anything."

"Are you considering marriage with me?"

Being coy was as alien to this young woman as frugality was to the regent.

He had not admitted to anyone—not even to himself—that he was considering marriage to Miss Rebecca Peabody. But she knew. Could she know him better than he knew himself? "I'm considering it," he said with great honesty. "I must tell you, though, that a marriage without mutual affection and intimacy holds no appeal to me."

It was a moment before she made a response. "Would you consider marrying me if I promised to be open to that at some time in the future? After a deep bond of friendship had the opportunity to form?"

He felt his chest expanding. Though he'd had no intentions of begging for her hand, such an idea now held appeal. "I would consider it, but I must first tell you some things that might change your mind about wishing to marry me."

Her brows lowered. “What things?”

“You know I have six sons?”

She nodded. “What are their ages?”

“They range in age from three to nineteen.”

“I assure you I love little boys. In fact, I like them much more than I like girls—owing to the fact they're all I've ever been around.”

Would she still feel that way once she became acquainted with his rambunctious sons? “My sons are really good lads, but they're always into mischief. They've run off more nurses, governesses and housekeepers than I can count.”

“How do they run them off, my lord?”

He frowned. “The last one left after she found worms in her garment drawer.”

Miss Peabody giggled. “The woman should have locked her chamber door.”

“My sons should not have gone into her room,” he said in a stern voice.

“Were I their mother, I would have to be a firm disciplinarian.”

“Exactly what they need.”

“And I adore worms.”

He burst out laughing. At that very instant he wished to ask her to marry him. Because of the worms. But he couldn't offer for her until she knew the obstacles that would face her should she become his wife. “In addition to my seven children, I'm also responsible for two other people. I'm guardian to my sister's son, a wastrel named Peter Wallace who is two and twenty, and I'm responsible for my daft uncle who's been banished to the dowager's house.”

Her brows lowered. “Pray, my lord, why did you banish your uncle?”

Aynsley really did *not* want to tell her. “He has a peculiar habit that is most offensive, especially to females.”

“What habit is that, my lord?”

He swallowed. “He believes he’s a kissing bandit.”

“Do I understand you correctly? He tries to steal kisses from females?”

He nodded ruefully.

She did not say anything for a moment. Then she said, “I sincerely hope his peculiar propensity does not run in your family, my lord.”

He laughed. “I assure you, Miss Peabody, I do not accost women for the purpose of stealing kisses.”

“I’m very glad to hear that.” Her lips pursed, she shook her head. “Has your uncle always done this peculiar thing?”

“No. That did not commence until his eighty-fifth birthday.”

“Oh, I see. His senses are in the same place with his head of dark hair and unlined skin?”

“Regrettably.”

“And now that he’s banished, I suppose he lacks the mobility to bother the females at Dunton Hall?”

“Usually. But he occasionally chases them about the park in his bath chair.”

“The poor old dear.”

“You would not say that were he leaping at you with pursed lips and groping arms.”

“No. I daresay I wouldn’t.” Now she met his gaze. “Is there anything more, my lord? Any skeletons in your closet?”

His gut plummeted. "Yes." He swallowed.

Her eyes rounded. "Pray, my lord, what odious offense have you committed?"

"I have turned my back on God."

She did not say anything at all for a full moment. "There is nothing I can do to remedy so great a loss," she said at last. "Only you can open your soul to receive the Holy Spirit's grace."

"I don't even know if I believe anymore."

"Then I am very sorry for you."

They stood there, illuminated by the fire, its heat rushing over them as tensions mounted. Finally, she spoke. "What of your children?"

"They do not attend church, either."

"I see." She nibbled at her lower lip. "Would you object if...if the woman you marry encourages your children to embrace God?"

"I would not object."

Silence filled the room like a heart that no longer beat. For a man as proud as he, it had been difficult not only to have laid before her his faults and his family's foibles but also to beg her understanding, even her acceptance. That she still stood there querying him bespoke her compassion, a compassion he'd known she possessed in great store.

He had a strong wish to marry this woman and bring her back to Dunton Hall. How could a woman who liked worms not be perfect for his boys? Miss Peabody now knew the worst about him. Would she still consider plighting her life to his?

There was only one way to find out. He must ask her.

Chapter Four

She was prodigiously glad she had worn her spectacles. Otherwise Rebecca would not have been able to observe the profusion of emotions that transformed his lordship's face. He had gone from amusement, to gravity and now to something altogether perplexing. Contemplation. Nervousness. Anxiety.

Her heartbeat drummed. Was he thinking about asking her to become his wife? His nervousness transferred to her as if by lightning bolt. He drew her hand into his, and she noted the twitch in his lean cheek and the slight descent of his brows as her pulse began to pound.

"I think, my dear Rebecca," he finally said, "we might just suit."

Close to an offer of marriage, but not close enough. Surely he was not going to force her into making a second proposal! With a defiant tilt of her chin, she gazed up at him. "I am very much aware of that fact, my lord. Why else would I have risked such humiliation?"

The corners of his mouth lifted as he moved even closer to her and murmured, "You did not humiliate yourself. Do you have any idea how magnificent you were that day?"

Magnificent? She was astonished that he could have thought her so. She wished to protest, to remind him of how rudely he had met her proposal, but the moment demanded soft words. It suddenly became clear to her that while he had initially balked at her offer, she must have made a profound impression upon him. "If you believe that, my lord, I believe you've been unable to purge me from your thoughts."

"How well you know me, Rebecca." His voice was low and gentle. And he did not seem so very old. Even if he was three and forty.

They stood facing one another, hot and flushed from the fire, the reflection of flames flickering in his green eyes. He was possessed of such a very fine face, it was a wonder she had failed to observe that fact when she had met him two years previously. Though too lean to emanate ruggedness, his face of smooth planes, high cheekbones and aquiline nose exuded a restrained power that was softened by his curved mouth and gentle, mossy eyes.

No man had ever held her hand like this before. Those long, warm fingers of his possessed a gentle strength. He lifted her hand to his lips, and her breath came quicker. When he lowered his mouth to her hand, she suddenly knew what it must feel like to rise in one of those balloons over Hyde Park.

He then did a most peculiar (but totally poignant) thing. He placed her hand over his heart and covered it with his own. "Will you, my dearest Rebecca, do me the honor of becoming my wife?"

Intense emotions washed over her, sweeping her up

in a roaring tide. Lord Aynsley was not the cold, aging peer she had anticipated. He was possessed of great tenderness.

As she went to accept his offer, she was horrified to find her voice hoarse and shaky and—worst of all—tears spilling from her eyes. She could not remember the last time she had cried. She thought perhaps it had been back in Virginia when her father died.

His brows lowered, and Lord Aynsley drew back to regard her with worry. "Have I offended you, my dear lady?"

She managed to shake her head. Sniff, sniff. "I'm never such a pea goose."

Mirth flashed in his eyes. "Could it be that the bookish, pragmatic Miss Rebecca Peabody is a sentimentalist?"

"You need not worry on that score, my lord." She swiped at her moist cheeks and squared her shoulders. "I assure you I can be practical, firm and *not* given to emotional displays."

"Does that mean you will accept the challenge of being my wife, of being mother to my children?"

The tears gushed. She was mortified. Not trusting her voice, she merely nodded.

He stepped closer, placed firm hands on her shoulders and spoke in a soft voice. "You've made me very happy."

"You may wish to retract your offer when you learn some things about me."

"Such as?"

"I disapprove of the English system of aristocracy."

He nodded. "As is your right."

"On that principle, I should not like to be addressed as a lady."

"Now see here, Rebecca. You cannot waltz into Britain and try to single-handedly change a system that's been in place a thousand years!"

"I'm not foolish enough to believe I can change the system. I merely refuse to be addressed as Lady Aynsley. And...I shouldn't feel right referring to your children as Lady This and Lord That."

He stiffened, glaring at her. "I flatter myself over my willingness to embrace progressive ideas, but I'm also proud to carry on the Aynsley title that's been in existence since the days of the Conqueror. I would have to insist my wife honor our family."

"By being addressed as a lady?" There was mockery in her voice.

"There could not be another woman in the three kingdoms who wouldn't be proud to be a countess."

"Then marry one of them!" She started for the door.

His extended arm barred her progress. "Surely we could come up with a compromise."

She gave him a quizzing look and did not speak for a moment, then her voice softened. "I suppose that *is* what a real marriage entails: give and take?"

He nodded gravely. "And mutual respect."

"But I do respect *you.* I just find it ridiculous that some completely useless men garner respect because of something a long-dead ancestor did."

"While I understand your feelings, I should have to insist that you be known as Lady Aynsley in Society."

Her slow nod was barely perceptible. "In our home—that is, *if* you still want to wed me—could we dispense with the titles? Then I wouldn't feel like such a hypocrite."

His eyes twinkled. "See, my dear, you are already learning about marital compromise. I should like us to use first names. It fosters intimacy."

She drew a deep breath. "Speaking of intimacy…"

"We will not share a bedchamber until such time when you become agreeable to such a prospect."

"Thank you." Her voice was almost a whisper. "You're sure you still want to marry me?"

"I'm sure."

The firelight was obscured when his head lowered to hers. Her heartbeat thundered. He was going to kiss her! Before she could mentally process what was happening, his lips softly settled over hers. She had thought he would merely drop a kiss, then lift his head, but it seemed Lord Aynsley wished to prolong this intimacy.

She eased away from him.

Lord Aynsley smiled that rascally smile of his. "One day, my sweet, you will enjoy being kissed. Of that I am certain."

It was Rebecca's wedding day. She was to marry a man she scarcely knew. She would travel to a strange new home and would seldom see the sister from whom she had rarely parted. She should be petrified, but strangely, she was not. Of course, she would miss Maggie dreadfully. And the children. But she was eager to meet the children who would become her own. The very prospect brought a smile to her lips.

The Warwick carriage slowed in front of St. George's, and Maggie stroked her arm. "It's not too late, pet, to turn back."

Rebecca smiled brightly upon her sister. "I've told you countless times. I very much wish to wed Lord Aynsley."

"But it's not right to marry a man you're not in love with."

"I may not be in love with him now, but I assure you I could never find a more suitable mate. He and I discussed this and decided that once we know each other better we quite possibly could fall in love."

Rebecca really did not believe that. Falling in love was for pretty little maids who cut their teeth on Mrs. Radcliffe's novels, not for unromantic bluestockings like herself.

"Should you not have gotten to know one another *before* deciding to get married?" Maggie asked as the coachman put down the step.

"Lord Aynsley possesses all the qualities I could ever desire in a husband," Rebecca said dismissively.

The coach door swung open, and Rebecca moved to get up.

Maggie seized her arm. "You are sure?"

"I'm sure." If only she felt as sure as she sounded.

Even as she walked down the nave of the church, she trembled. Was she doing the right thing? She certainly did not seem to be marrying for the right reasons. Here, in the house of the Lord, she felt a fraud. The Lord knew she was not in love with Lord Aynsley.

Her eyes met his. And it was as if her nervousness evaporated. His kindliness was so utterly reassuring. As she continued down the church's nave, she felt the Lord's presence.

This union would be sanctified by God and His church.

She came to stand beside Lord Aynsley, then met the bishop's somber gaze as he began to pray aloud. This was only the fourth wedding she had ever attended, and—understandably—none of the others had ever so profoundly affected her. This was the first time she had come to understand the religious significance of the sacrament of matrimony, *the joining of this man and this woman in holy matrimony.*

The bishop continued on with the service, uttering words she'd heard before but never thought would apply to her, the spinster Rebecca Peabody.

A few minutes later, the bishop instructed Aynsley to take Rebecca's right hand and asked Rebecca to repeat after him: "I, Rebecca, take thee, John, to be my wedded husband, to have and to hold from this day forward, for better or for worse, for richer, for poorer, in sickness and in health, to love, cherish and to obey, till death us do part, according to God's holy ordinance; and thereto I give thee my troth."

She almost felt relieved once she'd uttered the words. Their marriage was sanctified.

When he'd watched his frightened bride move down the church's nave, too nervous to even look at him, he'd experienced a rush of tender feelings. He wanted nothing so much as to reassure her. When her gaze finally met his, he knew the deep connection between them was as irreversible as the tide.

She had never looked lovelier. She had left off the spectacles, which he had come to feel were as much a part of her as her lovely dark eyes and her mane of lustrous dark hair. She had chosen a dress as white as snow, which contrasted beautifully with her dark features and which was adorned with pale blue ribbons.

While he wasn't a religious man, he was not unaffected by the service. The solemnity of the occasion, the recitation of vows before the bishop and others who had gathered, gave the service profound significance.

After placing the Aynsley emerald ring on her left hand, he continued to clasp her hand while pronouncing the words prompted by the bishop: "With this ring I thee wed, with my body I thee worship and with all my worldly goods I thee endow: In the name of the Father, and of the Son, and of the Holy Ghost. Amen."

Following the wedding breakfast, the Warwicks walked as far as Aynsley's carriage with the newlyweds, then the two sisters embraced. As his bride's eyes misted, a surge of protective emotions filled Aynsley. He vowed to do everything in his power to ensure that the life awaiting her in Shropshire be more rewarding than anything she had previously known.

"Come, my dear," he said, setting a possessive hand at her waist, "we've a long journey ahead."

"And I daresay his lordship does not wish to travel with a watering pot," Lord Warwick quipped.

Maggie affectionately swatted at her husband. "You of all people should know my sister is never a watering pot."

A smug smile tweaked at Aynsley's mouth. He alone knew of the great untapped depths of his wife's feelings, feelings she betrayed by weeping when he offered for her. He hoped one day he could awaken the emotions that smoldered deep within her.

He handed his bride into the carriage, then came to

sit opposite her. He very much wanted to gaze at the young woman who had become his wife. The coach pulled away, but Rebecca could not remove her gaze from the window that linked her to the sister who watched from the pavement. After they rounded the corner, he said, "I vow to make it up to you."

She glanced up at him, a look of query on her face. "Pray, my lord, make up for what?"

"John. Say it, Rebecca."

"John," she whispered.

A smile eased across his face. "It's my hope that your life at Dunton will be so satisfying you'll scarcely spare a thought for your sister."

She smiled. "I do hope you're right. I'm vastly looking forward to meeting the children. You must tell me all about them."

"You won't meet the three eldest boys for some time."

"I want to know all about them. Please start with the three oldest."

"The oldest is Johnny, Viscount Fordyce." He unconsciously lifted his index finger. "He's nineteen, almost twenty, and at Oxford. Next," he said, raising a second finger, "is Geoffrey, who is a year younger. In physical resemblance they are like twins, except that Johnny's eyes are brown and Geoffrey's, green. They're now separated, as Geoffrey is a captain in the army."

"Oh, dear, is he in the Peninsula?"

Aynsley nodded, a frown furrowing his face.

"Then I shall pray for his safe return. Tell me, is their hair brown, like yours?"

He chuckled. "Mine used to be brown, but I daresay the gray's predominant of late."

"I hadn't noticed."

Because she had taken so little notice of him. He was every bit the dullard Dorothy had always said he was. For Rebecca, he was merely a means to an end—the end being her highly desired independence.

He would refrain from telling her how completely he understood her, just as he would refrain from telling her he knew of her alter ego. She must come to trust him enough to make an unprompted admission. He hoped she would soon. He prized honesty above all. Especially since he knew firsthand how a wife's deception could ravage a marriage.

"And the next son?" she asked.

"That would be Mark, who's twelve and at Eton."

"Johnny, Geoffrey and Mark—all away. Now, tell me about the lads who are still at Dunton Hall."

"Spencer is eight." Aynsley started counting on his fingers again. "Like my daughter and the baby, he is blond. In between Spencer and the baby is Alex, who is quite a unique lad."

She looked puzzled. "In what way?"

Thinking about his precocious six-year-old made him smile. "For starters, he is the only one of the seven to be possessed of red hair."

"I adore red hair."

Red hair and worms. A woman after his own heart. "Unfortunately, he also possesses a redhead's fiery temperament."

Her eyes flashed with good humor. "He fights with his brothers, no doubt."

"Right you are. He's also the only boy who would rather be reading a book than playing cricket, and he is prone to using language his siblings don't understand."

"Big words?"

"Exactly."

"You could be describing me as a child," she said with a laugh. "Why do you refer to the youngest as 'the baby' when he is three years old?"

"For the obvious reason that he *is* the baby. There is also the fact that he is less...intellectually developed than the other boys were at three years."

Her brows lowered. "In what way?"

He frowned. Aynsley had been worried for some time about the little imp who'd so easily wiggled his way into his father's heart. "He's only just started to speak in sentences, and he lacks...how shall I put this delicately? Bladder control. He's forever having accidents."

"I daresay the little dear only needs a mother's love."

Love? Was he hearing correctly? Miss Rebecca Peabody—or actually, the new Lady Aynsley, though she detested the title—had used the word *love.* His heart melted at the thought—the hope—that this enigmatic girl-woman who sat across from him would come to love Chuckie and his other children. "I believe you're right," he said. "He's the only one who never knew his mother."

"If I recall correctly, she died shortly after his birth?"

His face was grim. "She died of a fever when he was just four months old."

Rebecca winced. "And what is the little lamb's name?"

"His name's Charles, but we've always called him Chuckie."

"I'm very glad that he's speaking in sentences."

As was he. "There is one more thing."

Her fine brows arched.

"I'm troubled that he lives in his own world."

"His own world?"

"Allow me to explain. He's always dressing in costumes and calling everyone he knows by names other than their given ones, names he's dubbed them. And he doesn't seem to care for his own name. The last time I was home, his 'name' was James Hock."

"I wouldn't worry about that, John. From what you're telling me, I gather that Chuckie's possessed of a lively mind and acute intelligence."

"He is intelligent, but I don't understand why the lad keeps having all those blasted *accidents.*"

"I daresay he's just too busy to take time out to..." She stopped, shrugged, then redirected her thoughts. "I don't profess to be an expert on children, but I think your concerns are not warranted."

"I hope you're right."

He settled back into the squabs and regarded his bride. She really looked quite fetching in her snow-white muslin that was trimmed in sky-blue ribbons. It was the same dress she had worn to their wedding ceremony that morning. She had been so incredibly pretty—and horribly scared. Fortunately, she was more relaxed now. The peach blush had returned to her cheeks, and her stiffness had unfurled.

"What of your nephew?" she asked.

He stiffened. "More often than not, I'm out of charity with Peter."

"He's how old?"

"He reached his majority last year and quickly went through every farthing he could get his hands on."

"So he lacks maturity, steadiness and—I think—your affection?"

"I wouldn't say that about the affection. If it weren't for Emily, things might be different."

"Emily's your daughter?"

"Yes. She thinks she's in love with Peter."

"And you find him ineligible?"

"I gave him a chance. After he was sent down from Oxford—for sottishness—I secured a post for him with Lord Paley at the Home Office and told Peter if he could live on the three hundred a year from the Home Office coupled with the two hundred a year from my sister, I would allow him to marry Emily."

"I take it he was not successful."

"Not at all."

"He could not live within his means?"

"He lost heavily at Brook's, then the moneylenders got their hooks into him, then he did the unthinkable."

Her eyes rounded.

"He left his post without so much as a fare-thee-well and fled back to Dunton, professing that he couldn't live without Emily."

"And his foolishness did not elicit disgust in your daughter?"

"She thinks I've been too harsh on him. He was very close to his mother—my sister—and Emily says I should have been more compassionate to him when he came to Dunton after his mother's death."

"How old was he then?"

"Fifteen."

"A most difficult age."

"He wasn't a bad lad," Aynsley defended. "And despite all his weaknesses, I cannot deny that he truly loves my daughter. Whatever I heard of his heedless activities in London, bedding loose women wasn't one of them." He shouldn't have said that in front of Rebecca. She was such an innocent. He looked up at her. "Forgive me."

"I beg that you not apologize. We are, after all, man and wife. I wish your speech with me always to be unguarded."

This was the first time Rebecca in the flesh—not through her elucidating essays—seemed more woman than girl.

"I can understand your wish that your only daughter marry a man more worthy."

At least his wife understood his fatherly affection. "The problem is my daughter says she wants no one else."

Rebecca nibbled at her lower lip. "Will she have a Season in London?"

"I mean for her to. She will resist."

"There is the fact that another man might not love her with such constancy as Peter."

The same thought had plagued him. Above everything, he wanted what was best for Emily. "Though I'm a wealthy man, I've seven children to provide for. Emily's dowry will not be large enough to compensate for a wastrel husband."

"Being a parent is no simple matter." She went to say something else, then clamped her lips.

He studied her pensive expression. The nibbling on her lower lip. The thick fringe of long, dark lashes that swept against the creamy skin beneath her eyes. He had become so accustomed to her spectacles he never noticed them anymore.

A moment later she said, "I want very much to be a good mother to your children. Do you think they will resent that I shall try to replace their own much-loved mother?"

He wished to soothe the worry he saw on her face. "The three youngest have little memory of their mother. I should think they would be most receptive to having a mother of their own."

The lively smile she tried to suppress told him she had warmed to the idea of being a mother, even though her voice strove for nonchalance. "And the four eldest will, quite naturally, cling to the memories of their own mother," she said.

"Most likely. But I daresay you will lift a huge burden from Emily's shoulders."

His bride eyed him thoughtfully for a moment. "Emily is very dear to you, is she not?"

"Very."

"You said she is a blonde?"

He nodded.

"I expect she's quite lovely."

"You'll have to judge for yourself. I find her so."

"As does Peter, obviously. Tell me, how long have they fancied themselves in love?"

"I can't remember a time when she didn't insist that she'd grow up and marry him."

"Oh, dear, a mind-set like that is not easy to break."

"That's what worries me."

She resumed peering out the window, and neither of them spoke for the next half hour. Then she turned back to him and said, "I should like to learn more of you."

That she was thinking of him was his first chink into her stiff formality. He gave her a warm look as he moved from the seat facing her to sit beside her. Her lashes lowered modestly as he drew her hand into his.

"What would you like to know?" he murmured. Was this to be the breakthrough he sought?

Chapter Five

As Aynsley asked his question, his green eyes twinkled in harmony with his dimpled grin.

"About the reforms you intend to promulgate."

"There are so very many."

"Indeed there are. It's hard to know where to begin to eradicate all the injustices."

He gazed from the window at a soot-covered old chapel until it disappeared from view. "I've given the matter a great deal of thought," he finally said.

"Which matter?" she asked.

"Reforms. The hierarchy of reforms."

As much as she had contemplated reforms, she had failed to consider the sequence in which they needed to be implemented. "Go on."

"Before the social ills like penal reform and abuses of laborers can be addressed, we need to correct the defects in the representative system."

The sheer brilliance of his words stunned her. Why had she never considered reforms in such a light before? Ideas raced through her mind so rapidly she had difficulty isolating one. She was still reeling from the wisdom of ranking the implementation of reforms when he had bedazzled her with his choice for first priority. "Oh, yes, I see it so clearly!" she said. "Under our present system, a handful of powerful landowners like you control Parliament, and they're not likely to welcome changes that reduce their own power in order to benefit the lower classes." She looked up at him with awe. "Are you familiar with the Great Compromise in America?"

"I am. A pity Englishmen would so resist such a perfect democracy."

She was impressed—and delighted—that Lord Aynsley was so well-informed on political theories and practices. "There would be great resistance to abolishing the king or the House of Lords," she said, "but do you not think the House of Commons should be set up along the lines of America's congressional representatives? One representative for every so many voters? I know Commons now *supposedly* represents particular areas of England, but you and I both know that's a complete farce. The geographic areas do *not* reflect the population, and there's no residency requirement for the members who serve in Commons."

"I do agree with everything you've said. We're now in a transition from an agrarian society to an industrialized one, and our elective system—inadequate at its inception—is sadly outdated."

She had never before felt so fully alive, so excited, never before spoken face-to-face with anyone as intelligent or like-minded as Lord Aynsley. John. It suddenly did not seem so very odd to address this man by his Christian name. "There would be a great deal of resistance," she said.

"We must remember the 1780s and '90s in France." His voice was solemn.

"You think the English people will revolt?"

"It's a possibility. They will certainly want a government that's more democratic. The manufacturing centers of Birmingham and Liverpool—which aren't so very far from Dunton—don't have a single borough in Parliament even though they have large populations."

"While some boroughs are inhabited only by sheep!"

"We must work to change that."

We? It was almost as if he knew of her essays, knew she was determined to work to bring about change. She felt wretchedly guilty for concealing her alter ego from the man she had married.

"In Parliament," he added.

She squeezed his hand, surprising herself. "I know I'm just a woman and incapable of influencing political thought, but I appreciate that you do not find me a muttonhead, that you're willing to discuss these matters with me as you would with a man."

He turned to her, their eyes locking. Her heart began to beat unaccountably fast. "And I appreciate that you are *not* a muttonhead," he said.

She giggled. "I'm trying to determine if you just complimented me."

His rakish smile returned. "I complimented you, Lady Aynsley."

She scowled.

"Forgive me. I should have called you Rebecca."

"Indeed you should have, *John,* but I forgive you because you are a beacon of light in the dimness that is the House of Lords." It suddenly occurred to her that marrying a peer came with an unexpected bonus. Her husband, as a member of the House of Lords, was in a position to actually work toward progressive changes.

She wondered if in the years which stretched ahead of them he would come to seek her counsel. Would he ever solicit her opinion? This marriage business was beginning to sound promising—certainly much preferable to being the peculiar spinster residing in the home of the staid Tory statesman Lord Warwick.

"Are there any peers in the Lords who could be persuaded to our way of thinking?" she asked.

"Let me put it this way. There are many who I think could be swayed."

"I do hope you can start gathering support for the overhaul of the elective system."

He looked at her with flashing eyes and a wicked smile. "You do, do you?"

She offered a lame nod. "I would be willing to do anything in my power to assist you." What an impotent offer! As if there was something a twenty-eight-year-old female bluestocking laughingstock could do. How she wished she could tell him she was P. Corpus and would use her pen to enlighten the masses. Despite that she and her new husband shared so many progressive views, she did not know him well enough to admit her authorship. What if he forbade her to ever write again? She was now obliged to obey her husband. To give up her writing would be to nullify her entire reason for marrying him! Admitting her authorship was too great a risk.

"I shall take that under advisement," he said.

"Your statement about the hierarchy of implementation of reforms brings to mind a most interesting essay I read. It was written by P. Corpus. I hope you are in agreement with his ideas, for he seems to me to be a very wise man." Her pulse accelerated as she gazed up at him, fearing he would not agree.

"For an idealist, but he lacks pragmatism."

"All visionaries lack pragmatism. That can only come with the universal acceptance of their ideas."

"A most mature observation," he said.

Under her husband's praise she soared like a phoenix. "I'm rather interested in political reform."

"To which of Mr. Corpus's essays do you refer?" her husband asked.

"The one about classification of crimes."

"Oh, yes, where he proposes that punishment should suit the crime. Lesser punishments for lesser offenses."

"That's the one. His idea is so simple, one wonders why no one else thought of it sooner."

He did not say anything for a moment. If he maligned P. Corpus she would...well, she didn't know what she would do, but it would make her decidedly angry.

"I much admire the man's writing," he finally said.

For which she was exceedingly grateful.

Until quite late that night they rode on, munching from the basket his cook had prepared, and they never lacked for a topic to discuss. They spoke of labor unions, the Corn Laws, the stodgy lords who controlled Parliament, and were in complete agreement on P. Corpus's plan for penal reform.

A few hours after dark, the coach rolled into the inn yard in Milton Keynes. This had been the most exciting day of her life—not because it was her wedding day but because she had found a man she had not thought could exist.

* * *

A light mist was falling. Aynsley did not wish to expose his wife to the damp until they were assured of procuring rooms. "I shall require a private parlor for dinner as well as rooms for myself and Lady Aynsley for the night," he told the coachman when that servant threw open the carriage door.

"Very good, my lord."

"Next to each other," Aynsley added, "and don't forget to mention we'll need a hot meal."

Once the coachman returned after procuring the rooms, Aynsley stepped down from the carriage, then offered Rebecca a hand. As she stood beside him he swept his greatcoat around her and pulled her close as they sloshed through the muddy inn yard toward the buttery glow of a lantern beside the timbered door of the Cock and Crown.

They were shown to the cozy parlor, where a welcoming fire was blazing in the hearth. They warmed themselves in front of the fire until a serving woman brought them a pot of hot tea, then they sat across from each other at the trestle table, which was lit by a candle.

He watched his bride as she clasped her hands around the cup's warmth, the candlelight bathing her face in its golden glow. She looked much younger than her eight and twenty years, and despite the brilliance that resided within her, she elicited a protectiveness in him. It was akin to that elicited by his children—yet altogether different.

It occurred to him that he would be spending the rest of his life with this woman. The prospect was almost overwhelming. What if he had acted too rashly? What did he really know about this woman? The memories of Dorothy's perfidy clouded this moment. Would Rebecca be capable of such duplicity?

"Have you any regrets, Rebecca?"

"Over what, my lord?"

It pleased him that she'd forgotten and addressed him as she had before she'd confessed to her ridiculous abhorrence of titles. "Over this speedy marriage of ours. What could have prompted you to…to honor me with your proposal when a considerable period of time had elapsed since we had last seen each other?"

"I will be honest with you, then. Please don't be offended."

She was going to admit her P. Corpus persona! "I assure you I won't."

"For some time I'd been thinking of how much more freedom is given to a married woman. I was beastly tired of never being permitted to go where I wanted without approval from my sister, who would then demand that a maid—or some type of chaperone—accompany me. I had decided that being my own mistress had vast appeal."

"That's it?"

"Hear me out. There's more. I was also having a great deal of difficulty living in Lord Warwick's house. I'm sure it will come as no surprise to you that he and I disagree on almost everything. Our disagreements were becoming more heated, and I felt I was tearing apart my sister's happy home." She paused to offer him a smile. "I'm sure you're wondering why I selected you."

Their eyes met, and he nodded.

"I'm not going to say I had been attracted to you because that would be a lie. It was just that as I started enumerating eligible men, I instantly discarded every unmarried man I knew. Except you. I cannot tell you why. I think it was the children. I knew you had needed a woman to serve as mother to your children, and the more I thought on it, the more I wished to undertake such a charge. I felt as if the Lord were guiding me to you. To you and your children."

Thankfully, the serving woman entered the chamber, saving him from having to reply. He would not have known what to say, he was so stunned. He hadn't thought of God in a long while, but now he did. He, too, could feel God's hand in this marriage. Why else would a sensible, pragmatic man like himself have agreed to so speedy a marriage with a woman with whom he had scarcely ever communicated?

After they ate, Aynsley turned to his wife, one brow hiked and a grin pinching his cheek. "A most peculiar wedding night this is."

"Thank you for being so understanding."

He lifted her hand to brush the back of it with a sterile kiss. "Don't give the matter another thought. Earning your trust is all I ask. For the present," he added wickedly.

A parlor maid carrying a candle led them up a flight of dark, narrow wooden stairs to their chambers. "These rooms at the top of the stairs are fer yer lordship and ladyship," she said. "They should be nice and toasty now. Yer servants have already laid yer own linens on the beds." She curtsied and took her leave.

His gaze flicked to his bride, who stood in her doorway. "Tomorrow will be another long day. I shall ask to be awakened at dawn. We'll dress and eat, then hopefully push off by seven." *My, but you're pretty. And uncommonly intelligent.*

"A very good plan."

* * *

The first night of their journey Rebecca had been too exhilarated to sleep. For that is how she felt now. After eight-and-twenty years of utter loneliness and a melancholy acceptance that she *was* different, she had at last found someone who thought like she did. She even began to believe that with Lord Aynsley she could salvage a semblance of a normal life.

Throughout the long night she had recollected every word of every one of their conversations and mentally added new topics to discuss with her husband the following day.

On the second night of the journey, her body cried out with fatigue, but she could not sleep then, either. But this time for entirely different reasons.

Now she found herself wondering about Lord Aynsley the man. Had he loved his first wife terribly? Had theirs been an affectionate marriage? The very thought of him with someone else ignited a strange sensation. Good heavens! Was it jealousy?

She also thought about his confession that he had shut God out of his life. *Please, Lord, help me help him find You again.*

She felt completely at ease with her husband and was coming to know him as she had never known any man. She had learned of his fondness for plum pudding, his disdain for men who could not hold their liquor, and she had come to relish the ready grin she seemed so capable of eliciting from him.

He was coming to know her well, too. The last day of their journey he sat across from her in the carriage, a concerned look on his face. "You did not sleep well," he said.

His words jarred her from reverie. "How did you know?"

That rakish grin on his face, he studied her. "I'm coming to know your face rather well."

The interior of the coach at once seemed a most intimate place. She felt as if all that mattered in the world was enclosed within that cubicle, that nothing else existed. This was uncomfortable territory for her. Equally as disconcerting was the way he continued to watch her so intently.

Did he stare at her because he found her wanting? If he'd been able to determine she had not slept, the evidence of her sleeplessness must show in her face. "I must look wretched," she finally said. What was happening to her? Rebecca never gave consideration to her appearance.

"Not at all. You're lovely."

Men never said she was lovely. "You, sir, will put me to the blush." She could now add blushing to her areas of expertise.

"I'm sorry you've been unable to sleep," he murmured. "I expect the mattress is not what you're used to."

"I'll be fine once we get to Dunton. When will we arrive there?"

"Before dark."

Her thoughts flitted to her new home, and she realized she would take the chambers occupied by the former Lady Aynsley. "Will I be given…your wife's rooms?"

"*You* are my wife, Rebecca."

It suddenly seemed very hot within the carriage. Intimate. Did the intimacy account for her sudden urge to pry? She vowed to be less personal, but her resolve dissipated before five minutes had passed. "What was her name?" Rebecca asked.

"Your predecessor?"

He had cleverly chosen not to call the former Lady Aynsley his *wife*. "Yes."

"Dorothy."

"Do you miss her dreadfully?"

"It's been a long time. I can't even remember what her voice sounded like."

How neatly he had avoided answering her question. "Were you utterly heartbroken when she died?" *What's wrong with me?* Rebecca never dwelled on *personal* matters. She'd always concerned herself with ideas, not people.

"She's dead, Rebecca. You're my wife now, and we'll make a new life. It's very important to me that you're happy."

It didn't seem that her happiness had ever mattered to anyone else before. Maggie, of course, loved her, but had never understood her. In that instant, in that cozy carriage, Rebecca came to believe that she did matter to this man who had honored her with his name. "I've never been happier," she whispered.

"I wonder if you'll feel that way a year from now." His voice softened. "I sincerely hope so."

That afternoon they passed through Birmingham. Aynsley had always found the city's jungle of bulging, belching, blackening factories oppressive. Now, he wished to gauge Rebecca's reaction. She seemed unable to remove her face from the glass as their carriage jostled over the filthy streets, and it was not until the city's unhealthy haze was behind them that she spoke. She turned from the window to face him, an incredibly solemn look on her face. "My heart bleeds for those people."

A morose nod was his only response.

After several minutes had passed, she asked, "Have you ever been inside one of those factories, seen the workers toiling?"

Until the day he died he would never forget his horror of watching a young man with body black from head to toe and upper arms as rounded and firm as cannonballs stoking one of those monstrous fires. The floor he stood on was so hot that Aynsley had been unable to stay in the sweltering chamber for more than a few seconds. He swallowed. "Once."

"Did you not feel excessively guilty?" she asked.

Her question stunned him. How could she understand him so perfectly? Guilt was exactly what he had felt that day. Guilt that he could walk away and live in luxury in an oak tree–laden parkland. Guilt that he was at liberty to do whatever he pleased whenever he pleased. Guilt that he consumed the products manufactured at those huge iron monsters.

But he did not wish to own his guilt—or any of his emotions—to this woman. It was not in his nature to discuss his feelings with anyone. He had certainly never done so with Dorothy, who found such talk—and her husband—exceedingly boring. He never allowed any of his friends to glimpse into the idealist side of him. Yet in a very short time he had grown close to this woman. "The visitation was not all negative. A positive came from it."

"Your commitment to reform?"

"Yes."

"I wonder how many children are employed at those factories?"

"Quite a few."

"I do hope you'll work to outlaw such a practice."

He stiffened. "I will own, my dear, that I feel beastly sorry for the poor mites, but it's far better to be drawing a wage than to be begging in the streets."

She glared at him. "Do you mean you *favor* the employment of children?"

"As a matter of fact, I do! I employ several lads at the mines I own, and they are handsomely compensated. Most of them are in fatherless homes where theirs is the only income with which to feed their families."

"I can think of no worse place for a young boy to work than in a mine. Have you no conscience?"

"I most certainly do! That is why I pay the lads the same as I pay their adult counterparts."

"Their daily wage is *not* what I was referring to! You should be ashamed to admit you expose mere children to such hardships."

His body went rigid and his mouth folded into a grim line. "Let us speak of the topic no more. It appears we shall never agree."

"Then I am very sorry."

Those were the same words she had uttered when he told her he had turned his back on God.

And both times her words made him feel small.

Chapter Six

Not far from the Birmingham environs the sky returned to blue, and a verdure landscape replaced the proliferation of sooty row houses. "We'll be at Dunton in a few minutes," he told her.

She pressed her face to the glass again. "I don't see any houses yet, only..." She stiffened. "Acres and acres of rich farmland. Don't tell me you own all this land."

"Then I won't."

She whipped back to face him. "Do tell me. Is all this yours?"

He shook his head. "No. It's ours."

"Oh, my goodness, you must be very rich."

He smiled. "We're very rich." He gazed from the window and saw Dunton's gray stone walls and turreted roof silhouetted against the waning sunlight. The grand old pile still had the power to fill him with pride.

"That's it?" She pointed toward the home where he and his father before him had been born.

"It is."

"Oh, but my goodness, it's magnificent!"

"I know I risk your censure for my pride, but I cannot deny I'm very proud of Dunton Hall."

"Now I understand," she said, her voice quiet, almost reverent. "I feel terribly proud that it's going to be my home."

Her words buoyed him. "If you will peer from the glass on the other side of the carriage, you can glimpse your wedding present."

"My wedding present?"

He nodded. "A small farm that I was able to purchase very cheaply recently. I thought you might enjoy a little piece of land to call your own." He hoped, too, that one day she would pass it to her child, a child born of this marriage.

She nearly flew across the seat and gaped. "The land between the hedgerows?"

"That's it, my lady."

This once, she did not upbraid him for addressing her in such a manner.

"Oh, John, it's beautiful! It's the most wondrous present I've ever received." As the coach turned, she met his gaze. "Thank you."

A moment later the carriage halted in front of Dunton, and the footman rushed to lower the step and assist them in disembarking.

As the newlyweds stood on the gravel drive, he smiled down at her. "Your new home, Lady Aynsley."

She bristled. "Just because I said I was proud to call Dunton home does not mean I shall be proud to be known as Lady Aynsley!"

"Forgive me."

"Of course, I know it cannot be easy for you to change something that's been second nature to you for three and forty years." She gazed up at Dunton's solid walls. "It's so…big."

His hand went to her waist. "Which should in no way discourage an efficient woman like you. You did, after all, single-handedly catalog the whole of Lord Agar's library. I expect you'll have this place running as smoothly as a man-of-war in a matter of weeks."

She gave a decided tilt to her chin. "Indeed I sh—"

The door burst open and Chuckie came flying to him. "Papa! Papa's here! Will you give me a piggy-back ride?"

"Not just now." Though Aynsley was inordinately happy to see the little fellow—who loved piggyback rides above almost everything—he wished his youngest son could have dressed in a more…acceptable manner. He scooped the lad into his arms. "My goodness but you've grown! You're quite the big boy since last I saw you." Then he turned to Rebecca, whose eyes twinkled with merriment.

"This must be Chuckie," she said.

Chuckie gave her a most perplexing look and would not speak.

"Say hello to your new mama," Aynsley said.

The lad shook his head. "I don't want her."

"Charles Allen Compton, that is a terrible thing to say to this lady who has been longing to meet her little boy."

"I'm not Charles Allen Compton. My name's James Hock."

"Not this again," he said through gritted teeth.

Her smile not faltering, Rebecca stepped closer.

Chuckie buried his face into his father's chest. "I don't wike her eyes."

"Oh, the poor little lamb," she crooned. "I expect he's never seen someone wear spectacles before." She took them off. "Look at me now, Chuckie. My eyes are perfectly normal."

His head shifted a fraction of an inch. When he saw she no longer wore the glasses, he turned to face her, his gaze riveted to the spectacles dangling from her hands.

"Don't my eyes look normal now, pet?" she asked.

He would not answer.

"While I admit on the outside my eyes look normal, on the inside, they are most deficient. If a penny were lying at our feet I would not be able to see it—unless I was wearing these silly-looking things." She handed him the glasses. "Here, look through them."

Chuckie perked up and reached for the spectacles, wasting no time in holding them up to his eyes. "I can't see good."

"That's because you already have good eyes," she said.

Even though the spectacles were much too large for his small face, in a matter of seconds he had fastened them to his ears and squirmed from his father's arms to rush into the house.

"Tell your brothers," Aynsley called after him, "they have permission to take leave of lessons with Mr. Witherstrum to come meet their new mother."

The door slammed in their faces.

"Pray, my lord," she said, "why does your son wear a bucket on his head?"

"He thinks he's in the Horse Guards."

"I see. The bucket is his helmet."

"Exactly."

"So that also explains why he's got a pair of white stockings crossing his chest."

Aynsley frowned. "He does not perceive that anyone could doubt him a soldier in his majesty's army."

Rebecca's interaction with his youngest child could not have pleased him more. She obviously possessed an inherent understanding of children.

A pity Emily was no longer a child.

He drew a deep breath as he and his wife climbed the steps and entered Dunton Hall. He dreaded facing his daughter. The very day before his wedding he had received a letter from Emily that only thinly veiled her displeasure over his marriage. Understandably, it would be difficult for her to see another woman supplant her mother, difficult to relinquish the reins of running the hall.

No sooner had a footman closed the door behind them than he glimpsed his lovely daughter slowly descending the broad staircase hugging one of the walls of the hall's great entry corridor. Her snail's pace was a complete departure from the way she normally flew into his arms after he'd been away.

He set his hand at Rebecca's waist and beamed up at Emily. The sight of her fair loveliness always filled him with pride. "Here comes my daughter."

"Oh, how I wish I had my spectacles," Rebecca lamented.

Emily's eyes narrowed as she reached the bottom step and faced Rebecca. "Pray, if you need spectacles, do wear them."

Anger surged within him. How dare his daughter speak so rudely to his bride. But as much as he wanted to rebuke her, he did not want to add fuel to the flames.

He did not want to do anything that would make poor Rebecca more uncomfortable than she already was. "Charles Allen Compton!" he thundered. "Come at once with my lady's spectacles."

A flurry of footsteps thumped above them, and Chuckie—spectacles slipping from his nose—pounded down the stairs, both brothers at his heels. Thank goodness Spencer and Alex were dressed as the gentlemen they were. Lamentably, nothing could be done about Chuckie.

"Here, Mother," Chuckie said to the new Lady Aynsley, placing the spectacles in her hand.

Her lovely face contorted with fury, Emily snapped, "She is not your mother!"

He could no longer ignore his daughter's hostility. "That will be enough, Emily. You are not to dictate how your brothers will address my new wife."

Rebecca, still managing to smile despite her chilly reception, donned her spectacles, whisked her gaze over Emily and said, "Oh, Emily *is* beautiful. I knew she would be."

"How very kind of you, my lady," Emily replied stiffly.

"I beg that you be less formal with my wife. She prefers *not* to be addressed as *my lady.*"

Emily rolled her pale blue eyes. "I can hardly call her mother."

"Of course, you can't," Rebecca said, "but I'd be ever so much more comfortable if you would call me Rebecca."

"As you wish, Rebecca."

"And these, my love," Aynsley said, peering at the boys, "are my middle sons."

Rebecca eyed them. "Don't tell me. The one with the blond hair is Spencer, and the handsome lad with red hair is Alex."

Both of them bestowed smiles on their stepmother—for which Aynsley was exceedingly grateful.

"I've been waiting in rotund anticipation for this elucidating meeting, my fair lady," Alex said.

"He means profound anticipation," Emily corrected, her eyes narrowed to slits.

"As have I," Rebecca replied. "I'm so very fortunate to have a ready-made family for I'm exceedingly fond of lads."

Emily gave her an icy glare, went to say something, then clamped her mouth shut.

He had never been more uncomfortable in his own home.

The door burst open and Peter came striding in, dirt from his dusty boots leaving a trail across the white marble floor. "Uncle! You're here." His glance flicked to Rebecca. "This must be the new Lady Aynsley. Welcome to Dunton. I hope you will be very happy here."

Rebecca nodded as she bestowed a smile upon him. "Thank you. You must be Peter Wallace."

Aynsley stepped forward. "Dearest, may I present to you my nephew, Peter Wallace."

"I am delighted to make your acquaintance."

"Now," Aynsley said, "I beg to take leave of all of you. I wish to show Lady Aynsley our chambers."

He did not even want to think of how outraged Emily would be to have another woman move into her mother's former bedchamber. As angry as he was over his daughter's blatant ill manners, his heart softened toward her. She had lost her mother; now she must feel she was losing her father, too. He had to assure her she would always be his cherished daughter.

"Will all the children dine with us?" Rebecca asked.

It had never occurred to him to allow children at the dining table. "I suppose they could this once. It is, after all, a special occasion." He drilled Chuckie with a stern stare. "But you, Master Charles, must be on your best behavior. No accidents."

Chuckie hung his head, nodding. "Did you bwing pwessents?"

"You will have your presents after dinner."

At the mention of receiving a present from her father, Emily's mouth curved into a smile. Her first. His presents had never disappointed. He hoped that success would continue.

"There wasn't time to redecorate the countess's chambers," Aynsley said as he swung open the door to the most beautiful bedchamber Rebecca had ever beheld. Gold silken draperies had been opened, and a wall of tall windows filled the creamy room with light. Everything was gilt and ivory and gold silk. Much too sedate for Rebecca's taste, but lovely nonetheless. "You must feel free to redecorate in a manner consistent with your taste. It can be your first function as lady, er, mistress of the manor."

She stood frozen in the room's doorway, her gaze slowly fanning across the utterly feminine chamber with its French dressing table, ornate looking glass and a magnificent bed draped in more gold silk. "It's so beautiful." Then she turned to him. "I declare, I feel such a fish out of water. I never thought that marrying you would bring...all of this. I just wanted a home of my own—and many children to nurture."

He frowned. "But not a husband."

Without being aware of what she was doing, she reached out and stroked his arm. "I'm coming to learn that having a husband such as you could be the best part of being married." Good heavens, what could have made her say such a thing? She moved into the chamber, going straight to one of the windows.

He came to stand behind her.

There was even more to appreciate outdoors. In the distance a verdant walking trail circled a serpentine lake, beyond which was a thicket. "I shall never want to go back to London," she said. "This is wonderful." She turned to him. "As lovely as the countess's chamber is, I shall redecorate it to suit my own taste—that is, if you can afford it." She didn't give a fig about decorating, but she suddenly found herself possessed of a strong desire to eradicate any signs of her predecessor from this room.

"I assure you *we* can afford it." He strode toward a door on an interior wall. "This is your dressing chamber. It connects with mine."

It seemed so peculiar that she and this man would live together as man and wife. *Almost.*

It was also difficult to credit that the man with whom she'd been so comfortable for the past three days owned a hefty portion of Shropshire and commanded his children with stern authority. This powerful man seemed a stranger now.

Then he gave her that rakish smile, and he was once more the man who had shared her carriage, the man who had won her deep admiration. "You, my dear, will need to rest and change out of your traveling clothes for dinner. We eat at five."

When he escorted her into the dining room, she once again felt like a fish out of water. The size and grandeur of the chamber only served to remind her of the disparity of their backgrounds. She had brought nothing to this marriage. What did she really even know about being a mother? Indulging Maggie's sons was nothing like being responsible for Lord Aynsley's. And she was well aware of Lady Emily's resentment. Quite naturally, the girl would not want a stranger replacing her mother, nor would she welcome that stranger who would supplant her as mistress of her home. Rebecca could see that Emily's authority for running Dunton Hall could only be relinquished in the tiniest of increments.

When Chuckie had called her *Mother,* she had positively melted. It affected her even more profoundly to realize this was the first time in his short life he'd had someone to call *Mother.* She had made a vow to herself on the spot to be the kindest of mothers to the adorable little boy.

The children, all of them dressed impeccably, were already seated at the long dinner table beneath three multitiered crystal chandeliers that lit up the chamber almost as brightly as daylight.

With effort, she refrained from laughing when she saw Chuckie seated there. He was so small his head barely protruded above the table's surface. As she drew nearer she saw that he was perfectly dressed with a freshly starched cravat around his little neck. "I declare," she said, "I believe Master Chuckie needs a very large book to sit upon if he's going to sup at the big persons' table."

"That's what we told him," Spencer said, "but he was not obliging."

"My name's not Chuckie!" the child protested loudly.

"It is, too," Alex argued.

Chuckie's face clouded. "Is not."

"Yes, it is!" Alex yelled.

Aynsley leveled a stern gaze at Alex. "Enough."

The boy clamped shut his lips.

"I beg that you procure a tall book to elevate Master Chuckie," Rebecca said to the footman.

"Grandpapa's *Plutarch's Lives!*" Emily said, rising. "I'll fetch it."

Rebecca favored the lady with a smile. Did Emily fear the footman could not read? More likely, he would have no idea where to look for one particular title among the many hundred in her husband's library. Rebecca turned back to Chuckie. "How very handsome you look tonight, Mr. Hock."

Chuckie beamed. "Thank you, Mother."

"She's not your mother," Spencer said.

Alex glared at his elder brother. "There, my brother, you're wrong. She actually is our mother, our stepmother."

"See," Chuckie said. "She is my mother." He looked up at Rebecca with his enormous blue eyes.

"Our Heavenly Father has sent me to be your mother because He needed your other mother with Him," she explained. She quickly glanced at Lady Emily, who was lugging a voluminous tome and placed it beneath her youngest brother.

When Rebecca took her seat at the foot of the table she realized that for the past three years Emily had undoubtedly occupied it. She turned and addressed her stepdaughter. "How kind of you to save this chair for me. I cannot tell you how honored I am to take it." Her gaze leaped to Aynsley at the table's other end, though her view of him was partially obstructed by a large silver epergne laden with fruit. "And how honored I am to be your countess, my lord." It was important to her that Emily not think her a scheming fortune hunter, that she realize Rebecca's true sense of humility.

Halfway through the soup, Rebecca addressed Emily. "Pray, Emily, do we have you to thank for Master Chuckie's most agreeable appearance?"

Emily sighed. "It was no easy task, I assure you."

"The lad is, I'm told, particularly fond of his Guards uniform."

"See, Alex, I told you people can tell I'm in the Gawds," Chuckie said.

Alex shook his red head vigorously. "Our new mother is just being nice to you, imbecile."

"You are *not* to call your brother an imbecile," Aynsley scolded. "Apologize."

"Pray, forgive me *Mister* Hock." Alex's eyes narrowed.

Sitting on his linen-covered book, Chuckie glared at his sibling like an overbearing monarch. "I don't even know what an abacile is."

"It's imbecile, you idiot!" Alex said, then sheepishly peered at his father from beneath lowered brows.

His father uttered but three words. "To your room."

"Yes, my lord." A now-remorseful Alex scooted from his chair and cowered from the room.

It took every ounce of restraint Rebecca could muster not to protest, not to beg that Alex be allowed to stay at the table during their first meal together. But she could not undermine her husband's authority. Especially in front of the children.

After he was gone, she said, "I beg that you allow the children to dine with us again tomorrow night, my lord, for I'm determined that all of us will enjoy a meal together."

"I shall take that under consideration." He looked at the sons who remained. "It will depend now on the conduct of Spencer and Chuckie."

"I don't know who Chuckie is," the tiny lad said.

Rebecca and Emily exchanged exasperated glances. "My youngest brother most decidedly has a mind of his own."

"I daresay I was a far more trying child than Chuckie because I went for a very long time refusing to answer to Rebecca. I wished to be Robin. In fact," she said with a laugh, "I wished to be Robin Hood. I was excessively enamored of him."

Everyone at the table laughed. "That's Alex's favorite book. He says he's read it thirty-eight times," Emily said.

Rebecca and her husband peered at one another. "You told me before you met him," Aynsley said, "that you thought Alex had a great deal in common with you when you were a child."

"But she's not a carrottop like Alex," Spencer added.

"You're not to call your brother a carrottop," Aynsley said. "You know how he dislikes that."

Spencer frowned. "Yes, Papa."

"Papa?" Chuckie said.

"Yes?"

"Can Alex have his pwesent after dinner?"

Rebecca threw her husband a pleading look.

"What do you think, Lady Aynsley?" her husband asked.

"I beg that you allow him to. You must realize the lads are not accustomed to dining with adults."

"Very well."

"And," Rebecca met Aynsley's gaze, "oblige me by addressing me by my Christian name when it's just family."

A look of distaste on his face, Aynsley said, "Very well, madam."

Peter broke the long silence that followed. "Tell me, my lady, were you also in the habit of reading every waking hour as Alex does?"

"I still am. My sister marvels at how I can climb stairs while reading."

More laughter. Except from Emily, who glared.

After dinner they retired to the drawing room—another opulent room with some half a dozen silken sofas beneath full-length Gainsborough portraits and Italian masters. Aynsley's glance darted to Alex as he strode into the room, a contrite look on his face and a very thick book in his hand.

"Do you play the pianoforte, my love?" Aynsley asked Rebecca.

"Very poorly."

"One who reads incessantly, I daresay, has little time to develop other talents," Emily said.

Rebecca smiled. "How right you are. My ladylike accomplishments are most inferior."

"But," Aynsley defended, coming to place a firm hand on her shoulder, "her ladyship is possessed of other accomplishments. I am told her organizational skills are remarkable, and I believe her more than a competent writer." Dash it all! He wasn't supposed to know of her writing talent.

"You could tell that from the single letter I wrote you?" his wife asked.

Thank goodness she had penned that one note to him back in London. Though its purpose had been to inform him she was accepting his invitation to the opera, it had cleverly been put to verse. "My dear, one cannot hide so great a talent."

Rebecca shrugged, then eyed her stepdaughter. "I beg that you play for us, Lady Emily. Your father has told me how much pleasure he derives from your musical talent."

"Very well." Lady Emily moved to the pianoforte with grace and elegance.

While she was playing, he reached into his large sack and began to distribute the children's gifts. Alex was inordinately happy to receive four new books, and Spencer delighted in the gargoyle statue for his bedchamber. Chuckie waited patiently—well, actually not so patiently if one considered that he could not resist the urge to jump up and down—while his brothers got their presents.

"And for you, Chuckie…" His father paused.

Leap. Leap. "What? What?"

"I've brought you a new uniform." He pulled from the bag a little red coat with shiny brass buttons, epaulets and crossed white sashes.

Chuckie squealed and rushed to try it on. Amidst protests from his siblings, he peeled off all his clothes.

Emily turned scarlet.

Alex and Spencer—along with their elder cousin—laughed hysterically.

Aynsley himself had to force back the propensity to smile. "You could have put it on *over* your shirt," he said in a stern voice. "It's not proper to remove your clothing when you're in the drawing room. Especially in front of ladies."

Chuckie was not listening. He was too intent upon buttoning up the jacket over his bare chest. "I got to get my swowd." He went to dash off.

"Not until you put your breeches on!" his father scolded. "Come here at once."

Chuckie stopped, pivoted and scooped up his breeches but could not take time out to put them on.

His brothers continued to wail with laughter.

It was all Aynsley could do not to join them.

He finally allowed himself to meet his wife's gaze. Her cheeks dimpled with a deep smile, and her eyes flashed with humor. "I believe Chuckie likes his present," she said.

Aynsley shrugged and shook his head.

"As you can see, my lady," Peter said, "the lads will need some motherly instruction on proper behavior."

Emily glared at her cousin, but he was still looking at Rebecca. "I don't suppose you've had the opportunity to meet Uncle Ethelbert yet?"

"Does she know?" Emily asked her father.

All eyes leaped to Rebecca.

She nodded. "Yes, I've been told of your uncle's exceedingly peculiar habit."

Aynsley picked up the bag and strode to the pianoforte where Emily sat. "For you, dear love, I've brought some lengths of lace and silk. Rebecca's sister, Lady Warwick, assisted me in making the selections."

"Unlike my wretched self, my sister is cognizant of what is fashionable," Rebecca said.

He handed the bag to Emily.

Her mouth gaped open as she removed the fabric from the sack. "Oh, my goodness, I've never seen such lovely fabric." Her glance flicked from her father to Rebecca, to whom she spoke. "I am greatly indebted to Lady Warwick for this is the very kind of silk and lace for which I've been so desirous. I cannot wait until Mrs. Egerton fashions these into gowns."

She stood and draped the fabric over her rose-hued dress and began to waltz around the room.

"What a beauty you'll be in those gowns," Peter said.

For once, Aynsley was *not* out of charity with Peter's remark. "Lady Warwick assures me dresses of such fabric will be all the rage during your come out."

Emily stopped and glared at her father. "I don't want a come out. I prefer to stay at Dunton."

Aynsley's face was grim. "And I prefer that you go to London."

Without a word, she neatly folded the fabric and returned to the pianoforte where she began pounding at the keys in a most agitated manner. In her own way, his daughter was every bit as obstinate as Chuckie.

Rebecca had gone to sit on the sofa near the boys. "What are you reading, Alex?"

He looked up from the tome he'd brought. "Homer."

She smiled. "There are some very exciting stories there, if I recall."

"I like it very much," he said. "Of course, I'm reading an English translation. I have not yet sufficient command of Greek."

"I know Greek," Spencer boasted.

"You do not!" Alex shouted.

"I do, too!" Spencer's fist balled and he slugged his brother.

Alex kicked him.

"Boys!" Aynsley frowned.

Like two soldiers at review, they straightened up and directed remorseful looks at their father.

"But Spencer lied," Alex said. "He can't read Greek, except for infantile words."

"Infantile. Imbecile. Why can't you use normal words?" Spencer demanded.

Alex glared at his brother. "You're such a baby."

"I'm two years older than you are!"

If his sons kept up at this rebellious state, Rebecca would be sure to take the next post chaise back to London. "I beg that you boys show your new mother that you can comport yourselves as gentlemen," Aynsley implored.

The door banged open, and Chuckie, waving a crudely fashioned wooden sword, burst into the room. His father was relieved that he'd restored his breeches.

"Papa says you have to sheathe your sword when you're in the drawing room," Alex told his younger brother.

Slashing the stick in the direction of his brothers, Chuckie ignored the admonishment.

"A pity you could not commission a small-size helmet for him," Emily lamented. "One grows tired of seeing that ridiculous bucket stuffed over his head."

"It's not a bucket," Chuckie protested.

"It is, too," Alex said.

His brows lowered, Aynsley effectively silenced Alex with The Glare. "You don't always have to have the last word, Alex."

Alex's lips puckered into a pout. "Yes, my lord."

Whether to make peace or to make mischief, his daughter directed her attention to Rebecca. "Tomorrow I'll guide you around Dunton. I'm sure you're anxious to *change the guard,* so to speak."

"How very kind of you to offer," said Rebecca, dispelling his uneasiness. "I look forward to learning all about Dunton Hall, but my work is cut out for me if I'm ever to manage as capably as your father tells me you do."

When Aynsley walked with his bride upstairs an hour later, he felt as if he'd come from an Iberian battlefield. He was exhausted and irritable and excessively disappointed in his boys' behavior. "You must see how badly my children need discipline. I only hope that you won't change your mind about staying at Dunton."

"I assure you I will not. Not ever. I told those boys the Heavenly Father had sent me."

"But you haven't met Ethelbert yet."

She stopped on the tread and whirled to face him. "I knew *everything* when I agreed to marry you. Do you think I'm a flighty girl prone to changing her mind?"

He touched her chin. "There's nothing flighty or girlish about you."

She resumed the climb. "I'm gratified that you understand that."

They reached the second floor and strolled toward

their bedchambers. "May I come sit with you for a few moments? There are a few matters I'd like to discuss."

"Of course."

They went to sit in front of the fire on a silk brocade settee. "I wished to discuss my children," he began.

"Our children now."

Her simple declaration was a balm for his perpetual loneliness. The thing he had missed most with Dorothy's death was losing the one person who loved their children as he did. Though the marriage had never been a love match, love for their children abounded. Could the potency of those feelings transfer to his new wife?

He studied her as a painter would his subject. Only the most extraordinarily gifted artist would be able to capture the juxtaposition of brandy highlights in her coffee-colored hair or the rosy hue tingeing her cheeks from the fire's blaze. He wondered how a painter could do justice to the sweep of long, thick lashes that framed her eyes like an ebony garland. "I had hoped the children would be on their best behavior for you," he said. "Unfortunately, they were not."

"You're too demanding. They're good children. Really."

"And Emily? What is her excuse for her abominable conduct toward you?"

"Her conduct certainly was not abominable. It's natural that she might resent that I'm here to displace her—and worse yet, I might be trying to displace the mother she dearly loved."

His wife made a good point. Two, actually. "Doesn't she know it's for her own good? I want her to marry and have a home and children of her own."

"I imagine she thinks she could marry Peter and never have to leave Dunton."

"And when I die? When Johnny's wife—when he takes one—usurps Emily's authority here?"

Rebecca held up her hand and winced. "I beg you not to speak of that!"

Her aversion to thinking of his death gave him a measure of pleasure. He shrugged. "I must apologize for my daughter. I shall have to speak to her."

"Please don't. It needs but time. She doesn't know me. No doubt she sees me as a fortune-hunting woman who's going to be a wicked stepmother."

The notion was so far removed from the truth he had to laugh.

"And I want to talk to you about your unnecessary sternness with the boys," she said.

"I thought you and I agreed—back in London—that discipline was what was needed."

"That was before I met the little darlings."

"Don't tell me you're going soft?"

She shrugged. "Let's just say I think you're excessively stern. You don't want the boys to fear you—or to hate you. Banishing poor Alex from the dinner table was terribly harsh. All he did was speak his mind."

"He called his brothers names!"

"Hardly a mortal sin. You must remember he's a middle child. He's likely jealous of Spencer because he's older and has had more experiences, and he cannot compete with Chuckie for cuteness and lovability. He has to draw attention to himself by being superior at something."

"So he's superior by using big words to ridicule his brothers?"

She nodded. "And by reading. Reading is his vehicle to amassing more knowledge than Spencer."

He could not argue with her. She made too much sense. He settled back against the settee and sighed. "If I hadn't stopped them, their fisticuffs would have broken the furniture and everything else in the drawing room. Surely you don't think I should have allowed them to go at each other."

She put hands to hips. "Of course not! Physical outbursts should never be tolerated. Besides," she added, her voice softening, "they might have hurt one another."

He had to laugh. In fact, he was filled with happiness over his bride's brimming affection for his children. He could not remember the last time he had felt happy. "Well, at least we're in agreement over something concerning my offspring."

"I don't object to you correcting Alex when he disparages one of his brothers, but I think your excessive anger was unwarranted."

Could she be right? Was he being too stern a disciplinarian?

"If you want them to love and respect you, you must be less severe," she said.

He could see the wisdom in what she was saying. "I shall try, but how will I ever get them to behave in a more gentlemanly manner?"

"Let me work on that. You, sir, have other important matters to dwell on."

"Like parliamentary reform?"

"Yes."

"The most pressing thing on my agenda is showing Lady Aynsley over the grounds of her new home. Do you ride?"

"I've had very little opportunity to do so in London, but I practically lived on horseback in Virginia."

"Good. Are you an early riser?"

"I am."

"Then it will be my pleasure to take you riding tomorrow morning."

"And afterward, when I'm counting linen or some such thrilling task, what will you be doing?"

"I have many papers that demand my attention." He stood and gazed down at her. "In fact, my library beckons. I'll start tonight."

She stood and walked with him to the door. "Good night, dearest," she murmured.

A rush of tender emotions washed over him as he looked down at her and—without intending to—bent to kiss her.

She did not push him away. She put her hands flat against his chest and kissed him in return. When he pulled away, he gently pushed up the spectacles that had slid down her nose. "Good night, dear one."

Instead of departing her room into the corridor—and thus announcing that Lord and Lady Aynsley did not sleep together—he left through their connecting dressing rooms.

Any doubts he may have had about hurrying into his marriage had been soundly dispelled this first day back at Dunton. How very good it felt to have a partner with whom to share his life—and his children.

Were it not for Emily's hostility, his happiness would have been nearly overpowering.

Chapter Seven

Rebecca stood like a statue and watched Aynsley go. Their kiss had left her stunned. Kissing had never been something that appealed to her. But when Lord Aynsley's head had bent toward hers it seemed perfectly natural that their lips should come together. What was *not* natural was her response to the action. She had not been repulsed, and she had actually participated in it!

When he pulled back, she was embarrassed. Would he think her a loose woman? But when he'd called her *dear one,* she realized their bond was sanctified by their wedding ceremony, a bond that would meld their lives together until death separated them. Together they would raise the children. She was astonished over how quickly the lads had won her complete affection, how powerful was her sense of protectiveness toward them.

Emily, however, would be a challenge.

Later—after she'd donned her nightclothes and lay in her bed in the darkened chamber—she prayed. *Please, Lord, help me be a good mother. Please guide my hus-*

band back to You. And please help me to love Emily as if she were my own daughter.

After breakfast, she and Aynsley walked hand in hand across Dunton's verdant park toward the stables. A single gravel path cut in identical halves the broad lawn surrounding Dunton Hall. Tall, classical statues stood as if they were sentries every twenty feet along the path. "These statues are Roman antiquities my father brought back from his grand tour," Aynsley explained.

Next, they strolled along one side of the picturesque lake. "It's purely ornamental," he told her.

"You mean the lake is man-made?"

He nodded.

"I must say, the English certainly know how to landscape." As soon as the words were out of her mouth, she glimpsed a rather formidable-looking two-story structure built of the same gray stone as the house. "What building is that?"

"The mews."

"Dear heavens! How many horses have you?" She did not know stables could be *that* large.

"*We,* my dear."

No one could be more unworthy than she. "You're much too generous, dearest." She felt more self-conscious than ever to be using such an endearment to this man, especially since the kiss of the previous night. "You did not answer my question." They entered the stable.

"Because I've never thought about it. Stanley, my steward, keeps up with such matters. I suppose there must be around thirty—but not all of them suitable for mounting. Today, you'll ride Emily's." He paused at a stall occupied by a white-footed chestnut.

"She's a beauty," Rebecca said.

"For today, she's yours. I'll select you a mount of your own someday soon."

Within a few minutes a groom had saddled the horses, and Lord and Lady Aynsley began to canter to the western portion of the property. From a distance, he showed her the acres farmed by tenants, and from a hilltop they looked down on the humble village of Wey. They raced through an apple orchard, galloped along the perimeter of the rolling sheep pasture and finished the tour of Aynsley lands by leading their horses to drink at the serpentine lake, which was spanned by a hump-back stone bridge. "I've always wished to walk on one of those bridges," she said.

He dropped the reins and offered his hand. "Then let's."

At the bridge's crest they stopped and propped their elbows on the stone baluster while they gazed over the sparkling blue lake. Directly in front of them on the other side of the lake a domed folly was flanked by two clusters of evergreens.

When he tossed a pebble, she was mesmerized by the ripple. "I cannot believe the sun has favored us today." She smiled as she looked up into his pensive face.

"I was hoping it would be a fair day for your first impression of Dunton."

He spoke of Dunton with the same pride that infused his voice when he discussed his children. She could well understand how such a lovely piece of property could instill such powerful feelings. Just knowing it was her new home gave her a wondrous sensation. "You love Dunton very much, do you not?"

"I do. I'm always happiest here."

"Then your work in Parliament is even more commendable." She took the opportunity to stare at his profile—the perfectly straight nose, the tiny cleft in his chin, the firm set of his jaw. She realized he was quite handsome.

"It's an obligation I feel strongly, even though I loathe having to leave Dunton to go to London."

"I understand—even more now that I'm here. I wish we never had to leave."

His brows lowered as he turned to her. "Surely you cannot be so attached to Dunton so soon?"

"Anyone would be. It's so…so peaceful and comforting and solid. It quite gives one a feeling of utter contentment."

"That's exactly how it affects me."

"Then we have much in common. In fact, if it weren't for your odious support of children laboring, we would be completely compatible. I do intend to do everything I can to change your tolerance of that beastly practice."

"I am not going to be a puppet for you or any woman, Rebecca."

She could tell she'd angered him. "It's not being a puppet. It's seeing the light."

"Seeing the light sounds suspiciously religious to me. If you think to change me in that regard, too, you'd best think again." He stalked away and took up the reins.

"Do I come with you?" she asked, feeling like a child who'd just been punished.

"Yes. It's time you meet Ethelbert."

They rode in silence. She felt guilty for angering him, but if she had it to do over again, she would do the same. That was her problem. She could never compromise her convictions. Or her faith.

The dowager house was closer to the main road than Dunton Hall and was set several hundred yards away from the main house. It was neither grand like Dunton Hall was nor was it constructed of stone. It was a typical wattle-and-daub cottage with thatched roof and trellis over the doorway. She fleetingly thought of how cozy and comforting it would be to raise a cherished family within its walls. Goodness gracious! What was getting into her? The former Miss Rebecca Peabody never thought about such things. Always, her mind whirled with political theory and the wisdom of Greek and Roman scholars.

Her husband assisted her from Emily's horse. "You are prepared for my uncle's peculiar practice?"

She nodded. But how did one *really* prepare for being accosted by an elderly lecher? Her heart began to beat unaccountably rapidly as they walked down the path to the cottage's front door.

A manservant let them in, bowing profusely at his employer. "So good to have you home, my lord."

"It's good to be back, Davis. Where's my uncle?"

"He's in front of the fire, your lordship."

They went to the drawing room, and she waited in the doorway while Aynsley strolled up to his kinsman. "Hello, Uncle, I've brought my new wife to meet you."

The white-haired Ethelbert, his eyes wide, spun around in his bath chair and began to roll across the chamber with prodigious speed. A smile fixed on his well-lined face, he raced toward her, his eyes dancing with every churn of his wheels.

She braced herself for his assault.

"Uncle! You must behave yourself!" Aynsley called as he made an attempt to intercept Ethelbert.

But he wasn't as quick as Ethelbert's well-honed skill with the invalid chair. The old man was not so much an invalid that he could not leap from the chair as soon as he reached the object of his attentions. "I must welcome the new lady with a kiss," he announced as he flung his frail body at Rebecca, his lips puckered as he clasped his arms around her.

She twisted her face away from his onslaught while patting him on the back. "It's very nice to meet you, Ethelbert," she said in her most authoritarian voice, "but I must insist that you return to your seat at once."

To her astonishment, he complied with her request.

Meeting her husband's eye, she shook her head ever so slightly, then turned a bright smile upon Ethelbert. "Should you like us to take you for a stroll outdoors?"

"Indeed, I would."

She saw the thin blanket on the sofa and fetched it. "Let's just put this over your lap so you don't catch a cold." She tucked it around him. Because he was so thin, she feared he would be sensitive to the day's chill. "There now. Comfy?"

He nodded as Aynsley began to push his bath chair toward the door.

It occurred to her that in his somewhat childlike state he had an inordinate attraction to females. Perhaps he'd missed there being no Lady Aynsley these past few years. "Tell me, Uncle Ethelbert," she began as they continued down the path toward the lake, "would you like to have dinner at the big house tonight?"

"What's that you say? Speak up, gal."

"I said," she shouted, "would you like to have dinner tonight at the big house?"

"Indeed, I would."

"You must promise to stay in your bath chair," she said.

"And you're not to attempt to kiss any ladies," Aynsley scolded, his voice elevated.

"You must listen to your nephew."

"He's a dull stick, just like his father," Ethelbert said. "Both of 'em as dull as a pair of wooden spoons."

She cast a bemused gaze at her husband. "Do you, indeed, take after your father?"

"Regrettably. My uncle is right."

"Uncle," she said. "I believe you mistake a high degree of propriety for dullness, and they are vastly different."

"Well of course, they both have a lot of property! They were both earls. But they weren't different. Two peas in a pod, they were."

She couldn't help herself; she began to giggle.

Aynsley joined her.

The next half hour was spent speaking in highly elevated voices to the poor man who still could not hear but every fifth word they uttered. By the time they returned him to the dowager's house, they were exhausted.

As Aynsley wheeled him up to the cottage door, he leaped from his bath chair, threw both arms around Rebecca and planted his lips upon hers.

She gently eased him away. "My dear Ethelbert, you must not be kissing the ladies tonight." She could well understand why his behavior had sent the last housekeeper packing.

"Yes, Uncle," Aynsley replied. "You're to be on your best behavior tonight."

* * *

There was one more thing Aynsley wished to show Rebecca that morning.

"Thank you for your superb handling of Uncle. I believe you've completely won him over." He gave her a leg up and handed her the reins.

"He's a dear. I do hope he will behave tonight for I do not at all like the idea of excluding him from the dinner table, and I know we must if he cannot comport himself in a proper manner."

He mounted his horse. "I'll own I don't like excluding him, either, but I have to be sensitive to Emily. She was not quite fifteen when I barred Uncle from the big house. She was much too frightened by his rash actions and too young to be exposed to his unacceptable behavior."

"I'm not blaming you. I'm sure I'd have done the same."

"Before we return to the hall I should like to show you your farm."

"I wasn't going to let you forget. It's undoubtedly the best present I have ever been given. I'm not into jewels as much as most women, but the idea of being given a living thing—land—is so elementally gratifying."

Somehow he'd known it would please her. Dorothy, on the other hand, would have been incensed over such a gift. "It's terribly small, there's no house on it, and it's completely barren because the neighbor who sold it to me was elderly and unable to farm it anymore. He's dead now."

"I don't need another house, and the fact it's barren gives me an opportunity to start from scratch. Not that

I have half a notion of what I'm going to do, but I look forward to learning something new."

A few minutes later they pulled up in front of her fallow farm. The road they were on formed one of its boundaries, and hedgerows formed the other three. "It's not quite two hectares."

The smile on her face could have warmed the coldest winter day. "Next to Dunton, it shall quite be my favorite place on earth." She turned to him. "Next to Dunton, is it not the most perfect place?"

"You must be blessed with the ability to see good where there's only bad. Speaking of the bad, I must tell you that you may not find Dunton's cavernous rooms and cold stone floors so fine on a dreary winter day."

"On those days I plan to sit before the fire in my chamber, drinking hot chocolate and peering out my casements as snow blankets the landscape."

"You almost make me regret spring is just around the corner."

Having someone who shared so many of his own ideas was a novel occurrence. A pity she did not trust him enough to reveal her secret. Would she, too, practice the deception at which Dorothy had been so very adept?

Rebecca's hand gripped the mellow wood banister as she and Emily climbed a staircase in the Tudor section of the house. "Pray, how many staircases *are* there at Dunton?"

Emily paused. "I've never counted. Let me see…"

"This is the third one I've seen!"

"I believe there may be eight."

What have I gotten myself into? Rebecca had to

school herself not to act like a wide-eyed child in front of Emily—though it was most certainly an apt description of her. It was obvious from the girl's icy demeanor that she was not satisfied with her father's selection of a bride. Even though Rebecca didn't give a fig about rank, she knew Emily did. And the girl undoubtedly looked down her aristocratic nose at her stepmother.

They began to walk along a long corridor on old oak floors that were laid in a herringbone pattern. "The portraits in this section date to the Tudor period," Emily told her as they strolled past many aged portraits of bearded men dressed in tights. On the opposite wall hung portraits of unsmiling women whose necks were encircled in stiff white collars.

"It's hard to believe a lovely girl like you could have sprung from these stern-looking women," Rebecca said. "There's not a blonde in the bunch."

"I believe the blond hair came from Mama's family. Most of the Comptons have had dark hair, and many of the earlier ones even had brown eyes."

Rebecca slowed down and gazed at one portrait of a bejeweled, black-eyed woman with a headdress and a stunning ruby necklace lying against milky-white skin. "Now this lady *was* beautiful."

Emily's mouth yielded a tight smile. "That is actually the first Countess Aynsley. She was a reputed beauty."

"Indeed she was."

They continued along until they came to a great room with walls of oak, floors of stone in the same gray as Dunton's exterior and ceilings that soared more than thirty feet overhead. A mustiness hung in the air. "As you can tell, since you are knowledgeable about Tudor architecture, this is the great room where banquets were once held. When Mama was alive we used it as a ballroom. Now, it's not used."

"I daresay you weren't old enough to dance here."

Emily's pretty face fell into a frown. "No, I wasn't."

"Should you like to once more have balls at Dunton?"

"I grew up dreaming of them."

"Then we shall have to have one—after you are presented."

Emily stiffened. "I have no desire to be presented."

"You have communicated that to all of us, but your father also has made it clear he intends to see that you have a Season in London."

"He's being very obtuse!" Emily's stride quickened as they swept through the great room.

The next room was a chapel that was intimate despite its high, vaulted ceilings. No more than twenty could be seated on its old wooden pews. Rebecca strolled down the tiny nave, knelt before the gilded crucifix that hung on the sanctuary wall between two arched Gothic stained-glass windows and began to pray. *Dear Lord, I thank You for this day. I thank You for bringing me to this man and his family, and I pray that You will guide me with Your wisdom.*

Her gaze lifted to the windows. The blessed Virgin Mary was on the left, England's patron saint, St. George, on the right. A sense of peace and deep contentment washed over her as she returned to a standing position and faced Emily. "What a wonderful place! Do you come here often?"

"Oh, dear me, no! I daresay it hasn't been used since the Dissolution."

"What a pity," Rebecca murmured.

Emily opened a rounded wood door and began to leave the chapel. "Papa's rather a heathen."

"I mean to change that."

Her stepdaughter whirled at her. "You can't just come in here and change things."

The harsh tone of her voice wounded Rebecca. "As to the physical, I plan to change very little. I will redecorate my private chambers because I believe it would be painful for you children to see another woman occupying a room that so distinctly bears the stamp of your dear mother. But as to the spiritual, I'm giving you notice that I hope to be the instrument that reunites God with all the Comptons."

Emily made no response as she led the way back to the Georgian section where their tour had originated. They began to mount still another staircase—this one as wide as a room and constructed of marble. "Would you like to see the nursery?"

"Indeed I would."

It was located on the third floor. Emily explained that the servants' rooms were also on the third floor. Which helped explain to Rebecca why the ceilings here were so much lower.

Chuckie was playing with tin soldiers on the carpeted floor. Knitting in a nearby rocking chair was his nurse, a kindly old woman they referred to as Beaver. They both looked surprised when the door creaked open. "Did you come to play soldiers with me?" Chuckie asked Rebecca, his bright blue eyes filled with hope.

She felt dreadfully guilty to disappoint him. "Not just now, my sweet. Emily's showing me around my new home, but I promise to come play with you very soon."

Emily spoke through gritted teeth. "You do not know what you're getting into."

"I daresay you're right, but the poor lamb must hunger for other children to play with."

"It is a shame. He's my only brother who was not paired with another of his own age."

Rebecca wondered if Dorothy would have given birth to another child, had she lived. Before they left the chamber, her gaze skimmed from the old wooden children's table that could accommodate from six to eight youngsters, to a bookcase crammed with slender, dog-eared volumes to the basket filled with toys, including a doll that must have been Emily's some years previously. At the far end of the room was a stage complete with curtains.

They said their farewells, and Emily proceeded to show her all the family members' bedchambers, along with closets for silver, linens and even the larder.

A highlight of the tour was seeing the more recent Compton family portraits. These hung in places of prominence for everyday activities—over the chimneypiece in the drawing room (the last earl) and the dining room (the last countess). *Dorothy.* John's wife. Why was it she thought of him as John while gazing at her predecessor? It was as if she wanted to reaffirm an intimacy with this woman's husband. Goodness gracious, could she possibly be jealous? In her entire eight and twenty years, Rebecca Peabody—now Rebecca Compton, the Countess of Aynsley—had *never* been jealous.

She did not want to be conspicuous gazing at the picture of Emily's mother. Besides, she had memorized every detail of the woman's face the previous night at dinner. Then, she'd been too shy to ask who the woman was. But she had known the handsome woman with wavy blond hair and eyes the same blue as Emily's and Chuckie's must be Dorothy.

And now she understood that she had—completely against her will—been imbued with a new vice.

Chapter Eight

Rebecca had been so busy since her arrival the previous afternoon, she'd had no opportunity to see Pru or to learn if she was happy with her new accommodations. Rebecca felt guilt that she could live wherever she chose—a choice never offered to a servant.

As Pru helped her dress for dinner, she inquired about her chamber.

"Oh, my lady, my chamber here has a fire as well as a window with a view of the lake. His lordship provides well for his servants."

Rebecca had flinched at being called *my lady,* but this once thought not to rebuke her servant. She was ever so relieved that Pru was not resentful about being displaced.

Just as she was clasping the pearls about her mistress's throat, Pru's hand stilled. "I declare, what can all that noise be?"

Rebecca had a very good idea. The sudden pounding of feet outside her chamber and a shrieking remarkably like Lady Emily's normally icy voice had burst into Dunton's stately quiet like a cannonball.

When she heard a babyish whimper, Rebecca leaped from her chair and bounded for the corridor. "Pray, what is going on?" she demanded as she threw open the door.

Chuckie skidded to a halt and eyed his stepmother. "She's being mean to me."

Rebecca tossed a sympathetic glance to Emily. "I cannot believe your sister would ever be mean to you."

"I was merely—" Emily started.

"She was, too, mean! She won't let me wear my wegimentals to dinner."

While Rebecca had no objection to Chuckie's wearing of regimentals to dinner, she could see that taking his side would further alienate Emily. "Come here, Mr. Hock," Rebecca said in her sternest voice.

Rubbing away the tears, Chuckie obliged.

Rebecca had to school herself not to drop to her knees and take the precious child in her arms, but the children needed to learn she was a figure of authority. "You sister is obviously concerned that your regimentals not get soiled by the food. What would you wear to battle tomorrow if your fine red coat has to be cleaned?"

"Then I won't spill my food tonight!"

His brothers, who had come to investigate the ruckus, guffawed. "You have the table manners of a swine," Alex said.

"I daresay that's why Miss Hatfield left," Spencer added. "She could not stomach watching you eat."

Rebecca effected a frown. "Now, boys! That's a wicked thing to say. I'm certain Miss Hatfield found Chuckie delightful."

The lad being discussed drew one last sniff and bestowed a radiant smile upon Rebecca as he began to divest himself of the bright red regimental coat.

"You can't disrobe in the presence of ladies," Spencer admonished.

"But I've gots to keep my uniform clean for tomowow's important battle."

In the battle being waged in this corridor, Rebecca had scored a victory.

Minutes later Aynsley knocked on her chamber door to escort her to dinner. His glance flicked to the pearls. "Careless of me to have neglected to get you the Aynsley jewels. You'll have them tomorrow." He proffered his arm, and they left the chamber. "How did your tour go?"

The tour of Dunton with Lady Emily that morning had been as enjoyable as getting a tooth extracted. Though her stepdaughter refrained from disparaging her, the girl's complete dislike of Rebecca was apparent in her chilling demeanor. But nothing would be served by imparting this information to Lord Aynsley. Rebecca wished to always foster the positive, banish the negative. "I enjoyed it very much. Dunton's far more grand than I'd expected, and it's obvious it's been run by an efficient and capable staff."

He shrugged. "You'll have to procure the services of a new housekeeper and a governess."

"The governess will have to be most qualified. The last one certainly was, if Alex's reading ability is any judge. Isn't he awfully young to read such big books?"

"I don't mean to boast, but he read very well at five. He had begged to sit in on Spencer's lessons, and despite his youth, he caught up with his brother quickly. So, I do believe the last governess must have been most capable."

"I do hope I can find one worthy of such brilliant

charges." She paused on the stairwell landing and gazed at his face, which was illuminated by a wall sconce. "I shall look forward to my first official duties as mistress of Dunton." But how would she wrestle the controls from Lady Emily's greedy palms? It was not a question she need pose to her husband. She not only wanted him to be proud of her, but she also prayed fervently that he would never regret his decision to marry her.

"I don't know if it's such a good idea to have the children eat with us," he said.

"After tonight, they can go back to eating in the nursery." She held her shoulders high and favored him with a smile. "I am determined to be so good a stepmother that I shan't lose my dinner no matter how much squishy squash or pulverized peas end up on Chuckie's cravat."

He burst out laughing.

In the dining room, the children—dressed in their Sunday best—had taken their seats. Alex and Spencer sat on one side, Emily, Peter and Chuckie across from them. Rebecca could well understand why Peter could not remove his adoring gaze from Emily. She looked especially lovely in a pale blue gown that captured the color of her eyes.

"How splendid you children look tonight," Rebecca told them.

Emily glared at her youngest brother, who teetered on the towering book. "I pray their table manners don't discredit their agreeable appearance."

"I declare," Rebecca said, scooting in her chair at the foot of the table, "what is that heavenly smell?"

"That's Cook's special French sauce," Aynsley said with pride.

Emily sighed. "Cook's the only dependable upper

servant we have." She smiled at her father. "I daresay that's because Papa pays her most handsomely. He lives in fear someone will snatch her away once they taste her French sauce."

During the soup course Spencer and Alex were on their best behavior, careful not to speak while eating—or in their case, slurping—their food. They also refrained from disparaging each other.

Aynsley cleared his throat and addressed his daughter. "Em, your stepmother will be relieving you of the burdensome mountain of responsibilities you've had to cope with of late."

"I pray that I'll be able to run things agreeably, with assistance from the new housekeeper, of course."

"Have you any prospects?" Emily eyed Rebecca. "It's not easy to entice prospective staff to relocate to the wilds of Shropshire."

Rebecca shrugged. "I have this afternoon dispatched letters to my sister and my best friend, Lady Agar. It's my hope they'll learn of someone from their vast network of acquaintances."

Peter chuckled. "Let us hope none of them have knowledge of Uncle Ethelbert."

At the mention of the eccentric uncle, both Rebecca and Aynsley exclaimed.

"The poor fellow must have forgotten," Aynsley said, shaking his head. "His memory's not what it used to be." He directed one of the footmen to go down to the dower house to collect Ethelbert.

Lady Emily's mouth gaped open. With narrowed eyes, she glanced at Rebecca, then at her father. "Surely you're not allowing him to eat with us!"

"If the children can sit at this table tonight, I see no

reason to exclude my uncle," Aynsley said, the tone of his voice dismissive.

Spencer and Alex exchanged amused glances. "We should not apostelate about Uncle Ethelbert," Alex said.

"Expostulate," Emily corrected.

"You're such a fraud," Spencer said to Alex, "using words so big you don't even understand them."

"I know more than you," Alex said as he kicked his brother.

"That's enough, boys!" their father said, his voice irritable and harsh.

Rebecca could see she would need to curtail the lads' disagreements. Their father particularly desired harmony; therefore, she would do everything in her power to see that he got it. Her voice stern, she said, "I shall have to implement a plan to encourage you to be more solicitous of one another."

Emily harrumphed. "Good luck."

Rebecca proceeded to empty the contents of her reticule onto the table.

The boys' eyes grew wide when they saw the pile of sparkling pence. "Now, let me see," she said, "what day of the week is it?"

"Friday," both boys uttered.

She nodded. "Then on Friday next you will be released from your lessons so that you may go into Wey and purchase pasties or comfits or whatever you like with these pence."

"We get all of those?" Spencer asked.

A broad smile transformed Alex's face. "We really get out of our lessons?"

She nodded. "Each of you shall have ten pence every Friday."

Spencer beamed. "Truly?"

Rebecca nodded. "Indeed you will."

His red brows drawing together, Alex asked, "What is the *caveat?*"

"How clever you are, Alex," Rebecca said, meeting her husband's amused gaze, "for there is a *caveat.*"

"Because I know Latin, I know what a caveat is, too," Spencer boasted. "Pray, milady, what is the *caveat?*"

Milady? Though she had specifically asked not to be referred to as a countess, she could only allow herself to address one offense at a time. She sighed. "Every time one of you speaks or acts unkindly to the other, I take away a coin."

Alex's lower lip worked into a pout. "Then I'll never get to go to Wey."

"I have much more confidence in you than you have in yourself," Rebecca said.

"Can you possibly understand how thoroughly Spencer aggravates me?"

"What does aggwevate mean?" asked Chuckie, whose cravat was the receptacle of more soup than his mouth.

"It means to make mad," Emily said.

"I for one am going to be most tolerant of my brothers," Spencer announced, bestowing bright smiles on each of his brothers.

"Prevaricator!" Alex shouted.

Rebecca reached out and withdrew a coin. "This pence goes from Alex's pile to my pocket."

Alex's eyes narrowed.

"Milady understands your big words, Alex." Spencer helped himself to sturgeon, then spooned some of

Cook's famed French sauce on it. "Prevaricator, indeed! Why can you not just say liar?"

Milady again. Not once the previous night had she been referred to by that title. Had the boys made some kind of pact to call her that?

"See, you called yourself a liar!"

"I did not!"

"Boys!" Their father drilled them with an angry stare.

"Yes, milord," a repentant Alex said.

"Pray," Emily said, glaring at Rebecca with hostility, "does my father approve of your bribery?"

"My wife has been given authority in everything that occurs at Dunton."

"I only wish to ensure that things run smoothly," Rebecca said.

Emily glowered. "Are you saying the house has not been running smoothly under me?"

"No. Of course not. Your father's very proud of all you've done."

"But I'm not proud of your demeanor now. I beg that you show your stepmother more courtesy," Aynsley said.

"My dear," Rebecca said to Aynsley, "I assure you Emily's been delightful." While Rebecca thoroughly disapproved of lying, she must do so now in order to shield Emily—as well as Emily's adoring father. She vowed to never do anything that would jeopardize the bond between them.

Chuckie gazed at Rebecca. "Mother?"

"She's not your mother," Spencer snapped, then met his sister's approving nod.

It took no great deductive skills for Rebecca to realize Emily had instructed her brothers *not* to refer to Rebecca as *Mother*. Rebecca smarted from the hostility in the boy's voice. "I explained this last night. I'm to be his earthly mother."

"Because our real mother's been called to heaven," Alex added.

"I'm sensible that you lads have fond memories of your mother, and I shan't wish you to ever forget her." Rebecca gazed at Chuckie, and her voice softened. "Chuckie, the dear lamb, never knew her. I'm honored more than I can ever convey to serve as mother to him—and to each of you. But I understand if you choose not to address me as such."

Just then a footman rolled Uncle Ethelbert into the room.

"Just make a place for him next to me," Aynsley instructed.

The great-nephews and Emily offered the elderly man polite greetings.

"Have you met the new mistress, Uncle?" Spencer asked.

"No, no. Not distressed at all. Been wanting to come up to the big house."

Alex and Spencer could only barely refrain from bursting into laughter.

Aynsley's quick glare sobered them. "As it happens, boys, your stepmother personally invited our uncle to dine with us tonight."

Despite that Ethelbert sat at the other end of the table, he seemed unable to remove his gaze from Rebecca, which made her a bit uncomfortable.

Finally Ethelbert turned to address his nephew, and though they sat next to one another, he shouted. "John, my boy, you should tell that new wife of yours not to wear those blasted spectacles. Never in my life saw a pretty lady in spectacles."

Aynsley looked exceedingly uncomfortable.

"I don't believe I have, either, Uncle," Rebecca agreed, her voice raised. "Spectacles *are* ever so unattractive, but I'm blind as a bat without them." It did not escape her notice that Emily—her eyes flashing with merriment—sent Peter a smug smile.

Rebecca could not face these challenges without the Lord's help. *Dear God, please don't let my patience with Lady Emily wear thin. Help me love her in the same way her true mother did. I ask this in Jesus's name. Amen.*

During the remainder of the dinner the boys were relatively well behaved. Only once did she have to pocket one of Alex's coins—for calling Chuckie an imbecile.

"But you said I wasn't to call Spencer names!" Alex defended.

"If I recall from last night, your father was decidedly distressed when you spoke ill to Chuckie, was he not?"

Alex refused to reply.

Just before the sweetmeats were about to be laid, Rebecca heard a trickling sound, like the pouring of wine, but there was no wine at the table.

Emily suddenly shrieked and darted toward Chuckie. "Grandpapa's *Plutarch's Lives!*"

Then Rebecca understood the source of the noise. "Oh, dear."

"Chuckie had an accident!" Spencer shrieked, shooting Alex a smug smile.

Emily yanked Chuckie from the now-soaked book.

A footman rushed to help, but Rebecca, who'd left her own chair, waved him off. She lifted the tome from

Chuckie's chair, careful to keep it several inches away from her. Drip. Drip. Drip. She hurried to the hearth and set the opened book there to dry. Then she turned to the footman. "I beg that you see that Master Chuckie gets on dry breeches then accompany him to the scullery. He must procure a bucket of soapy water and something with which to scrub the chair and floor. If he proves incapable of carrying the bucket, you may help him."

A squishing sound could be heard with each step as the little boy trailed the footman from the dining room.

Outrage in her voice, Emily addressed Rebecca. "Surely you don't think Chuckie capable of cleaning his mess!"

"His…mess will be properly cleaned later. For now, the boy must be charged with cleaning his messes. It is hoped that once he perceives the cleaning of his *accidents* causes him to miss his sweetmeats—or his fun—he will avoid such accidents in the future."

Emily directed a scathing gaze at Rebecca. "You really don't know much about children, do you?"

"Emily!" Lord Aynsley was furious. "You will apologize to my wife!"

Rebecca rapidly shook her head. "No, no, please. She's right. I don't know much about children, though it seems to me that those who do, have not succeeded with the lad's *accidents.* Why not try something different? I'll be the first to back off if it's not successful."

Peter smiled at Rebecca. "I think it sounds cunning."

"Found some money?" Uncle Ethelbert shouted, eyeing Peter.

This time neither Alex nor Spencer could hold back their giggles. Even Emily had a difficult time concealing her smile.

"No, Uncle," Peter said, his eyes flashing, his voice elevated. "I said, I think Lady Aynsley's plan very cunning."

Ethelbert's gaze shifted to her again.

"Can I get you some plum pudding, Uncle?" Peter asked, his voice raised.

"Two please."

"Ethelbert has quite the sweet tooth," Aynsley said, eyeing Rebecca.

Chuckie, who had set about scrubbing his chair in a most careless manner, tossed the brush back into the bucket, hopped upon the soaking seat cushion and attempted to reach across the table for his own serving of plum pudding. When he realized his arms weren't long enough, he began to climb upon the table.

That was when Emily stopped him. "Get down right now! What do you think you're doing?"

"I've gots to get my plum pudding before Effelbert eats it all up."

"You cannot climb upon the table!" Emily scolded.

"I don't think mess makers should be allowed plum pudding," Aynsley said.

The last thing Rebecca wanted was for Chuckie to hold his father in animosity. She gave her husband a pleading look. "But he *has* cleaned his mess."

"Very well." Aynsley got to his feet, snatched up his youngest son, then returned to his chair to allow Chuckie to eat the plum pudding while sitting on his father's lap.

After dinner, courtesy of Mr. Walter Scott, Rebecca had the opportunity to ingratiate herself with the lads by reading to them one of Mr. Scott's adventure stories. When she finished the chapter, she tucked each of them into their beds, promising to read the second chapter the following night.

Before she left the chamber Spencer and Alex shared, Alex said, "Thank you ever so much, milady. No one has ever read to us before. Even though I love to read myself, being read to is an ever-so-exciting experience."

Milady again. The first night Alex had referred to her as *Mother.* Rebecca could see Emily's hand in the change. "Did your nurse not read to you when you were smaller?"

"Never," Alex said.

"My mother died when I was a babe. I used to wish I had a mother to tuck me in and read to me at night. I suppose that's why I want to do this with you lads." She turned back toward the door.

"I thank you, too," Spencer added.

With the children in bed, she came to her husband's library. He immediately left his desk and moved to the sofa near the fire. "Come, let's sit by the fire, my dear."

It was such a comforting room with its book-lined walls, dark woods and a fire that hadn't gone out since they'd arrived at Dunton Hall. She inhaled the mellow smell of wood burning, which was so much nicer than the wretched coal fires of London.

She collapsed beside him. "I'm ever so sorry I've made a muddle of things."

"You most certainly have not! I'm the one who should be apologizing, apologizing for my daughter's inexcusable behavior. You will likely not believe that she's never behaved so wretchedly before. She's always displayed the most delightful manners."

Rebecca knew how dearly he loved Emily, and she did not want to be the cause of any friction between them. "I do believe you. She has so many amiable qualities. I daresay she's just having a difficult time adjusting not only to relinquishing her authority here but also fearing I'm trying to replace her own mother."

"I don't care what her reasons are, I'll not have her behave in such a manner. I'm going to have a good talk with her tomorrow. I plan to take her riding in the morning."

"I have no objections to you taking her riding, but I beg that you not tell her how to treat me. I *would* like her affection but only if it's earned—not forced. Please give me your word that you won't chastise her."

He was silent for a moment, his thinned lips twitching. "I don't like it, but if that's what you want, I'll agree."

"Good. Now tell me, did you approve of Ethelbert's conduct tonight?"

Aynsley started chuckling. "For the most part—but I'm sorry for the comment about your spectacles."

"If I were vain, his words might have offended me, but you must own, I'm one of the least vain women in England. I'd like to think I bring many more useful qualities to this marriage in place of a pretty face."

"Indeed you do, but you mustn't discount your face. It *is* pretty."

His comment embarrassed her. She must change the subject. "The boys loved *Ivanhoe* ever so much."

"What lad wouldn't? You have very good instincts about what pleases lads."

"I do hope they will be pleased when I tell them they'll start attending Sunday church services." Her lashes lifted, and she met his gaze. "You must help me by setting a good example. Your attendance is compulsory."

He frowned and did not reply for a moment. "For a marriage to be a successful partnership, I must support you, and you must support me. It's all about comp—"

"—romise," she finished, remembering her own compromise that she would allow herself to be known as Lady Aynsley in Society, even though such titles went against her principles. "So, you will accompany us to church?"

"I will."

"Should I have first discussed with you my methods of discipline? Emily was not pleased with my bribery plan or with Chuckie's scrubbing punishment."

"Emily is not their mother. She'll be having babes of her own before too long. You are older, more mature and have some excellent ideas. You also have my full support."

"Thank you. Now, we've spoken enough about the children. You must tell me what you've been working on in the library."

"I had some correspondence with fellow members."

"About proposed legislation?"

His eyes twinkled as he regarded her. "Yes. Lord Sethbridge has asked for my support for his bill to raise taxes."

"Oh, dear, that's difficult."

"Yes, it is. The only way I could support him would be in exchange for his support of a franchise-expansion bill."

"How exciting!"

"Would that it were. It doesn't stand a chance of passing." He looked tired, and because of that, he looked his age. Had the cares of his home worn on him?

Her first obligation now was to lift any burden from him. She vowed to do everything in her power—with assistance from the Heavenly Father—to win over *all* his children and to love them as dearly as he did. Already, she knew she loved the lads. *Please, Lord, help me love Emily.* "What about in Commons?"

He shrugged. "Chances of the franchise bill passing are better there."

"Then we'll just have to drum up support in that quarter." She began to yawn. A pity she was so tired. She would have liked to start a new essay that very night promulgating the expansion of the franchise.

"You've had a very long day," he said.

She got to her feet. "Yes, I am very tired, and I can tell you are, too. Can you direct me to a book on agriculture?"

"Indeed I can." He went to the bookcases and quickly produced a thick volume. "This is my favorite. It discusses the newest methods in agriculture. Should you like one on animal husbandry, too?"

"I think not. My farm, as you know, is quite small. I shan't want to try too many new things." She took the proffered book and brushed her lips across his cheek without even thinking about what she was doing. "Good night. Pray, don't stay up too late. You look as if you could use a good night's sleep."

At the landing at the top of the steps she came abreast of Peter. "I beg a word with you," he said.

She indicated a bench there in the corridor, and they both sat down under the buttery glow of a wall sconce.

"I don't know if you're aware of the fact Emily and I wish to wed."

"I am."

"I would be ever so indebted to you if you could put in a good word about me with my Uncle Aynsley."

"It's not words that will cull his favor, but actions."

"That's the pity of it. I am incapable of action, having no money coming my way until next year."

"Then how could you expect to take a wife?"

"We had hoped to stay on here."

"Though it's not a subject I care to discuss, Aynsley worries that Emily will have no home if he should die because Fordyce's future wife would probably not be agreeable to the arrangement."

He hung his head. "I know Emily deserves her own home—and a wealthy husband."

"She may not care about wealth now, but that's because she's always been indulged. The hardships of being poor, you must know, could ruin even the best marriage."

The poor fellow looked utterly dejected when he nodded gravely.

"I will use every opportunity I can to put in a good word for you, but you must be prepared to demonstrate your maturity."

"How?"

She got to her feet and looked down at the top of his tousled brown hair. "Let me think on it."

That night as she was reading her agriculture book by the light of the candle beside her bed, she realized in just what way she could solve Peter's problem.

Chapter Nine

The following morning Rebecca attempted to put pen to paper. It was the first time she had tried to write an essay since the day she had taken a hackney to Lord Aynsley's in order to make her bold proposal. Since that day, radical changes had affected every facet of her life. It was time she got back to doing that which gratified her the most, that which was the impetus to this marriage in the first place.

Since that day in the carriage when her husband—it was still difficult to think of Aynsley as her husband—had explained the significance and immediacy of working first for the extension of the franchise, she had known that must be the topic for her next essay.

To her astonishment, though, she did not seem to be as consumed with the burning desire to write about political reform. There was too much going on in her life. Also to her astonishment, the words were not flowing to her pen, despite the high degree of passion the subject elicited in her. Never before had she been at a loss to convey her progressive ideas.

She had chosen the morning to write in order to

avoid seeing Aynsley. The previous night she had decided she would wait until he and Lady Emily went riding in the morning, then she would speak to Peter. At this time, she did not want to share with her husband the nature of the proposal she was going to make to his nephew. If Peter rejected it, it might prejudice Aynsley against the young man.

It had been half an hour since Aynsley and his daughter had departed, but still she had not written a single word. Had she been called to do so, though, she could describe in the most accurate detail every delicate petal and wispy branch on the wallpaper she had stared at for those thirty minutes.

Finally, she tossed aside her pen. She might as well go down for breakfast.

Just before entering the sunny morning room, she asked one of the footmen to tell Peter she desired him to join her for breakfast.

When he came to her, she took what was most likely her first *real* look at him. Physically, he did not resemble his uncle so very much. They were the same height, and both were somewhat fair, but Peter's skin tended to freckle, where Aynsley's did not. His hair was a lighter brown than Aynsley's, too. There was, however, something about the young man that very much resembled her husband. Not the physical, certainly. Something much harder to define. She realized he carried himself in the same proud manner as Aynsley.

It occurred to her, too, that he did not dress with the dandyism embraced by other men of his youthful years. No high jacket points framing his face. No boldly colored waistcoats. No opulent buttons adorning his coat. His clothing bespoke the quiet good taste of his uncle's.

Because he was in the country, he wore tan superfine breeches with a brown woolen coat and plain but finely made brown boots.

He helped himself to a steaming cup of tea and came to sit opposite her at the small table in front of a window from which the lake could be viewed. "You wished to see me, milady?"

"Please call me Rebecca. As an American, I disapprove of the English class system."

"That's an opinion I hope you do not share with Lady Emily. She's very proud, and…"

"…and I can ill afford to rouse any more hostility from her."

He shrugged. "You mustn't think ill of her. She's normally the most amiable, courteous thing imaginable."

"I completely understand her reasons for not being overjoyed by her father's marriage." She looked up from buttering her toast. "It wouldn't have mattered who he married, she would have been upset."

"Just give her time."

"I assure you, I've made no rash judgment against her." She poured more tea into her delicate porcelain cup. "But that's enough talk about me and Emily." She peered into his eyes and realized they were the same green as Aynsley's. "I wish to talk about you."

"Me?"

She nodded. "I've been thinking about your future. First, I must know if it's truly your desire to marry Emily, if you're willing to do anything to demonstrate your worthiness."

"Marrying her is what I desire more than anything on earth." There was earnestness in his lightly freckled face. "And, yes, there is nothing I wouldn't do to win her hand."

"Then I daresay we must improve your prospects, or should I say your lack of prospects? You must demonstrate to Lord Aynsley your dependability."

"How can I do that?"

Her heartbeat drummed. She stared out the window. A strong wind was stirring the trees, and sunlight dappled on the surface of the distant lake. What if he laughed at her proposal? She drew a breath. "A lot of well-born gentlemen serve as secretaries and stewards to aristocrats—often extremely capably running the lives of the titled men who employ them."

"I cannot be a secretary. I have the most abominable penmanship."

"Have you ever thought about being a steward?"

"I must own, I've often envied them. Getting to ride over property and boss people around. It's far better than sitting in some stuffy office. The problem is, I have no experience in such matters. No gentleman would turn over his profitable estates to someone like me."

"That's true. What you need is to prove yourself on a small project first."

He shook his head. "The pity of it is I can't leave Dunton. I don't have enough money for my essential expenses."

"You wouldn't have to leave Dunton. Are you familiar with Mr. Abington's farm?"

His brows lowered. "You mean what used to be a farm, don't you?"

"Indeed. Did you know your uncle has purchased it?"

"Why would he need it?"

"Actually he bought it for my wedding present."

"What in the blazes can you do with it?"

"My aim is to make it a profitable endeavor—that is, with the right steward. I need a man to come in there and make something out of nothing."

"It's too small to support a qualified steward, and it would be a year or more before there would be any payoff."

"I would like for you to be my steward. If you could show your uncle that you could transform a barren piece of land, it is my belief that he could then entrust you with the running of one of his large estates."

"But I don't know the slightest thing about agriculture!"

"Neither do I, but my husband gave me a farm. I borrowed one of his agriculture books last night and found it to be very helpful. You see, until I hit on the idea of having you as my steward, I had planned to do it myself."

"But you're a countess!"

"I like challenges and payoffs. Besides, in all endeavors success hinges upon the ability to surround oneself with capable people."

His eyes brightened. "Aynsley's got some very experienced tenant farmers from whom I could learn. Can I see that book on agriculture?" His excitement was not unlike Chuckie's when he first saw his bright red military jacket—which pleased her inordinately.

"Of course." She rang for a footman, and when he came, she told him to tell her maid to give him the agriculture book that was in her mistress's bedchamber, then take it to Mr. Wallace's chambers.

"Would you like marmalade on your toast?" she asked Peter.

"That would be most kind."

She spread the orange jelly on two pieces of toast, one for each of them.

After they ate, they decided to go look at the farm.

"We can walk," she said, "but I'll warn you first that it's very windy today." She donned her rose velvet pelisse, tied on a bonnet, and they set off for the farm.

"It's exactly one mile from Dunton Hall to the Wey Road," he told her.

She knew the farm was just opposite the road from Dunton. As they walked, it occurred to her how unfair was the English system of primogeniture. Peter obviously loved Dunton Hall, and even though his mother was the old earl's daughter, she could never possess—or pass on—the home she'd been raised in. And of Aynsley's six sons, it was likely only one of them would be able to enjoy ownership of their home.

And what a splendid home it was! She had never thought she would ever call such a palatial house her home. It would be many weeks before she could move about its labyrinth of corridors and not get lost. But as grand as it was, the land it sat on was even more magnificent. From any point in Dunton Hall, she could look out a window and see nothing that did not appear to be virgin land. Even if such a view had been contrived by a gifted landscape artist, she did most certainly appreciate it.

The very lane they now walked upon was shaded by an oak alley that must have been planted a century or two earlier. It would take no very great imagination to know that as far as she could see everything would be green in a matter of a few more weeks. Already, barren branches on trees were beginning to leaf out, and deep, vibrant green was beginning to be restored to the broad lawns.

When they reached the fallow farm, she stayed on the Wey Road and surveyed her little plot of land. Peter strode some twenty feet onto the property and knelt. He attempted to dig in the earth with his bare hands, but it proved impossible. The only thing growing on the hardened earth was weeds.

"It is like a blank canvas," he said, shrugging as he got to his feet and walked toward her. "There's really not a lot to see. What I need to do is go and talk with Uncle's tenants. I mean to get educated."

Every man, in Rebecca's opinion, needed a purpose. And now Peter Wallace had one.

All the way back to Dunton Hall, he chatted excitedly. "Have you told my uncle about this idea of yours?" he asked.

"No. If you hadn't been interested, he could have assumed you had no intentions of improving your prospects—which, you must own, would not demonstrate your worthiness for winning Emily's hand."

He looked down at her with soft eyes. "Thank you."

Off in the distance, on the lawn that lay between Dunton Hall and the grove, Lord Aynsley and his daughter were riding toward them.

"I believe Emily and her father will be proud of you."

"I would prefer that we don't tell them."

She eyed him, her mouth open. "What do you mean?"

"Wouldn't it be capital if I could surprise them at harvest time?"

"But they'll see the transformation."

"Which you will explain as the work of the steward you've engaged."

She came to an abrupt stop and faced him. "I will not lie to my husband." Already she felt guilty that she'd not been honest about P. Corpus.

"I'm not asking you to lie, only to avoid being forthcoming about the identity of your steward."

She started to walk toward the riders, conscious of their gazes on Peter and her. "But won't you be away from Dunton a great deal? How will you explain that?"

"It's my plan to be away every day. I fancy the idea of tilling the soil myself."

"You cannot be serious! You're a gentleman."

"A gentleman who's tired of being called lazy. I need to prove myself. I need to show Uncle I'm good enough for his wonderful, beautiful daughter."

Rebecca thought the words he'd just spoken the most romantic she'd ever heard. And—even more astonishing—Rebecca never thought about romance. "How, my dear boy, will you explain your absence?"

"Lady Emily knows I'm horse mad. She'll have no trouble believing I've been riding."

"All day, every day?"

He grinned. "I'll make myself convincing."

"And when you come home covered in soil?"

As his uncle and Emily came closer, he frowned. Then he turned to her, smiling. "I know! I'll keep *farming* clothes at our farm."

Our farm. She could not have hoped for a more enthusiastic reaction from him. Emily was very fortunate to have someone love her like that. What was getting into Rebecca? Once again, she was thinking about love.

"Well," Peter said, his voice low, "will you help me keep the secret?"

"I will do my best."

He smiled down at her.

They reached the front of Dunton at the same time as Emily and her father were dismounting.

"Despite the wind, it's a lovely day for a ride—as well as a walk," Aynsley said to Emily, smiling as he moved to Rebecca and brushed a kiss upon her cheek.

"Indeed it is." Rebecca eyed Emily. "How did you enjoy your ride?"

Emily gave her an icy glare. "It was most pleasant, but I daresay not as amusing as what you and Peter have been doing. You two look exceedingly happy." She then spoke to Peter in a scolding voice. "Whatever did you and Rebecca find so amusing?"

"Nothing more than the beauty of the day." He smiled at her. "Speaking of beauty, you are stunning today."

She truly was in her sapphire velvet riding habit. "Indeed she is," Rebecca said. "I should love to have so lovely a costume. Of course, the blue is perfect with your eyes."

Aynsley set a hand to Rebecca's waist. "You should have one in red."

What was getting into Rebecca? She could not remember a time when she had ever set her mind to the contemplation of clothing! And here she was, coveting a velvet riding costume.

Before dinner that evening Aynsley knocked on Rebecca's dressing-room door. When there was no answer, he took the liberty of entering the small chamber that connected their rooms. She and her maid were talking in the chamber beyond. He knocked. "May I enter?"

"Please do, dearest."

Dearest? Of course, she would use the endearment

in front of the maid. Servants talked among themselves. She would, as would he, prefer that everyone find theirs a proper marriage. A consummated marriage.

She sat before her dressing table in a snow-white dress that looked spectacular with that rich dark mane of hers and her equally dark eyes. They made a stunning contrast with her perfect white teeth.

Her gaze darted to the velvet case he carried, then she addressed her maid dismissively. "Thank you, Pru. You've made me most presentable for dinner."

Once the maid was gone, he came closer. "How lovely you look tonight, Rebecca, but I daresay the dress needs more adornment."

Her brows lowered as she looked suspiciously at him.

He set the box on her dressing table and opened it. "Should you prefer sapphires, rubies or diamonds?"

"Those are the Aynsley jewels?" There was astonishment in her voice, and she seemed unable to remove her gaze from the glittering gems set in distinctive designs.

"Yes. They're yours for a lifetime."

"My dear man, I do wish you would refrain from speaking of your mortality! I do not like it at all. First it was *when Fordyce inherits* and now it's this business with the jewels. I daresay if you were not an aristocrat you wouldn't forever be talking about your demise."

She was awfully cute with her solicitousness toward him. But he still could not resist pulling her leg a bit. "Don't worry, my dear wife, I'm sure Fordyce will allow you to live in the dower house with Uncle Ethelbert after I've passed on to my great reward."

She hurled her hair comb at him. "You odious man!"

His eyes sparkling, he picked up the comb and replaced it beside the jewel box. "Seriously, my dear wife, have you decided which jewels you'll wear to dinner tonight?"

"Oh, my goodness, surely you can't be serious! I'm to wear something this enormously valuable to dinner with just you, Emily, Peter and Uncle Ethelbert?" She eyed the opened box. "I should think things that precious would be reserved for court presentations or for visits with foreign royalty."

"I assure you that the countesses of Aynsley have always dressed for dinner in the family jewels."

"Always?"

He shrugged. "For the past three hundred years."

She rolled her eyes. "Do you realize in the place where I was born, no men even existed three hundred years ago? Not even a mere two hundred years ago."

"Then I daresay I shan't mention that the Comptons came over with the Conqueror. We've only been earls three hundred years, but the first baronet goes back much further."

"How reassuring," she said facetiously. She began to poke about in the jewel box. "Do you think the diamonds would be too formal?"

"No, but I rather fancied you in rubies. I think they'd be striking with the white gown."

"Then I trust your judgment. I have no sense of style whatsoever. I daresay when Emily needs a trousseau I shall have to turn her over to Maggie."

His gaze swept over her. "Did your sister select the gown you're wearing tonight?"

"Do you like it?"

"I do. It's elegant."

"Then, of course, Maggie selected it. I am hopeless when it comes to fashion."

He chuckled. "That's all right, love, you have other attributes." Now why had he gone and called her *love?*

She frowned. "Having cataloged Lord Agar's library is hardly serving me well at Dunton Hall."

"Your organizational skills will be invaluable. Remember, you've been here but three days." He did not want her to be discouraged. True, his daughter was making things difficult for her. If only Rebecca hadn't made him promise not to chastise Emily.

He needed to reassure Rebecca. "You do seem to have a keen understanding of lads. I've been meaning to compliment you on knowing how thoroughly lads like getting out of their lessons every bit as much as they like to buy comfits."

"Why, thank you."

"And they adore stories by Mr. Scott."

"You must own, even little girls would have to like his stories."

"True, but not as much as boys." He reached for the ruby necklace and draped it around her slender neck and bare white shoulders, coming to clasp it at the back of her neck. "What do you think?" He stepped back to gaze at her in the looking glass she faced.

She was spectacular. And the rubies were perfect with the simplicity of her soft white gown. Her sister had done well, too. The scooped bodice of the dress swept up to a pair of tiny puffed sleeves—a perfect frame for the exquisite necklace.

Something must be wrong. She was completely silent. Did she not approve? Good gracious, did her aversion toward aristocrats extend to their family jewels? Then he realized she was dazed, awestruck.

Her mouth dropped open. "Maggie has nothing like this."

"Warwick's title is new and did not come with the lands and wealth of the Aynsleys."

She spun around and faced him. "Pray, John, do you keep the doors locked?"

He rather liked it when she called him John, especially when it came out naturally as it just had. Unforced. It showed a certain level of intimacy he wished to promote. "I don't think we have to worry about being robbed. If you will notice, the bottom drawer of your dressing table has a lock. Once these jewels are stowed there, that drawer will remain locked at all times. Your maid will always keep one key, and I will stash the other in a safe place. You will, of course, need to convey all of this to your maid."

She sighed. "Do you think Emily will think me pretentious?"

"Emily is well aware of how the Countess of Aynsley comports herself."

"How silly of me."

He proffered a crooked arm. "May I escort my lovely wife to dinner now?"

She stood and faced him, shyly smiling.

On the way downstairs he asked if she'd communicated with the boys that day. "A little. I asked Chuckie's nurse to let him enjoy the sunshine, but I did not think it right that he enjoy something denied Spencer and Alex. So, of course I had to ask that they be excused from lessons for a half an hour, and of course, I had to make myself go, too. The boys just ran around, but I think they enjoyed it."

He remembered how much he'd loved being out of

doors when he was a lad. How did she comprehend the mind of a lad so very well?

"I must own, I also had an ulterior motive."

"What, pray tell?"

"I wished to butter them up. You know what tomorrow is?"

He thought for a moment. "The Sabbath?"

"Indeed."

"I see. You wanted to prepare them."

She nodded.

"How did they accept the news?"

"They were excited. Perhaps not for the right reasons. I think their excitement was because they find Sundays at Dunton so boring and tedious. At least going into Wey and getting to be around other children is much more appealing than spending the day in quiet pursuits. You must know, Mr. Witherstrum encourages them to read Scripture on Sunday, and they do not find that very appealing. I shall have to make it so for them."

"If anyone can, I am sure you will."

"I think another reason they are not averse to going to church is because they remember fondly going there with their mother, did they not?"

"They did." Dorothy was not a good Christian, but no one cared more about appearances than she. How would it have looked if the Countess of Aynsley didn't take her proper place in the family pew at the front of the church? It was almost laughable how Dorothy and Rebecca were complete opposites. Rebecca didn't care about appearances, but she did care about her spiritual life.

They had reached the dining room. Since it was just the five of them this night, the candles in the chandeliers remained unlit, but two massive silver candelabrum lit the table.

"Have you told my daughter about church?"

"Not yet. I actually didn't have the opportunity to speak with her today."

When they entered the dining room, Peter stood. "Hello, Rebecca, Uncle." His nephew looked approvingly upon Lady Aynsley. And Emily did not like it.

Aynsley hated the demeanor that had come over his formerly excessively sweet, gracefully courteous daughter. It would serve her right if Rebecca could not stand the sight of her.

But he would hate that. Why had he allowed Rebecca to extract that bloody promise from him? What Emily needed was a good scolding.

"I see you're wearing Mama's jewels," Emily said.

"Emily! You know those are the Aynsley family jewels. They're rightfully Rebecca's now. Until—"

"Pray, dearest!" Rebecca interrupted. "I beg you not mention that dreadful subject."

His daughter at least had the decency to smile at Rebecca. "I completely agree with you, Rebecca, about Papa's dreadful propensity to always talk about when he's gone and Fordyce inherits. I, too, hate that talk."

He could have let out a huge sigh. His wife and daughter finally found a subject upon which they could agree.

Rebecca ladled clear turtle soup from the tureen into one bowl and passed it to Emily, then started on another. "By the way, Emily, our family will be going to church in the morning. Your father has even done me the goodness to agree to come. Are you not happy about that?"

Emily eyed him. "Truly, Papa?"

"Yes. It's time I set a good example for my children."

"Indeed it is."

When Rebecca came to his library later that night, he left his desk and came to sit next to her on the sofa in front of the fire. "So did the lads enjoy the latest chapter of *Ivanhoe?*"

"So much so they begged for me to keep reading, but I explained that the anticipation of a good story is almost as much fun as the reading of one. They agreed that the storytelling has made bedtime something to look forward to."

"Then that's a very good thing. Alex, in particular, used to cry when he had to go to bed. He took great satisfaction in telling us he was *nocturnal*."

She laughed. "That is so like Alex to toss out one of his big words!"

He could tell that Alex had won her affection. She could not hide her tender feelings for him as well as Chuckie. He wasn't sure about Spencer. The lad had to have offended her when he spat out that she was *not* their mother. Other than that, though, Spencer had been amiable to Rebecca.

A pity that he couldn't say the same about Emily. "I wish you'd reconsider that blasted pledge you extracted from me. My daughter needs a good scolding from a stern father. I don't at all like the way she treats you."

She met his gaze with those large almond-shaped eyes of warm brown and spoke softly. "I don't, either. I want her affection most heartily, but I'm obliged to earn it. Can't you see that's the only way it can come?"

He wondered how she could possibly have acquired such a breadth of knowledge about human nature. Had that come from those books she always had her face pressed against? He gave a reluctant nod.

"Tell me about the stage I saw in the nursery. Do the children do productions?" she asked.

He hadn't given the stage a thought in many years. In fact, he could not remember his children, not even his oldest boys, ever putting on a production. A pity. Some of his fondest childhood memories were from when he and his sister and their cousins had performed plays. "No."

"Don't tell me it's there from when you were a lad!"

"I daresay it was there many years even before I came into the world. Meg and I and our cousins staged many a play there. We would purge the attics for old clothing from generations ago. Of course, they were much too large for us, but we did not seem to perceive that." He shook his head. "And our poor parents had to come and sit on children's chairs and pretend to be a rapt audience." He chuckled.

"It sounds like wonderful fun. We'll have to encourage the children to do a play."

He agreed. It was funny how often his thoughts seemed to mesh with Rebecca's. "It might be difficult to find material for so few actors."

"Oh, I wasn't thinking about finding something. Why can we not encourage Emily to write a play? Perhaps she could take something simple like one of Jesus's parables and create a play from it."

"So my little Bible-spouter has an ulterior motive?" He regarded his wife with amusement.

She shrugged, the slight movement causing the graceful clusters of rubies in her necklace to twinkle. "I cannot shirk my parental responsibility."

She made him feel wretchedly guilty that he had neglected his children's spiritual development. Thank God for Rebecca.

And he really meant it. For the first time in a very long while he felt the stir of his relationship with his Lord being rekindled. Had God sent Rebecca to him?

Chapter Ten

The chapel of St. Andrews was lovely with the early morning sunlight filtering through the stained-glass windows and the creaking pews filling with freshly scrubbed villagers dressed in their finest. Aynsley had told her the church was three hundred years old. She could well believe it. Generations of the Compton family had worn indentations into the smooth wooden pew upon which they sat. The wood planks of the nave, too, wore thinner in the center where they had been trodden upon for three centuries.

Each one of the stained-glass windows on either side of the church bore a plaque beneath it that dedicated the window to the memory of a different member of the Compton family. The newest of these commemorated the life of Dorothy Compton, the Countess of Aynsley. Her sons Spencer and Alex paused in front of it and said a little prayer.

"What are they doing?" Chuckie asked Rebecca and Aynsley, each of whom held one of his little hands, as they entered the family's pew in the front row of the church.

Rebecca held her index finger to her lips, then whispered, "Remember what we told you? You're not supposed to talk in church."

He whispered back, "I forgot."

Rebecca met Aynsley's amused gaze, and they both smiled.

It was a few more moments before Emily and Peter came strolling down the center aisle. Since Aynsley's carriage was not large enough to accommodate everyone, the young couple had come in Aynsley's phaeton. All eyes were on the beautiful couple as they made their way to the front of the church. Emily, in her butter-yellow dress, was uncommonly pretty, and Peter, so much taller than she, looked handsome.

Once again, Rebecca met her husband's admiring gaze and smiled. He fairly burst with pride toward his lovely daughter. She thought, too, he welcomed the opportunity to display his family to the villagers of Wey, many of whom he'd known since he was a lad.

She knew, though, that such pride was no reason to come to the Lord's house. She hoped they all had come here this morning to offer praise to their Creator on His day.

They all scooted down to make room for Emily and her future husband.

Prior to the start of the service, Rebecca prayed fervently that her husband would be filled with the Holy Spirit. It was her duty as his wife not only to see to his material comfort but also to help him fulfill his spiritual needs. And as she did each night when she said her prayers, she asked the Lord to continue to fill her with love toward Emily, even when the girl was openly hostile to her. *Bless them that curse you, do good to them that hate you, and pray for them which despitefully use you and persecute you.*

When the vicar entered the sanctuary, his glance flicked to her husband, and a hint of a smile tweaked at his lips. Dressed in his silk vestments, he appeared to be close to Aynsley's age. Like her husband, he possessed a full head of brown hair that was brushed with gray at the temples.

The gospel that day, from Matthew 20, she knew well. In Jesus's parable, the workers who were hired last and worked the least were paid the full amount first. Thinking of the Lord's benevolence brought a smile to her face.

In the vicar's short sermon afterward he explained the parable to his small congregation that was comprised of all ages and all social stations. Rebecca wondered if there was special significance that on the day Lord Aynsley returned to his church, that particular gospel was read.

Please, Lord, I know my husband may be last in coming to You, but I beg that You allow him first into the kingdom of Heaven. I ask, too, that all of my stepchildren will welcome You into their lives from this day forward and that You will show them—and their father—the way to eternal salvation.

Spencer and Alex were on their best behavior and gave the appearance they were listening intently. Emily had no need to consult her prayer book. She knew all the prayers by heart. For the first time, Rebecca had the opportunity to view her stepdaughter in a favorable light. It was easy to see why Aynsley and Peter championed her. She could be delightful. *Please, God, I need Your help with Emily, too. I beseech You to banish any obstacles that impede us from loving each other as a mother and daughter ought.*

Chuckie was fascinated by all the new sights and sounds and people, including other children his own age. When the congregation prayed aloud, he pretended to say the prayers along with them, moving his mouth without words actually coming out. Rebecca almost burst into laughter.

Following the service, Rebecca and Aynsley and Emily and Peter stood on the steps in front of the chapel's timber door and greeted not only the vicar but also most of the villagers. No matter how amiable the conversation, Aynsley made it a point to introduce his bride to each person who came up to them. She hoped she could remember half of their names.

Rebecca watched helplessly as the boys proceeded to get their Sunday clothing soiled while playing with other lads on the church grounds. What kind of an impression would she make if she were to screech at the lads or admonish them? They weren't doing anything all the other boys in the village weren't doing.

She cringed every time she was addressed as Lady Aynsley, but true to the compromise she'd made with her husband, she smiled while being addressed as such. She even found herself once again addressing him as Lord Aynsley—which she had not done since they married.

She especially abhorred the frequent observation that she didn't look a day older than Lady Emily. "I am a great deal older than I appear," she continued to tell the curious. "The birthday after next I'll be thirty."

At least twenty times Aynsley said, "Yes, the lads *have* grown so fast. Every time I return from London it seems they've grown a foot each." And twenty more times he would respond to compliments over Emily's beauty.

Rebecca was able to observe Emily being charming and quietly gracious as she stood in the shadow of her outgoing cousin. Why couldn't Emily be like that with her?

On the way home, Rebecca was delighted that Chuckie chose to sit upon her lap. He commenced to sucking his thumb and wrapping a coil of her hair within his fingers as his drowsy head lay on her sternum. A contentment as deep and satisfying as anything she'd ever experienced rushed over her as she clasped this precious child in her arms and dropped soft kisses on his blond curls.

When she lifted her lids and realized Aynsley watched her with an inscrutable look on his face, her sense of well-being almost overcame her with emotions so profound she could not understand them. Certainly she had never experienced anything of such an emotional magnitude in her entire eight and twenty years.

Perhaps it was the confines of the carriage that contributed to the cozy effect. As grand and stately and solid as Dunton was, she thought she preferred just being in this carriage with her family.

For no longer was she an appendage to dear Maggie's family. Now she had her very own family. An honorable husband. Three lads she adored. A pity she and Emily could not feel the closeness for which she longed, but she trusted God to remedy the painful estrangement.

"How are you lads enjoying *Ivanhoe?*" their father asked.

"Ever so much," Alex said.

"Papa?" Spencer asked.

"Yes?"

"Could me and Alex get bows and arrows?"

Aynsley shrugged. "What do you think, Mother?"

"She's not our mother," Spencer said.

Chuckie shot up. "She is, too!"

The spell was broken. Her little world was not as perfect as it had seemed a minute earlier.

"It's irrelevant what they call me, but as to the question about archery equipment, I think it would be great fun for the lads—but only if you or another responsible man is always with them to ensure their safety."

"Then we could pretend we're Ivanhoe," Spencer said.

Alex pulled back on an imaginary bowstring. "I want to be Locksley!"

"I'll see if I can't get my hands on some," their father promised. He looked at Rebecca. "It appears you've selected a book my sons enjoy very much."

My sons. How she wished they were *our sons.* Would they ever come to think of her as their earthly mother? She truly did not want to replace their birth mother… or did she? She wished to always honor Dorothy. She wished for the children to never forget the woman who gave them life. But she also wished to take her place. She wanted to think of them as her own children, and she hoped that one day they would feel toward her the same as they would have toward their true mother.

She wanted her name on their lips when they were sad or glad. She wanted them to understand that whatever affected them, affected her. She wanted them to come to think of her as their mother, the mother God sent.

For she knew the Lord had called her to this family. Now why would He not remove all the impediments to a happy family?

These evenings after the children were tucked into their beds were coming to be his favorite part of the day. Not that he did not enjoy being with his children. He derived a great amount of pleasure from each of them, but he also enjoyed these evenings sitting before the fire in his library when it was just him and his wife.

She could discuss politics more intelligently than any man he knew. And they did so for hours on end without ever running out of things to say. Rebecca's contributions to the speech he was drafting to deliver to Lords were immeasurable.

This night he was working silently at his desk, Rebecca seated on a sofa near the fire while catching up on her newspaper reading.

"This says Mr. Wilburforce will introduce a measure in Commons which will limit child laborers. I certainly hope you will support his efforts in Lords."

He impatiently tossed aside his speech. "I most certainly will not! We've had this conversation before, Rebecca." He felt like he was reprimanding one of his boys. "While I do pity these children, you must understand many of them are orphans. If they weren't employed, they'd go hungry on the streets."

"It's a wretched society we live in that allows children to go hungry on the streets."

"You won't get any argument from me. I have the utmost empathy for orphans. In fact, I've established and maintain a rather large orphanage in the Capital, but it's merely a drop in the bucket. There are thousands of these wretches. My pockets are only so deep."

"Everyone, not just rich men like you, should do their part to take care of the poor orphans."

"That's a wonderful sentiment, but that's all it is—sentiment."

Her eyes narrow, her lips compressed, she glared at him a moment before she deigned to address him. "I cannot believe I am married to a man who will oppose the honorable Mr. Wilburforce."

"I never said I was going to mount an opposition to the man—I just cannot support him. I have always supported his antislavery measures, but you must own, that hardly affects the English pocketbook."

"How can you be so progressive in all other matters and so pigheaded about child labor?"

"You know very well I'm a pragmatist. Idealists never live to see their ideas fulfilled."

With a great, dramatic flair, his sulking wife took up her newspaper again and began to read it while attempting to ignore him. Except for the frequent huffs. And the crinkling of pages as she turned them much more noisily than she had before.

If she could act like that, so could he! He returned to writing his speech.

Perhaps fifteen minutes passed before she finally spoke. "I should like to see the working lads."

"What working lads?"

"The ones you employ in your mines."

"My dear woman, my mines are located in Wales."

She shrugged. "Shropshire's near Wales."

"My mine is more than six hours away."

Her "oh" sounded like it came from a young child.

They both went back to their singular pursuits. Which bothered him. He did not like any kind of friction between them. He liked it much better when their minds and thoughts meshed like those couples who had been married for decades.

Another half hour passed before he had to put a stop to this ridiculous bickering between them. Not that he was going to give in to her foolish demand. "Pray, my dear wife, could I interest you in a game of chess?"

She flung down her newspaper. "Indeed you could! I adore chess."

He moved to the sofa where she sat and proceeded to set up the chess pieces on the tea table in front of them.

"I propose," she said, her eyes flashing, "that we make a wager."

He raised a single brow.

"If I win, you will agree to support Mr. Wilburforce."

A sudden fury bolted through him. No woman had ever dared to tell him what to do or how to vote! One whack of his hand flattened all the chess pieces. Mumbling under his breath, he leaped to his feet. "I've had enough of your foolishness, madam."

Then he stormed from the room.

He dared not look at her face as he strode angrily across the chamber and slammed the door behind him. It would have been too painful to see a wounded look on her face. He was disgusted with himself for his angry outburst, for offending the poor woman whose concern had been not for herself but for unfortunate orphans.

Nevertheless, she'd made him angry with her meddling ways. Dorothy's meddling ways had once nearly destroyed his political career. He had vowed to never again go down that road. It had taken him years to repair the damage done by Dorothy's lies.

Even though it was a cool evening, he left the house and walked the grounds of the place he loved best—Dunton Hall, where he'd been born, where each of his children had drawn their first breath. This was where he had learned to ride and to read, and it was on this land that he would one day be buried—though Rebecca would not like for him to be thinking of that! The very thought brought a smile to his lips.

His strides long and swift, he did not even think of how bitterly cold it was or of the brisk winds that stirred up whistling noises in the surrounding trees. His thoughts were too melancholy. Perhaps this marriage had not been such a good idea. He'd never been happy with his first wife. What made him think he could find happiness with a second?

He had felt such a deep connection to Rebecca. He had hoped to awaken the passions he knew resided within her. He'd been foolish enough to believe she would also feel the connection, but she obviously did not.

Had she, she would have revealed to him her authorship.

Why was it his lot in life to be saddled with women who were intrinsically dishonest? He had thought Rebecca would be different. He had hoped theirs was to be a true partnership.

But she didn't even trust him enough to admit her alter ego. That had been eating at him like acid on rock, slowly yet decisive.

The farther he walked away from the main house, the guiltier he felt for his rash behavior to Rebecca. He supposed he'd already been on edge before she'd even come into the library that night. Because he'd brought Rebecca into his home, he was losing his cherished daughter. He'd always enjoyed an excessively close relationship with Emily, but the morning they had ridden, even though Rebecca was not with them, his wife sliced a rift between them that he feared would never be repaired. Emily had been solemn and distant, not the laughing, playful girl she had always been.

He'd made the mistake of bringing up Emily's presentation in London, and she'd launched into an angry attack at him—and Rebecca. "*She* wants to be rid of me, no doubt!" Emily had said.

"You do your stepmother a great disservice. She wants only what will make you happy, as do I," he'd told her.

"Then I beg you don't make me go to London."

His lips in a grim line, he'd told her he would give consideration to her feelings.

He loved Peter, really he did, but he loved Emily too much to wish her married to a wastrel.

The house was so far away now he could no longer see its lit windows. He had best turn back. The cold air stinging his cheeks, he continued to think about Rebecca. Before her, his life had been less conflicted. Utterly lonely, but peaceful nevertheless. Through her, he had glimpsed a sliver of potential happiness, and had rushed toward it like a blind old fool. And what had he gotten for his imprudent act? A deep chasm with his beloved daughter and a wife who thought to boss him as if he were a misguided child. A dishonest wife, at that!

He tried to tell himself this marriage was not bad. Rebecca did have a way with lads, and he truly believed she cared deeply for Chuckie and Alex. Against his will, he pictured her in the coach that morning after church, holding his youngest son on her lap. No one could have seen her and not believed she was Chuckie's natural mother. He could have wept with joy.

And now he could weep for altogether different reasons, reasons he himself could not fully comprehend.

As he came closer to the house, he wondered if he should ask Rebecca's forgiveness for his rude conduct. But with a certainty born of resolve, he vowed he would not. Though he knew his actions unpardonable, he felt even more strongly her meddling ways could not be tolerated. Early in this marriage, he must show her he was not some simpleton to be led around by a domineering wife.

It was still hard to credit that he'd married Rebecca. What had possessed him?

Long after he entered the house, long after he climbed the stairs, and long after he lay in his bed unable to sleep, he asked himself the same question. Why *had* he married the bossy Miss Peabody?

Rebecca, too, lay in her bed hour after hour pondering this marriage. When Aynsley had so angrily left her in the library, she'd been stunned. More than that, she'd been hurt and humiliated. Though she was irritated over his stubborn support of child labor, she had not been angry with him. She would never have mentioned the silly wager had she known he would have so violent a reaction to it. She'd meant it only as a jest.

The anger she had elicited from him could only have arisen if there were other, underlying impediments to them enjoying a smooth marriage. Her husband must already be regretting that they'd wed. But why now? There was, of course, Emily's disapproval. Had she said something to her father the morning they had ridden? Had he come to believe their marriage had been a mistake? Spencer, also, seemed to resent her. Twice now he'd snapped that she wasn't his mother. Though she must own, the rest of the time he'd been a perfect angel, the dear boy.

Did Aynsley regret the bedroom arrangements? Did he think her an unfeeling prude of a woman who could never love a man?

He obviously thought her a manipulator, and she could understand that a certain type of man would be resentful of such a woman.

But did he not know she was willing to make compromises? She wanted most keenly for this marriage to be a true partnership.

A deep melancholy had seeped into every pore of her body and robbed her of the ability to sleep. Since she had stood before the fire with Aynsley that night in Warwick's library, she had felt the Lord guiding her to this man and his children.

Had she been mistaken?

No, surely not! She recalled the words she said to her bridegroom before the priest on their wedding day. *I take John to be my wedded husband, to have and to hold from this day forward, for better or for worse, for richer, for poorer, in sickness and in health, to love, cherish and to obey, till death us do part, according to God's holy ordinance; and thereto I give thee my troth.*

She had felt God's presence in the church that day. Her vow was not only to John but to God. Had both of them forsaken her now? She began to weep.

Chapter Eleven

Aynsley was not in the morning room when Rebecca went down for breakfast. She had hoped to see him, to offer an apology. She could not remember a time when she had been more upset, and knowing that she was the source of their conflict increased her suffering tenfold. Why could she not hold her tongue? Why did she have to be possessed of such strong opinions? She was sure Aynsley must be wishing he'd married a meek, compliant woman. Certainly, he must be wishing he'd never married her.

She went to the cherrywood sideboard and poured herself a cup of tea. She eyed the toast and jams, but she had no appetite. In her state of agitation, she doubted she could keep anything in her stomach.

As was the family custom, the fast was broken each morning at a table that was only slightly larger than a game table and was situated against tall windows that afforded a view of the lake. Perhaps looking out over the rolling, peaceful landscape of Dunton would soothe her after her miserable, sleepless night.

Far in the distance toward the apple orchard she

could glimpse her husband riding with another man, a man she assumed to be his steward.

"Have you seen Peter?"

Rebecca spun around to face her stepdaughter, smiling. "No, I haven't."

Emily did not return the smile. "I can't find him anywhere. One of the footmen said he left early this morning. Surely he's returned."

Rebecca shrugged, though she had a very good idea where Peter could be found. She was not at liberty to reveal that information to the lovely blonde. "I've just come down. Have you eaten?"

"Not actually. I'd thought to join Peter." Her glance skipped to the rack of toast.

"Why don't you join me? I cannot think of a lovelier place to eat breakfast." Rebecca's glance swept over her stepdaughter. "How pretty you look today."

Emily wore a simple muslin gown sprigged with tiny blue flowers and tied under the bodice with a pale blue satin sash. Rebecca thought she looked like an angel.

Still, no smile was forthcoming from Emily. "But you're not eating!"

Rebecca sighed. "I have a digestive complaint this morning, but the tea's still nice and hot—and most welcome." It helped to clear her groggy head.

Emily helped herself to a piece of toast and patted marmalade on it before she came to sit across the table from Rebecca.

"I'm so happy to see you this morning," Rebecca began, "because I shall beg that you do me the most tremendous service."

The girl's fine golden brows arched. "Pray, what could I do for you?"

"I should like the lads—as well as you and Peter and possibly even Uncle Ethelbert—to stage a performance in the nursery."

"What kind of performance?"

"That's the rub, you see. I thought perhaps you could write a short play especially for the family."

"I cannot write a play!"

"I believe you can. Your father says you're a terribly clever writer. I will presume to suggest a topic, but bear in mind, it's only a suggestion." If only she'd been as diplomatic on the previous night.

Those fair brows of Emily's lowered. "What?" She did not appear to be in the least agreeable.

"I had hoped you could take one of Jesus's parables and possibly even give it a modern-day treatment."

The girl gave no reaction for several seconds. Rebecca feared she may have angered Emily with her presumptiveness.

"You know," Emily finally said, her eyes glittering like the sapphires they so strongly resembled, "I do believe I could do that! We could do the prodigal son. I would love for Uncle Ethelbert to be the father, but I daresay the poor man would not be able to remember his lines."

She was likely right. "I have every confidence you'll figure out something."

Emily's lips pursed with contemplation. "Perhaps I will. It will be such great fun for the boys. I believe I'll go start in the library. Is Papa there?"

"No, he's riding."

"Oh, that's right. It's Monday. He always rides with Mr. Stanley on Mondays." Rebecca remembered now that Stanley was the steward's name.

When Emily swept from the room, she almost collided with a footman who was bringing Rebecca the morning post.

Nothing could have been calculated that could get Rebecca out of her funk as easily as a letter from Maggie. Well, there most certainly was one thing, but a proud earl like Aynsley was unlikely to ever come apologizing to her. Her delighted gaze fell on the Lady Warwick seal, and she hurriedly tore open the first letter she had received from Maggie since she'd left London.

My Dearest Becky,
I'm not going to be selfish and fill these pages elaborating on my own misery over your absence, nor will I go into long, heartbreaking descriptions about how thoroughly your nephews miss you. I am, however, writing with glorious news! I have located for you a wonderfully capable housekeeper by the name of Mrs. Cotton. She's run Lord and Lady Bermondsey's London home for the past five years, but after visiting her sister in the country recently and learning that her asthma complaints completely disappeared upon leaving London's sooty skies, she is quite determined to take a position in the country. I took the liberty of engaging her on the spot. Lady Bermondsey, I must tell you, is prostrate. Unless I receive a negative response from you immediately, I will put her on a post chaise for Birmingham tomorrow. Aynsley could send his carriage to pick her up on Tuesday, the 16th.

Well, my dearest love, I've got to get this let-

ter off by the next post—which is just outside our door.
M

It was, indeed, glorious news. And the sixteenth was the following day! By Wednesday, they would have a capable housekeeper in place. She so hoped Aynsley would be proud of her. Not that she'd done anything more than beg Maggie to assist.

Now, if only she could engage a governess. Surely then she would have accomplished something that would make her husband proud. She perused the rest of the mail and was delighted to find a letter from her old friend Verity, now Lady Agar.

How gratifying it was that both Maggie and Verity had been thinking of her during her short absence from London. She broke the Lady Agar seal and unfolded the letter. Like Maggie's, this one was brief.

My Dear Lady Aynsley,
I have every reason to hope this letter brings you welcome news for it's my pleasure to tell you I believe I've found just the person to serve as governess to your stepsons. Allow me to tell you a bit about her. You will remember my brother Will and his bride, Lady Sophia. Well, Lady Sophia's old governess has just finished up with the last of the Devere children (you recall Lady Sophia was a Devere before she married), and being just in her middle forties, the governess is too young to retire. As it happens, she has been looking for a post.

Lady Sophia is uncommonly attached to her. Of course, Lady Sophia is such a dear she treats that maid of hers as if she were family. I thought it quite interesting that her maid, who is well into her forties, has just married my brother's longtime valet, who's of a similar age. Is that not romantic?

But back to the governess. All the Deveres adore her. In addition to being possessed of a sweet temperament, she is said to be terribly clever. She is fluent in French and displays a high degree of talent with both music and penmanship and spelling and arithmetic. She is the daughter of a rector, now deceased. Her name is Miss Mary Seton. She's currently still residing with the Deveres, and you can write her at their home on Half Moon Street.

I cannot believe my dearest friend in the world has deserted me to live in faraway Shropshire. When, my dear friend, can I expect to see you again in London? I pray that by now you are madly in love with your husband. Lord Aynsley, which I'm sure you've learned by now, is a most honorable man. I cannot recommend marriage enthusiastically enough. But, then, I am blessed to have the most wonderful husband God ever created. I do pray you will come to feel the same toward Ld A.

I eagerly await a nice, long letter from you telling me everything about your new home and family.

Affectionately,
V.

How wonderful! Rebecca reread the letter again. Miss Seton sounded perfect in every way. It was so nice to personally know a person who had actually been educated by the prospective governess. Lady Sophia, a perfect dear, was a high recommendation, indeed, for any governess. She seemed so very well brought up.

Rebecca raced to her chamber, sat at the gilded desk that she continued to think of as Dorothy's, then dashed off a letter to Miss Mary Seton, imploring her to come to Dunton Hall at her earliest opportunity. She also described the situation, as well as telling her a little bit about the lads and about Dunton Hall. Rebecca herself still marveled that she was mistress of such a grand house, still marveled over Dunton's grandeur. She hoped the new governess would enjoy living there half as much as she.

She was inordinately impatient to see her husband's reaction to her two pieces of good news.

After she posted the letter to Miss Seton, she returned to her chamber to write both Maggie and Verity nice, long letters describing her life at Dunton. That her desk was situated in front of a window delighted her. Aynsley had told her the lake was man-made under the direction of the landscape designer. She could almost believe it had been designed to be viewed from the many tall casements in her oversize bedchamber. But, then, she felt exactly the same when viewing it while sitting at the little square table in the morning room, and she would imagine the same gratifying view was available from Aynsley's bedchamber next to hers.

Completely unsummoned, she began to wonder if Dorothy and John—now why was she thinking of him as John?—freely went back and forth between each other's bedchambers. She understood they had often shared a bed, and the very thought of him with Dorothy made her feel…bad. This was an altogether unfamiliar experience for her.

Oh, my goodness! It was that wretched jealousy again! Never in her eight and twenty years had she experienced jealousy, and now it was consuming her on a daily basis! What in God's wide, wide world had gotten into her?

She forced herself to return to her letter writing. After nearly two hours, she had filled several pages that described to Maggie her life at Dunton Hall. When she realized that Verity's letter would contain the exact same information, she decided to add a little note to Verity on the end of Maggie's letter and beg that after Maggie read the letter she send it along to Lady Agar.

Just as she was signing the letter with much love, a knock sounded at her door. She could think of several reasons why it wouldn't be Aynsley, the most obvious being his anger toward her. He usually came from the interior rather than the corridor, which he felt would indicate a level of formality not appropriate for a married couple. It could not be Pru, either, because she always entered the chamber concurrently with her knock. Rebecca certainly could not expect any visitors since she did not really know anyone within a hundred miles from here. Exchanging names on the church steps did not count! "Yes?" She remained seated in front of her desk.

"May I come in?" It was Aynsley's voice. And it no longer sounded angry.

She threw down her pen and swept toward the door. "Of course, dearest!"

His face was solemn when he met her in the eye. "You're not angry with me?"

She set a hand on his sleeve. "No. I feared you'd be angry with me."

"Come, let's sit at the settee."

They sat before the comforting fire, facing one another. "I must apologize—" he began.

At precisely the same time, she blurted out, "I must apologize—"

They both began to laugh.

Thank You, Lord.

He took both her hands in his. "I've been beastly, barking at you simply for expressing your noble opinions."

"But I was much too overbearing. Understandably, no man wishes to be dictated to by a woman."

"You certainly have the right to express your opinions—even if they are in opposition with mine. A solid marriage must be based on being honest with one another."

Being honest with one another. Sweet heavens! Had he learned about P. Corpus? She felt wretchedly guilty for withholding something from him when he was making every effort to make this marriage a true partnership. How she wished she could open up to him about P. Corpus, but what if he forbade her to continue? She would be forced to obey his command. On the day of their wedding she had vowed to obey her husband.

Now she was withholding two important things from her husband. Why had she not refused Peter's request to keep silent about his management of her farm? How she would have enjoyed telling Aynsley about it. She thought he would approve.

"As your wife, I should honor your beliefs." She had started to add, "even if they're wrong," but had, for once, exercised the good judgment to keep her mouth closed.

"Oh, John, I hope we never again have such a dreadful disagreement. I cannot tell you how wretched it made me."

He squeezed her hand. "Me, too. As Stanley and I rode the property today, I felt as if a heavy gloom were hanging over my head even though the sun was sparkling."

"You have described my very feelings! I haven't eaten a bite all day."

A look of concern swept over his face. "We must remedy that. I propose a picnic at the folly."

It was as if the sun had suddenly broken through the darkest day.

As they neared the folly, she realized this was the closest she'd been to it. Corinthian columns—with no walls—supported its domed copper roof. The interior floors, as well as the bench they came to sit upon, were constructed of the same marble as the elegant columns. Her first thought upon sitting was that if this marble were in London, it would no longer be such a pristine white.

Like most everything at Dunton, the bench was situated to take advantage of a view of the man-made lake.

"How long has the folly been here? she asked.

There was amusement on his face. "What would be your guess?"

"I feel as if it must have been built by Mr. Capability Brown, which would suggest to me it was constructed during your father's tenure as earl."

"Right you are. Which I knew you would be."

She uncovered the picnic offerings, broke off a serving of crusty bread for him and took one for herself. "Oh, my dearest, I forgot to tell you the most wonderful news!"

"Which is?"

"First, I got a letter from Maggie, who has managed to secure for us a new housekeeper. She's been with Lord and Lady Bermondsey for these past five years, and she arrives here tomorrow!"

"That is, indeed, wonderful news." He would not have had to say a word, for the happy expression on his face bespoke his pleasure.

"It gets even better."

"Don't tell me you've managed to procure a governess, too!"

She nodded sheepishly. "That is, Lady Agar did."

"It's my good fortune to have married a well-connected woman."

That was the first real praise she had warranted from him since they had wed. She couldn't have felt happier had he said he loved her. Loved her? Now why in heaven's name would she go using the word *love,* even if it was only an internal thought? The former Miss Rebecca Peabody *never* thought about love. In fact, she had resigned herself to the reality that she was one of those women who would never experience love, never marry. Not that she was experiencing love, of course. Even if she was married.

But ever since the night she and…John had stood together before the fire in Lord Warwick's library, her life had been turned completely upside down from what it was before. She most assuredly was no longer Rebecca Peabody. And she wasn't precisely P. Corpus, either.

She hadn't managed to write a single word on an essay since John had offered for her hand.

Now she was a mother, whether the children wanted her or not. She was mistress of a home more palatial than any grand home she'd ever slept in. And she was John's life partner.

With the Lord's help, she prayed they would never be estranged again.

She proceeded to give him all the details about their two new employees. "Oh, I forgot another piece of good news."

"Perhaps I should get angry more often if I can return to such an abundance of welcome announcements." His eyes flashed mischievously.

"I pray you don't." She reached into the basket and plucked an apple for him, then another for herself.

"Geoffrey's coming home?" he guessed, a hopeful expression on his face. At times like this, he did not seem old enough to have a son fighting on the Peninsula.

She felt wretched that she'd gotten up his hopes. Her face fell. "Unfortunately, my news isn't *that* good, though I pray every day the Lord will watch over our soldier son, and that he'll be coming home soon."

His face was utterly somber. "Thank you."

"My last piece of good news regards Emily. I'm so proud of her. You will not believe how wonderfully she took to my proposal that she write a play based on a Biblical parable."

"You're talking about my daughter?"

"Indeed. She actually seemed excited. I expect she's madly working on it in your library at the moment."

"It's not *my* library."

How sweet of him! She was so unworthy, yet he really was so very good to her. "Emily told me that first day that you did not like to be disturbed when you were in *your* library, and she has certainly been at Dunton longer than I."

He shrugged. "I regret to say I can be a curmudgeon. It appears I shall have to apologize to Em, too. I enjoy sharing the library with my family—provided they're quiet and don't disturb my work."

"Your work is very important. I am most impressed with the speech you're working on at present. When will you deliver it?"

"Probably not until we present Emily."

"Oh, dear."

"She's complained again about her refusal to be presented?"

Rebecca nodded.

"Do you think I'm being too domineering because I want my daughter to have a Season as do all other ladies of her class?"

"I'm not going to take sides in this. I understand each side only too well. Do allow me to say that I hated my Season more than I've ever hated anything in my life. Granted, I was not a beauty, like Emily, nor was I the daughter of an earl. There is no doubt Emily would be a spectacular success."

"Thank you."

His affection for his children was so touching. "Not all young ladies enjoy such endeavors. The purpose of a Season, after all, is to land a husband."

"And Emily believes she has found her husband right here at Dunton."

She nodded in agreement. "Peter's a good fellow.

Really. And he does love your daughter very much. Do you know what he told me?"

"What?"

"That he wanted to marry Emily more than anything on earth."

Aynsley frowned. "You can understand why I wanted something else for my only daughter."

"Of course." Rebecca's arm swept toward the lake and arched to encompass all the area between them and Dunton Hall. "After all, she's been raised with such incredible privilege. It would be difficult to step down and marry a mere mister who has no property."

"Which is what my sister did, and I believe she came to regret it."

"I daresay your sister did not marry a man who had loved her almost since the cradle, though."

"True."

"Whether she has a Season is entirely up to you. You are, after all," she added with a smile, "the lord and master of all of us at Dunton."

"The Dunton curmudgeon is more like it." He did not look happy.

"It's difficult to achieve a delicate balance between affection and guidance. You, understandably, don't want to come across as a complete milksop."

"I have an aversion to being a milksop in any way."

"Yes, I learned that most painfully last night."

He offered her a smile. "This impromptu picnic was just what we needed."

"Indeed it was," she said, her voice soft. Being with him, sharing with him, seeing his anger dissipate, uncoiled the tightness and gloom that had been inside of her.

* * *

Rebecca's good humor carried over to the start of the dinner hour. As John escorted her to the dining room, she felt like a fairy princess. She wore the Aynsley emeralds, and they looked spectacular with her green velvet gown.

Not long after they sat at the dining table, her husband made the announcement about the procurement of a new housekeeper and governess, and Rebecca filled in with what she knew of their backgrounds.

"I daresay I've met the governess before," Peter said as he was cutting his grouse. "I was at Eton with one of the Devere sons and spent some time at their home." He shrugged. "Pity is, I can't remember a thing about the poor creature."

"I pray that you're not calling her a poor creature because our boys will be rough on her," Rebecca said.

Peter set down his fork and eyed her. "Surely you're aware of the fact those little *angels* have run off many, many governesses?"

"Unfortunately," Emily added, eyeing Rebecca, "what he says is true. It all started with Fordyce and Geoff, and now all the brothers feel they have a family tradition to uphold."

"Well, this father intends to put an immediate stop to such an unacceptable practice!" Aynsley said in his sternest voice.

After a considerable period of silence, Peter spoke. "And let's hope we can keep the housekeeper, Mrs. Cotton."

"You say this grouse is rotten?" Ethelbert shouted, pushing away his plate. "I just won't eat rotten grouse."

"Uncle," Aynsley said, "the grouse is *not* rotten!" He

raised his voice. "The new housekeeper's named Mrs. Cotton." Aynsley pushed the plate back.

Rebecca was happy to see that Emily was becoming more compassionate toward her great uncle. Emily smiled at him and began to speak in an elevated voice. "I'm writing a play in which I want you to act."

"Will I get to kiss the heroine?" he asked, a broad smile on his aged face.

As they all began discussing the play, Rebecca's attention strayed. For her, the dining room was dominated by Dorothy's portrait. She could not take a bite of food without staring at the blonde's elegant countenance. Rebecca wondered if the Aynsley jewels would look half so good on her own bony neck—not that she even wished to wear them now that she associated them with Dorothy.

She kept peering at the portrait, then at Emily. There was a strong resemblance between mother and daughter, but where Emily appeared delicate, Dorothy was formidable.

Rebecca had become more aware of the portrait with each successive meal. The first night she'd not known for sure that was Dorothy staring down at her—though from the fairly recent style of hair and dress she was almost certain the attractive woman in pale blue silk and lace had to be Dorothy. That first night Rebecca had too many other things on her mind to give the portrait much notice. Each night thereafter, though, she seemed more aware of it and was made more uncomfortable by it. And now she felt almost as if Dorothy were a silent guest at the meal, a silent guest even more hostile than Emily.

As John spoke to the others, Rebecca obsessed over

her predecessor. Had John loved her deeply? Had she been madly in love with him? Did he still grieve for the woman who'd given birth to his beloved children, the woman whose traits must remain in her progeny long after she had gone from this earth?

The more Rebecca dwelled on Dorothy, the more morose she became. If John were attracted to blue-eyed blondes, he must be very disappointed with Rebecca of the dark hair and almost-black eyes.

To sink her even lower, she had learned that Dorothy was the daughter of a duke. How exceedingly disappointed John must be in Rebecca. She'd brought nothing to the marriage except the ability to catalog a library! No wonder he'd gotten so upset with her didactic ways the previous night.

She tried to tell herself it was her lack of sleep that made her so melancholy, but then she'd feel compelled to stare at Dorothy, and the painting seemed to say, "You're not worthy to take my place. He'll never love you."

Love? Why did she keep thinking of love? The former Rebecca Peabody never thought about love. And love had never been part of this marriage. So, why in God's wide, wide world had John stooped to marry her?

"Why so quiet, Rebecca?" Peter asked.

Her glance flicked from him to Emily, who sat across the table from him and glared at Rebecca. "I daresay I'm just worn out. I was unable to sleep last night and haven't felt quite right all day."

"I didn't sleep well, either." John sent her a warm look. "I think we'll be early to bed."

Even though she was incredibly tired, she did not like the prospect of going to bed shortly after dinner and not enjoying private time with her husband. The evenings with him had become like a sumptuous dessert after a modest dinner, something she greatly looked forward to all day.

Was Aynsley sincere about wanting to be early to bed, or was he eager to have his library to himself—alone?

Chapter Twelve

Aynsley looked up from his desk when his weary wife came to the library after reading another chapter of *Ivanhoe* to the lads. Gone now was the sparkle he'd observed in her that afternoon when they sat in the folly beside the peaceful lake. He immediately left the desk and strode toward her. "Don't even think about staying here, madam. You need to go to bed."

"As do you, but there's something I must speak to you about."

The serious tone of her voice disturbed him. Was one of the boys sick? "What is it?"

"Please, let us go sit by the fire."

Once they sat down, he turned to her. "What's wrong?"

She drew a deep breath. He could see that she was trembling.

"Is something the matter with the children?"

She quickly reassured him. "No, they're all perfectly fine."

"Then it's you?"

Her face incredibly somber, she nodded. "I must tell

you why I'm so disturbed." She looked at the flames, then drew in another deep breath. "What I'm going to say will make me seem horridly selfish, and I fear I'll alienate the children, but I have to speak my mind."

"What's the matter, Rebecca?" he asked, his voice gentle.

"I cannot believe any other woman in the kingdom must eat dinner every night in her own home beneath a larger-than-life-size portrait of her predecessor."

Of course she was right! When a new countess came in, the old countess's portraits were consigned to the attics. How insensitive he'd been not to think of Rebecca's feelings! "Forgive me. I never thought of it. I'll have it removed in the morning."

"I fear Emily will hate me even more."

He wanted to reassure her, but she was likely right. Emily could be only barely civil to her stepmother. "I won't let her blame you. The removal of the portrait is *my* decision entirely. If my daughter blames anyone for the removal, she will blame me."

"Where will you put it?"

"Nowhere at Dunton Hall. Her portrait can return long after you and I have passed from this earth. For now, it will go to the heir. I'll send it to Oxford, and Fordyce can keep it in his chambers there." Aynsley took her slender hand in his. The poor girl. Her hand trembled. "I'm going to commission an artist to do your portrait."

She shook her head vigorously. "No, I haven't earned the right to have a portrait hanging at Dunton."

His brows lowered. "What can you mean? You're the Countess of Aynsley whether you wish to answer to that title or not. You don't have to *earn* anything."

"What I mean is," she said in a barely audible voice, "that I shan't merit a portrait until I could give birth to a child of Aynsley blood." Her eyes were downcast, as if she were too embarrassed to look at him.

Her words nearly knocked the breath from him. He knew he should say something, but he did not know what to say. At that instant he realized the prospect of having a child with his wedded wife held great appeal. Finally, he thought of a response. "Then we shall wait until then before I send for the artist." He was sure that day would come even if he didn't know when.

They both sat in silence, peering at the repetition of rising, flickering and falling flames, then he was aware of a whimpering. He spun toward her and met her watery gaze just before her face swooshed into her palms, and her shoulders began to shake with racking sobs.

He did not think; he only reacted. His arms closed around her as he hauled her into his chest, patting her and murmuring soft words.

"I—I—I am such a pea goose," she managed between huge sniffs.

"Whatever is the matter, dearest?"

"I don't belong here. I know you must wish you'd never married me. I'm so sorry."

He held her a bit tighter while shaking his head to emphasize his denial. "You are wrong. Not for a single minute have I regretted marrying you."

She began to bawl even louder.

"Have I done something to upset you?"

She shook her head. "I have no handkerchief, and I fear I'm ruining your fine coat."

He started to laugh. "My dear wife, you may blow your nose on my jacket for all I care. I have many more."

Sniff. Sniff. Then she, too, began to laugh as he tightened his arms around her, stroking and whispering soft words.

"Never forget, Rebecca, that night in Warwick's library it was I who asked you to marry me. Nobody can make me do something I don't want to do."

"But what have I brought to this marriage?"

"Much." She obviously confused wealth with intangible assets.

"I can't think of a single thing."

His gentle hands swept circles on her back. He rather liked the size of her. She was a bit smaller than average. "But I can. Were you not here, I'd be sitting in my library with nary a soul on earth with whom to share my life. Until we became reacquainted, I thought I'd die a lonely old man."

"Pray," she whispered in a soft voice, "I beg that you not talk about dying."

He smiled. "You see, that's another very good thing about having a wife. It's nice to know someone else cares for you." Now why had he gone and said that? She hadn't actually ever *told* him she cared for him.

"I do understand what you're saying. I thought I should miss Maggie dreadfully, but because I've got you—and I must own, your ideas and mine do not clash as mine and Maggie's do—I feel I've gained a best friend."

Even though having a best friend was *not* his motive in marrying her, he understood what she meant because he felt much the same. "I don't think I ever realized until we married how lonely I was."

She nodded, and he could feel the tension ease from her. "Me, too. Though I love Maggie most dearly, we had nothing in common. With you I feel…it's like the words at our wedding ceremony *a man shall be joined unto his wife; and they two shall be one flesh.*"

He was so touched by her words, it took a moment before he could find his voice. "We had much in common before you came to Dunton, as witnessed by our never-ending stream of shared ideas during the journey here. Now, I feel even closer. Because of the children. Raising children by oneself is difficult. I don't know how you've managed it in so short a time, but I know your affection for them is genuine. "

"Oh, it most assuredly is!" She straightened up and offered him a smile. "I was looking forward to being a mother, but I never imagined I would lose my heart so quickly."

He would not bring up Emily. Her animosity toward Rebecca would only send his wife back into hysterics. He took a good long look at her. The firelight was reflected in the spectacles that seemed to accentuate the red now in those soulful eyes of hers. "You look tired, and it's my fault you didn't sleep last night. Come, Lady Aynsley, it's time you go off to bed."

He was pleased she did not chide him for referring to her as Lady Aynsley, a title he rather liked.

"You know, another thing that's better at Dunton now that you're here," he said as they mounted the stairs, "is having my uncle back at the dinner table." Dorothy had forbidden the poor old fellow to even come up to the big house.

"You are making me feel so much better. Two months ago I never dreamed I'd ever have a family of my own, and now I find having a family even more fun than—"

She stopped, then shrugged. "Well, more fun than anything in my previous life."

He knew very well that she almost alluded to her essay writing, but she had stopped short. Why could she not be totally honest with him? This could never be a true marriage until he gained her complete trust.

That she would not be completely open with him once more sent him into curmudgeon mode. By the time they reached her chamber door, the smile that had been on his face was gone, and he brusquely brushed his lips across her cheek. "Earl's orders, madam, get a good night's sleep."

"Yes, my lord."

He could not deny it. He liked being referred to as *my lord.* Another source of friction in a marriage that held much promise.

She could not fall asleep despite the fatigue that made her body ache, despite the earl's orders and despite that she and John had repaired the previous night's rift. The previous night's melancholy was now replaced with a buoyant feeling unlike anything she had ever experienced.

Rebecca Peabody had always prided herself on her analytic mind. Rebecca, Countess Aynsley, was an altogether different creature. Numbers and theories were things she clearly understood. But these…these *feelings* were untried, unfamiliar and unwelcome territory. She had actually become a watering pot tonight! She had experienced a jealousy toward Dorothy that was so intense, it had made her feel as if she were the most inferior creature ever to draw breath. And this wasn't the first time since coming to Dunton that she had experienced jealousy—though in her previous eight and twenty years she could not remember ever having a jealous thought!

Even though she did not understand why she was becoming such a slave to emotions—which she most decidedly had never, ever been before—she rather fancied the pleasant emotions she was experiencing now. Dear John was going to remove Dorothy's portrait! Dear John did not regret marrying her. Dear John was no longer lonely.

Nor was she. For the first time in her life, actually.

Before she finally did drift off into sleep, she decided she would personally go to Birmingham in the morning to greet Mrs. Cotton. Sending only the driver was too impersonal. Mrs. Cotton must be shown how desperately she was needed, how grateful were the Aynsleys to have her.

Now that Rebecca thought on it, she was rather glad to be getting new servants. Servants of her own. Servants who would not owe their allegiance to the previous countess.

Forgive me, Lord, for being so wretchedly jealous of our children's mother and help me to be a better person.

When Rebecca awoke the following morning, her sense of well-being was still with her. She rang for Pru. "I wish for you to make me very pretty today."

"Yer always pretty, my lady."

Rebecca scowled. "Now what have I told you about addressing me as a lady?"

Pru frowned. "Seeing as that's how all the other servants refer to you, it seems only right that yer own maid would. Besides, I always fancied being lady's maid to a fine Lady Something. Yer sister hasn't ever minded being a countess." She laughed. "She liked it so much, she married two Lord Warwicks!"

"Her first husband, you will remember, was a counterfeit Lord Warwick, the scoundrel. If I ever return to Virginia, I shall certainly have his grave marker changed."

"A terrible man he was, deceiving your poor sister."

Rebecca had come to sit before her dressing table. "You, of all people, must know how unlike my sister I am. I am *not* attracted to titles."

The maid proceeded to style Rebecca's hair, chattering constantly. Rebecca felt guilty that she wasn't really listening. She was attempting to analyze her sudden interest in looking pretty. Looking pretty had never been something Rebecca Peabody had even spent any time contemplating.

But, of course, the newlywed Lady Aynsley was a different person. This Rebecca had a strong desire for John to think her pretty. There. That didn't take any prodigiously analytical mind. She merely wished her husband to find her pretty.

What happened to her burning desire to write a book on political reform? She hadn't even been capable of penning an essay promulgating something she felt very strongly about!

That would come later. Other things were more important now. Things like meeting the new housekeeper. And imparting to the new governess all that she wished for her to teach the lads. And taking time every day to ride with John. And read to the boys. And discuss reform with John in the library each night.

A pity she could not reach out and find some commonality with Emily. The play had been a start, but the little ground it had gained had eroded by last night. She'd felt her stepdaughter's glare throughout dinner. Hers and her mother's.

At least Dorothy would be banished today!

But Dorothy was not banished.

And Rebecca's sense of happiness was destroyed when she came downstairs and met her husband. A frown on his face and a letter in his hand, he asked that she follow him into the library.

"I fear I've got some disappointing news."

Her first thought was that his son had been killed in Spain. She was quivering, so her voice shook when she asked him what was wrong.

He closed the door of the library for privacy. "I have to return to London at once."

As thoroughly disappointed as she was, she was at least relieved the bad news did not concern Geoffrey or one of the other boys. She collapsed onto a sofa, very much aware that her husband had said *I* rather than *we*. He did not intend to take her. "Why?"

"Lord Sethbridge has sent a special messenger to beg that I come at once. He desperately needs me to help him pass the bill to raise taxes."

"But I thought you'd not made up your mind to support a tax increase?"

"It's a grave step," he said, shaking his head. "This war's been costly, and I cannot help but to wonder how much more of a burden the people can sustain. I know, though, that if we don't raise taxes, our troops won't get paid and our government won't be able to operate."

"If that's the case, every Member of Parliament who's there should feel compelled to vote for it. I don't see why you have to go. You're only one person." One person she did not want to do without. She was—dare she even think it?—*afraid* to stay on without him, without his support. He was her only advocate at Dunton.

"It may very well come down to one vote. Lord Sethbridge assures me that if I will support him, he will support my franchise bill."

"He will actually support it? As in voting *for* it?" That would be a coup, indeed, for Aynsley. "I thought he told you he could not personally vote for it, but that he might consider not standing in your way."

"He's always vehemently opposed such a measure—as do a majority of the Lords, but he's willing to compromise in order to get me back to London. In addition to my vote, he seems to think I may have some influence over other members." He shrugged, as if he did not credit such an opinion.

Even though social gatherings appealed little to her husband, his intelligence and solidity commanded the respect of other members of the House of Lords. Those same qualities—combined with his dislike of balls and routs—were the ones that had initially attracted her to him. "Lord Sethbridge's support for the franchise extension would be a very valuable thing," she said.

So, of course, her noble husband would go and do his duty. She should be ecstatic. Wasn't the expansion of the franchise one of those reforms she had been so passionate about? Hadn't the reforms been the guiding force of her entire existence? Hadn't the prospect of having a husband who was actually in Parliament—who had the power to enact reforms—been one of the huge pluses to marrying John in the first place? Why, then, did she feel as if she were losing her best friend?

Because she was. It suddenly occurred to her that

her husband had, indeed, become her best friend. She did not want to be separated from him.

He, apparently, had not given a thought to traveling to the Capital with her. She eyed him as he paced back and forth across the library, the expression on his pensive face inscrutable.

She fleetingly thought of begging to come with him, but she could not. She disliked putting herself in a position to be pitiable. And there was another reason, too, why she could not force her presence upon him. Early on in this relationship, she had been the aggressor. She couldn't risk alienating him again by being too forward. Hadn't he gotten angry with her just two nights ago because she'd attempted to tell him what to do?

If he wanted a meek, compliant wife, then she would attempt to be a meek, compliant wife. For the sake of her family.

The very notion of having her own family suffused her with a warm glow.

"I shall go immediately."

She whirled at him, her stomach roiling. "Why immediately?"

"Because if I go now, I can go in Sethbridge's carriage. It's here. I know you'll be needing ours to get the housekeeper in Birmingham."

In this morning's chaos she had completely forgotten about Mrs. Cotton. "How will you return?"

"You can send the carriage for me when I'm finished with my work."

Her stomach plummeted and her brows lowered. "How long does it take to cast one vote? Do you mean you won't be back at Dunton right away?" She hoped her voice did not sound as forlorn as she felt.

"Lord Sethbridge says he will try to get the vote this week, but it could take up to two weeks." He came to sit beside her. "I hate to have to cut short the honeymoon, and I hate to have to leave you here so soon."

Not nearly as much as I. She vowed to be strong. Hadn't she—when she was still Miss Peabody—assured him she could competently run his home and care for his children most adeptly in his absence? Isn't that one of the reasons he needed a wife? A strong, competent wife? "I shall manage most capably." She offered him a bright smile, even though she felt as if she could bawl. "I shall miss you."

His eyes locked with hers. There was a boyish quality about him despite the brush of silver in the hair just above his ears. "I will write every day."

"Every night before you go to bed you must summarize your day for me. If you'd like, I can do the same."

"I would like that very much."

There was a rap at the library door.

"That will be my man. He's been packing my things."

So his valet had known John was leaving Dunton before she knew. Her opinion was not to have been considered. He had already made up his mind.

The valet stepped into the chamber. "Your valise is ready, my lord."

Rebecca leaped to her feet. "Oh, my dearest, I must have Cook send along a basket for you!"

"Now see," he said, shooting her a crooked grin, "a wife is a very useful thing to have. I hadn't even thought of food, but two or three hours from now I would likely be starving."

While Cook was gathering food into a basket, Rebecca saw that the children were summoned to say farewell to their father.

Minutes later, when Aynsley began to stride toward the carriage, only Chuckie seemed as upset as she. He began to cry. Rebecca picked him up and comforted him. "As soon as Papa goes, I will let you ride in the carriage with me to get Mrs. Cotton."

As his tears evaporated, she and John exchanged amused glances. "Take care of yourself," she said. She took one last, long look at her husband as if to impress his vision upon her memory. His slightly long, casually styled hair was the same light brown as his soft leather boots. In spite of the stern face he put on, his patrician features could not conceal his natural congeniality.

His gaze fanned over the children. "I'm expecting all of you to be on your best behavior for Rebecca."

"Yes, my lord," the boys said in unison.

"And I'm counting on you lads to show the new housekeeper that the Compton family respects and values her." He drilled Alex and Spencer with a ferocious glare.

Their heads hung, they nodded.

Even though she felt like crying, she flashed what she hoped was a radiant smile upon him when he came close, one hand clasping at her waist as he leaned into her and brushed his lips over hers.

"I shall miss you most dreadfully," she said.

"And I shall miss all of you," he said, a grim set to his mouth.

Chapter Thirteen

Her first day without John was so full she had not been able to dwell on him. It wasn't until after dinner, after she had read the lads a chapter of *Ivanhoe,* that her spirits began to sink.

From habit, she went from the boys' chamber to the library. Though a robust fire blazed, and the room was always most comforting, now—without John—the room seemed unfamiliar. She went to his desk and ran a loving hand over it. How lonely the chamber was without him. How she wished he were here to speak of Parliament with her. She never tired of discussing his important work in Lords, never tired of discussing the reforms they both endorsed, never tired of discussing political theory.

What she and John shared went much deeper than common interests, though. The children had given a new purpose to her life, and her mutual affection for them bonded her even closer to the man she had married.

She stood in the middle of the library, her gaze sweeping over its dark, mellow wood, the faded red leather bindings on row after row of books, many of which had been in the Compton family for generations. As much as she loved this room, she did not want to be there tonight without him. Without John. Her husband.

She trudged up the stairs and to her bedchamber. She had much to impart to her husband. Tossing off her shoes, she went to the writing desk, Dorothy's desk, and took up pen and paper, while vowing to replace the opulent desk at the earliest opportunity.

Dearest,

As Chuckie and I drove in the carriage to Birmingham, my thoughts were with you. I found myself wondering how far you had gone, where you would be, when you would arrive in London. It was a lovely day for a drive, was it not? Chuckie adored looking out the window. He's most enamored of sheep. He was quite the little lamb himself, and I am happy to report he did not have a single accident.

As to Mrs. Cotton, I found her most agreeable. She told me she will be fifty next year, and if she were not possessed of silver hair, she would appear much younger. Her figure is trim, and her hair is neatly arranged. She is most energetic, brushing off the coachman's efforts to carry her valise, declaring that she was perfectly capable of carrying her own things.

When we got to Dunton, I showed her to her rooms—she was most happy with her accommodations—and told her that she needed to rest after the wearying travel, that I would show her the house tomorrow, but she declared she wasn't a bit tired and was ready to jump right in!

You will be happy to know she thought Dunton a lovely home—much less fussy than Lord Bermondsey's, she said—and she added that the Shropshire landscape suited her quite well. She pointed out that all our chandeliers needed a good cleaning. She seemed courteous to the staff she will head, and she complimented Cook on the menu, even telling her she would be happy to seek Cook's input as well as mine when drawing up the menus.

I have just realized one of my duties is to work with Mrs. Cotton on the menus, therefore I need to know all your favorite foods. Besides buttered lobster and plum pudding—which I am very well aware of.

Mrs. Cotton asked about our entertaining, and I confessed that we were positive hermits when in the country. After meeting all her staff and interviewing with them, she has determined we need one more chambermaid, so I authorized her to seek one. Do you object?

After dinner the children began to build sets for Emily's play. She has decided she will sew costumes for everyone in The Play. Everything should be ready for production when you come home. I confess I am most anxious to see it. The children are very excited about being actors. As clever as he is, dear Alex told me, "I would wager Papa won't recognize me in my costume!" It was all I could do not to laugh.

By the time you return, our new governess should be installed at Dunton.

The library without you makes your wife most

forlorn, especially when the children are in their beds and I wish to share a quiet time in that comforting room with their father. How I longed to have you there! It was so wretchedly lonely, I came to my bedchamber to write this letter.

I am eager to learn how your work in Parliament progresses. Pray, keep me well informed. I assure you, I hunger for all the details.

I worry that you won't take proper care of yourself. When you are excessively busy, you often forget to eat. Remember all of us at Dunton who care about you. I shall be a most morose woman until you return.

Most affectionately,

R.

The following day Rebecca continued to ease Mrs. Cotton's transition by going over the household accounts with her. It wouldn't do at all for Mrs. Cotton to learn what a short time Rebecca herself had been there. It was imperative to Rebecca that Mrs. Cotton see her as the competent mistress of Dunton.

Would John ever come to think of her in that manner?

Rebecca continued to feel melancholy. She could not understand why she was so very blue deviled. The sun favored them. The children were all well. The new housekeeper could not be better qualified and was also possessed of an agreeable personality. Tomorrow Miss Seton would arrive.

John's absence accounted for most of her sorrow, she knew, but her moroseness went even deeper. She was wounded that he had not considered taking his bride with him when he returned to London. She tried to console herself with the recollection of her own persuasive argument to him for marrying her. He needed a competent, intelligent, well-organized woman to oversee the running of his home and the upbringing of his children.

Now that he had wed such a woman—in a marriage that was not a complete marriage—why should he not wish to leave his family in her care?

She should not feel so hurt. But she did.

And because of the urgency of his trip to the Capital, he had forgotten about his promise to remove Dorothy's portrait.

Rebecca had never allowed herself to stare at the portrait because others were always present when she was in the dining room. Now that John was gone and all the others busy, she felt beckoned to the dining room, beckoned to peer at the portrait of John's dead wife.

The dining room's gold silken draperies had been opened, and the room filled with light. Rebecca came to stand before Dorothy's portrait. A Gainsborough.

Did Gainsborough never paint a woman who was not a beauty? The painting was executed about twenty years previously. Were Dorothy still alive, she would be a middle-aged woman. Rebecca took a most perverse—and she hated to admit, mean-spirited—satisfaction in hoping that Dorothy's lovely face had begun to sag and wrinkle, that the hair that was powdered in this portrait would have turned gray.

The resemblance between Dorothy and Emily was strong, but Emily was prettier than her mother. Despite Dorothy's fair blond, blue-eyed beauty, there was a quality about her that was more formidable than feminine. It took no great perception to understand that this self-assured-looking woman was a duke's daughter. There was an aura of privilege as well as arrogance about her aristocratic face.

Dear God, please rid me of these feelings of such intense jealousy.

While Rebecca stood rooted to the Turkey carpet staring at her predecessor and feeling wretchedly inadequate, Emily stopped in the doorway, malice on her face. "What are you doing?"

Rebecca felt like a thief snatching alms from the poor box. "I…I was noting how very much you look like your mother."

"Yes, I'm often told that."

"I have a question to ask you," Rebecca said, turning away from the portrait, her face flaming. "It's about the writing desk in my bedchamber—I presume it was your mother's—and I wondered if you would like to have it. The gilt is a bit too formal for my tastes. I saw one of a more simple design in the Yellow Room when I was showing Mrs. Cotton around this morning, and I believe I would prefer to have that one in my chamber."

Emily glared. "Then, yes, of course, I should like to have my mother's desk." She continued on down the corridor.

Rebecca started after her. "There's one more question I'd like to ask."

Emily spun around. "What?"

"Was your mother older than your father?" Now why had she gone and asked such an irrelevant, ridiculous question? What had prompted such a question in the first place?

Iciness stung Emily's voice. "As a matter of fact, she

was. She was three years older." Emily turned away and left Rebecca staring after her.

If John was now three and forty, and his eldest child was nineteen, he must have become a father at four and twenty and married at three and twenty. Therefore, Dorothy would have been six and twenty when they wed. On the shelf.

Like Rebecca had been.

There was one question that only John could answer, one question she would never ask, yet it was the question that had begun to plague her every moment.

Had John been terribly in love with Dorothy?

And even more painful…did he regret marrying Rebecca?

It seemed so strange to Aynsley after a lifetime of loneliness to be sharing a bond with someone. With a woman. Throughout his first day back in London, he kept finding himself saying, "I must share this with Rebecca" or "I must tell Rebecca that."

By the time he came to his bedchamber well past midnight that first night, he had no desire to go to bed even though he was bone weary. He could not allow himself to lie down until he imparted to his wife all that had occurred that day.

He removed his coat and boots, then went to the desk in his bedchamber where he began to pen the letter.

> My Dearest Rebecca,
>
> I came to Lord Sethbridge upon my arrival in London, and he apprised me of the fact we need eighteen more votes to pass the tax bill. He had drawn up a list of those lords still in opposition to

the measure, and he asked which ones I thought I could influence. While I believe he is possessed of an inflated sense of my consequence, I told him which men I would try to persuade to our way of thinking. Because the list was longer than I had anticipated, I may remain in London longer than I had planned.

I made it clear from the outset my efforts would be contingent on his support of my franchise bill, and he gave me his word to go against his personal convictions and vote for the proposal when the time comes.

I started my conquest tonight by attending a dinner at Lord and Lady Holland's. While they are decidedly Whig, Lady Holland assembles a good mix from all quarters. I counted twelve Members of Parliament at the (very large) table. I found myself wondering if you'd ever taken dinner there. It was just the sort of gathering I fancy you'd enjoy.

I actually introduced the matter of the tax increase, and the ensuing discussion was most lively. In fact, the remainder of the evening, each man, and many women, present weighed in on the matter. Lord Holland favors it, and I believe he and I managed to coax two fence straddlers to our way of thinking, and there are three more we will work on. So, whittle that list down to sixteen. For now.

When your sister found out I was in town (she was gravely disappointed you did not accompany me), she insisted on having me—and many others who hold government positions—to dinner tomorrow. I expect there will be many Tories there.

Hopefully some can be persuaded to support the tax increase. For the good of England.

I have not been so tired in a very long time, but I could not even think of going to bed until I wrote you, as promised. I miss being at Dunton more than words can say.

Yours,
Aynsley

She folded up the letter and pressed it to her heart. It was the kind of silly gesture a schoolgirl might do. What was coming over her? The former Miss Rebecca Peabody was becoming ruled by emotions—and profound feelings like nothing she had ever before experienced.

How dear was this letter to her! *His letter.* In his neat hand. That he had thought of her even though he was bone weary made her feel as if her chest were expanding with joy.

At the same time she missed him so acutely, it was almost painful.

Two days after Aynsley left, Miss Seton arrived. She was so highly valued by the Devere family, for whom she had been employed many years, that Lord Devere sent her all the way to Shropshire in the Devere carriage, which also carried all her worldly goods.

It made Rebecca sad that a woman who had lived more than four decades possessed no more than could fit into one valise and one portmanteau. How sad not to have a family of her own. Rebecca vowed to endeavor to make both Miss Seton and Mrs. Cotton feel valued as if they were an integral part of the Compton family.

Rebecca told Miss Seton her duties would not begin

until her first full day. On the day of her arrival, Rebecca invited her for tea in front of the fire in the drawing room.

"How many years were you with the Devere family?" Rebecca asked, to make her feel comfortable by talking about the familiar.

"For fifteen years. It was a privilege to have instructed all eight of the Devere children."

"And the youngest one is?" Rebecca studied Miss Seton so she could write an accurate description of her in tonight's letter to her husband.

"That would be Lady Sarah, who is now seventeen."

"I am acquainted with Lady Sophia, who would bring credit to anyone."

Miss Seton's plump face broke into a broad smile. "Indeed she would. She is as kind and intelligent as she is beautiful."

"I hope you will find our lads intelligent."

"*Our?* Lady Sophia told me you have just married Lord Aynsley."

Rebecca frowned. Just married? It seemed as if she had been married for a considerable period of time. And it did seem as if the lads should be hers. She certainly wanted them to be. "While it's true that I've not been married long, I think of my husband's dear children as my own."

"What are their ages?"

"While he has seven children, four of them are past the age of needing a governess. We have three lads at home still. Spencer is eight, and Alex is six. Chuckie's a bit too young for a governess. He's three."

"Very good. I had several offers of employment, but the reason I chose to come to Shropshire—besides the kind words Lady Sophia spoke about you—was the knowledge that you and Lord Aynsley are bound to have more children, so I will be able to make my home here for many years. I do not like being uprooted."

Heat began to sting Rebecca's cheeks. For someone who had never blushed until her twenty-eighth year, she was squeezing a lifetime's worth into the past several weeks.

What an incredibly intimate topic for the governess to introduce! Rebecca herself had not even thought on that subject recently. Miss Seton's comment left her momentarily mute. "Your desire to make your home with us, hopefully for the rest of your life, is just the very thing we have hoped for. I will do everything in my power to see that you will be happy here at Dunton."

"Thank you. Now what can you tell me about the lads?" For a woman who'd been an authority figure over others for more than two decades, Miss Seton was surprisingly soft-spoken, and her countenance was meek.

"I believe Spencer and Alex are both very intelligent. They are being tutored in Greek, Latin and mathematics by Mr. Witherstrum in the afternoons. They will come to you in the mornings. You will help with their French, penmanship, reading and music."

"How do the lads get on with each other?"

Rebecca smiled. "The fact that you ask that question tells me you must have experience with squabbling brothers."

"In my experience, brothers come to fisticuffs with one another on a weekly basis—not that I tolerate such behavior."

In her wildest imaginings, Rebecca could not picture Miss Seton being an assertive disciplinarian. "I believe a lot of the friction between Spencer and Alex results from Alex wanting to do everything his brother does—and not quite being able to measure up—"

"Because he's two years younger." The governess was nodding. "Exactly like my Stephen and Richard. They, too, were two years apart."

My Stephen and Richard. Those four words from Miss Seton's own lips were the most stupendous recommendation of her employment.

Rebecca knew Miss Seton was the perfect governess for her sons.

That night she eagerly picked up her pen and wrote to John.

Dearest,

I have every confidence you will shoot off a letter to me at the completion of every day you are in London because you know how much I share your interest in the workings of government and how much I long to hear of everything you are doing. Miss Seton arrived today. That she came in the Devere family carriage speaks to her worthiness. The Deveres valued her highly.

I like her very much. She's more meek than I would have expected, but the lady is possessed of a good heart, which is, to me, the most important recommendation. She called the Devere boys "my Stephen and Richard." Is that not a wonderful testament to her temperament? She may not be a stern disciplinarian, though she assured me she did not tolerate fisticuffs between her lads!

I do hope Spencer and Alex do not engage

in fisticuffs. As you know, I abhor violence of any kind.

Miss Seton was with the Devere family for fifteen years, and while I did not ask specifically, I think they were probably not her first family—owing to her age. She, too, is well into her forties. Unlike Mrs. Cotton, Miss Seton is a little on the portly side. I do hope our lads are inclined to like her as much as I do. And I pray they will comport themselves as the gentlemen they should be.

I do miss you dreadfully. Every room where I am accustomed to seeing you now seems wretchedly void without you. And as much as I have grown to love Dunton, I think I do not like it without you. Am I not most pitiable? What has happened to that strong woman I assured you I was?

I shall go to sleep happy now, knowing I will have your letter tomorrow.

With deepest affection,

R.

The next day's post brought another letter from her husband. She rushed to the library to open it, sitting herself right down at his desk to read it.

He was true to his word, apprising her of all that he'd been doing in London. She could almost hear his voice as she read the words he had written. She read the letter through two times. As she was finishing the second time, Chuckie entered the room.

"Mother? Is this the day you and I are going to go walking with Uncle Effelbert?"

Her heart melted like cheap tallows when he called her *mother*. "Yes, love. Would you like to go now?"

His head bobbed up and down.

When they arrived at Ethelbert's cottage, he leaped from his invalid's chair and smacked Rebecca on the cheek while throwing his arms around her.

She distanced herself from him by several inches. "Uncle, you are to be seated. We've come to take you for a walk." She had learned to raise her voice considerably when she spoke to the hard-of-hearing man.

"Hello, Uncle," Chuckie shouted—as Rebecca had instructed.

"Hello, lad. Would you like to ride on my lap?"

"Indeed," Chuckie answered, looking up at Rebecca for approval.

She nodded. "If you'd like, love."

Chuckie climbed onto Ethelbert's bony lap, and Rebecca pushed them out the front door.

Being with John's son and his uncle in some strange way compensated for his absence. Each of them had a part of John in them, and she was compelled to snatch whatever she could.

She was astonished at how much she missed him.

The following day she received another letter from him. Once again, she rushed to the library to read it at his desk.

My dear Wife,

I have now received two letters from you and could not be happier to learn that our home is fully and capably staffed. Pray, write me what the lads think of Miss Seton. I hope they are as happy with her as you seem to be. I would have preferred her to be a sterner disciplinarian. Lads are apt to take advantage of meek, middle-aged women.

It is well past midnight as I write this, and for the past few hours I've been eager to write to you and impart what has transpired today. I am still rather astonished at how successful I've been in my mission. I delivered five new votes to Lord Sethbridge today! Two of the Lords who were at the Hollands last night called on me today and pledged their votes. In addition, I coaxed three Lords at Warwick's tonight. When I left there, I went by Lord Sethbridge's.

He told me in the strictest confidence—and he, I and you are the only three in the universe who know this—that next year he will introduce the franchise-expansion bill, so I shall have at least ten months to use my so-called persuasive powers to bring around as many parliamentarians as I can to support it. Please understand that for now, no one else is to be privy to this information. I know I can share this with you, knowing it will go no further.

Do you suppose Lord Sethbridge knew something about me that I, myself, did not know? As you know, I am not a very social creature. Lord Sethbridge said it's my very reticence and he used the word "solidity," that make me command respect. I would never repeat any of the previous musings to anyone except you, and only because I perceive that you are somewhat partial to me. I do beg that you tell no one what I've just imparted. I would come across as one in possession of a most inflated sense of my self-worth.

If we keep up at such a rate, I may be home much sooner. As sorry as I am that you are melancholy in my absence, I confess the knowledge that you are, pleased me. Does that not make me a most selfish husband?

As it was a mild day, I hungered for fresh air, air like that in my beloved Shropshire countryside, so I went for a walk in Hyde Park, but I confess it made me wish you were by my side as when we walk through the paths of Dunton.

So I suppose I share your moroseness.

Please give my love to the children. Are you finished with *Ivanhoe* yet? What will you read next that will have the lads in such raptures?

I pray that Emily's demeanor is less chilling. Will you please let me write to her, begging that she be more civil? I'm very vexed with her.

I am very tired, so I will close. I wish I were at Dunton. With you.

With deepest affection,

Aynsley

The most grievous source of her displeasure was her loneliness. She longed for him desperately. Emily had become even more antagonistic. Without her father's presence, she was outwardly hostile to Rebecca. Each day in John's absence had become more intolerable. Rebecca was still sitting there at his desk, his letter in front of her, when her stepdaughter entered the library.

"Have you seen Peter?"

Rebecca was thankful she had not asked if she knew where Peter was because Rebecca could not tell a lie. "No, I haven't seen him."

Emily's icy glare fell on the letter. "Have you a letter from Papa?"

"Yes."

"Does he say when he's coming home?"

Rebecca shook her head.

"May I come and see the desk in your chamber, Mama's desk?"

"Yes, of course." Rebecca stuck the letter in the top drawer of her husband's desk.

As much as she could enjoy anything in John's absence, Rebecca had enjoyed walking with Spencer and Alex into the village. This was the day they had been excused from their lessons, awarded the pence they had earned by not arguing with each other, and spent their money on comfits.

She did not know if she could credit the ingenuity of her plan or Miss Seton's soothing, steadying influence for the improvement in their conduct, but the boys had made her very proud. This was the first Friday they both got to go, and it pleased her how well they got along with each other during the journey. Their happy spirits combined with the radiant sunshine on the crisp, cool day lifted the gloom that had settled over her for the past two weeks of her husband's absence.

It was late afternoon as they were returning to Dunton, which they could see in the distance. "I'll race you to Dunton Hall," Spencer said.

"But you're faster than me because you're older," Alex protested.

"So I'll allow you to start before me."

"How much?" Alex asked, one red brow shooting up.

Spencer shrugged, looking up at Rebecca. "How much do you think?"

"It's quite some distance still, which would allow

you to catch him rather easily, unless you wait until he reaches the edge of the park before you start," she said.

"But—" Spencer stopped himself in midcomplaint. "Very well. I still believe I can beat you!"

Alex took off running.

Spencer did not sprint away for at least a minute, possibly two, before his brother reached the lush green lawn.

Watching the sun sinking in the sky beyond Dunton and watching the lads who brought her so much happiness made her feel as if she, too, could run back to Dunton. How long had it been since she had run? Probably not since she had been Spencer's age.

As she came into the park, her heart fluttered. She thought she saw John on the steps in front of Dunton. Her heart began to beat prodigiously. It was John!

All of a sudden, she did begin to run, like a barefoot child on a summer day. Her face lifted into a smile. She continued to run as he swung his sons into the air, then he set them down and stood there facing her.

Now she could clearly see his face. He was smiling!

Next, she found herself in his arms, found her arms hugging him tightly, found her face lifting to his. His head lowered to hers, and she stood on her tiptoes to kiss this much-beloved man.

Chapter Fourteen

Even after the kiss—which seemed the most natural thing she had ever done—Rebecca could not remove her arms from her husband's torso. It was as if by holding him, she could assure herself he was, indeed, home, that by holding him tightly she could prevent him from ever leaving her again. "I can't believe you're home! This is the most wonderful surprise ever!" She nestled her face against his chest, her smile reaching toward the heavens, her hands linking behind his back.

She was actually shocked over the boldness that had sent her flying into his arms, that allowed her to hug him like a child with its rag doll. She was shocked, too, that her actions did not embarrass her. How could they? Greeting her husband like this felt so right, so natural. This was the man to whom she had been joined in holy matrimony, the man whose flesh would be her flesh.

Her husband drew her tightly against him as he tenderly kissed the crown of her head. "Had I known I would be welcomed in such a manner, I would have gone away sooner."

Still not ready to disengage from him, she said,

"How did you get here? I thought you were going to send for the carriage?"

"We voted for the tax bill the day before yesterday, and I was eager to be home. Since the weather was fair, I rode. With great haste."

That he admitted he was eager to be home compensated somewhat for his decision to leave her behind. That decision had hurt even more than his absence—and his absence had hurt a great deal. She had convinced herself he regretted marrying her, that he wanted to be away from her, that he still loved Dorothy. "You really missed…Dunton?" She had started to say *me* instead of *Dunton.*

He pulled away in order to meet her gaze. "Very much. I'm happy to be home." His head bent, and their lips came together. It was a light kiss, and it lasted but a second, yet it spoke more eloquently than a poet's words of love.

She finally managed to pull away from him. "I cannot tell you how happy I am to have you home, my dearest."

They held hands and climbed the steps to Dunton Hall together. She could not remember ever being happier than she was at that moment.

"The lads told me they walked into the village this afternoon and had enough coins to indulge in all the comfits they desired. How can this be?" he asked.

She frowned as they strode along the entry hall. "They could not go last Friday because they did not have enough pence, owing to their less-than-desirable behavior. I like to think that motivated them to be good lads this past week. Neither of them was penalized a single farthing all week."

"I'm very proud of them, then. Why did you not take the carriage into Wey?" He nodded at the footman who was lighting candles in the entry hall's wall sconces.

"The boys preferred to walk, and I must own, I rather liked the idea myself."

"You barely made it home by dark. Had you forgotten how early night falls this time of year?"

"We did cut it close." She gazed at the mock stern expression on his face. "The walk will have given them quite an appetite for dinner. Can they join us tonight? To celebrate your return?"

He nodded, smiling. "Very well. You certainly know how to spoil children. What happened to that woman I married, the one who said strict discipline was exactly what was needed with my rowdy boys?"

"She changed from being a sanctimonious spinster to a…" She swallowed, then lowered her voice. "I'd like to think to a mother."

He squeezed her hand. "You are, my dear. My children are blessed to have you." His voice lowered. "As am I."

Then he did not regret marrying her! Her joy knew no bounds.

Aynsley sat at the head of the long dinner table, his eye cast over those assembled, those he loved most. At his left, lovely Emily. She wore about her elegant neck her mother's pearls, the same Dorothy had worn in the Gainsborough.

The Gainsborough! His glance flicked to the wall where his first wife's portrait still hung. Poor Rebecca. He'd forgotten to have it removed. Making his new wife sit beneath a larger-than-life-size portrait of her predecessor every night was more than any bride should be asked to bear. He silently vowed this would be the last night she would have to endure it.

His gaze moved across the table from Em to his nephew, who sat next to Ethelbert. How had Peter's skin darkened so much in just a few weeks? Then his gaze moved to his three lads. Spencer and Alex next to each other, neatly dressed and freshly scrubbed and behaving remarkably well. Opposite them and next to Rebecca, Chuckie teetered on Aynsley's father's massive *Plutarch's Lives,* which he was surprised had not been replaced since the *accident* the last time his younger boys had dined with them.

But of all those gathered there, the one who drew most of his attention was Rebecca, who sat at the opposite end of the table from him. He did not delude himself that she was a great beauty, but there was no other woman on earth with whom he would rather share his life.

The coral gown she wore accentuated the hint of coral in her alabaster cheeks. Her rich, dark brown locks had been swept away from her youthful face in a most becoming fashion. If he was not mistaken, her beautiful sister wore her hair in the same fashion. He recalled how melancholy it had made him to dine at the Warwicks' and observe the sister who bore so striking a resemblance to his own bride. Peering at Maggie had made him long for Rebecca in the flesh.

Why had he not asked his wife to accompany him to London? He had to concede that he had not even considered it. With the new housekeeper and new governess both scheduled to arrive during the week of his departure, he knew the mistress of the house had to greet them and acquaint them with their duties at Dunton.

Also, he had become so accustomed to leaving his wife and children behind when he went to the Capital, he'd ordered his valet to pack his bag even before he'd told Rebecca the news. For so many years now—even when Dorothy was still alive—he'd lived so solitary an existence he was in the practice of making plans for one, never for two.

How incredulous it seemed that now, at the age of three and forty, he had finally found his life's companion.

Not until he'd reached London did he realize how deeply he would miss Rebecca. Each day there without her had been miserable. That she had felt the same—and willingly confessed her melancholy—had eased his own suffering as effectively as an apothecary's restorative.

How happy it made him to peer down the table at his sweet wife. The very memory of the stupendously satisfying welcome she had given him made him feel as if he could soar high over this candlelit dining room.

The purity and tenderness of her kiss had nearly shattered him. From the day he realized she was P. Corpus, he had known her huge heart capable of great love. Before he'd gone to London, he knew she loved his children. When he was in London, he suspected from her letters that she held in her heart a great fondness for him. Now that he had returned from London, he believed she had fallen in love with him. Did she even know it yet? Did she even understand the potency of her feelings?

He nearly lost his breath at the memory of their

sweet kiss. Equally as touching was watching her help Chuckie cut his roast beef.

It was so very good to be home.

"Now that you're home, Papa," Emily said, "we are ready to present our production."

"I am greatly looking forward to it. Rebecca said you've been sewing the cast's costumes yourself," he said.

She nodded. "My timing could not have been more perfect. I finished the last one this afternoon."

"Then will we have the privilege of seeing your masterpiece tomorrow?" He looked hopefully at her.

She glared at Peter. "Will you be able to honor us with your presence tomorrow, Peter?"

"Seeing as how I'm to be the star," he said facetiously, his eyes glittering as he watched her, "I shall be available tomorrow evening."

"Tell me," Aynsley said to him, "how is it you've become…darker in my absence?"

Peter hesitated a moment before he responded. "I have discovered I wish to be out of doors. No more idle days for me."

"Of course there's no title for you, young man!" Ethelbert shouted. "My nephew's the earl. Just like my brother was, God rest his soul."

"What I said, Uncle," Peter said in a much-elevated voice, "is I don't wish to be idle. No more sleeping the day away."

"So what are you finding to amuse yourself?" Aynsley asked his nephew.

"I would imagine it has something to do with horses," Emily said, narrowing her eyes with displeasure.

"I have always been horse mad, but I've learned my

lessons about wagering." He shook his head. "No more races at Newmarket for me."

Perhaps Peter *was* maturing. "A wise decision."

Spencer and Alex told their sister how much they had enjoyed their visit to Wey. Aynsley was surprised she did not show more enthusiasm. Surely she was not so jealous of Rebecca that she resented her successes with the lads! He was very disappointed in his daughter.

"Can I interest you and Rebecca in a game of whist after dinner, Uncle?" Peter asked Aynsley.

All Aynsley really wanted to do after dinner was to be alone with Rebecca. He had stored up so many things he wished to share with her.

And he was anxious to acknowledge the love that had grown between him and his wife.

"Certainly," he said. "We must allow Rebecca time to read to the lads. She goes to them every night before she meets me in the library."

"Are you still reading *Ivanhoe?*" Peter asked Rebecca.

"Indeed, I am."

"Papa, when will we get our bows and arrows?" Alex asked.

Aynsley smiled at his redheaded son. "I did not forget. I ordered some fine ones before I left London. You should have them in a few days."

The boys' faces brightened.

He drew in his breath. He'd been waiting for just such a pleasant moment as this to make the announcement that might offend his children. "Tomorrow I am sending the portrait of the late countess to Fordyce. I believe the heir should have his mother's portrait in his lodgings at Oxford, and after he inherits, I daresay the portrait will be restored to Dunton Hall."

Emily's head whipped around to face Rebecca. "You're behind this!"

"Emily!" He could not remember when his tone had ever been so severe with his daughter. "The idea is mine. Dunton has a new mistress now, and I demand that you show her the respect that is her due."

Peter scowled at her. "Your father's right, Em."

Rebecca spoke in a soothing voice. "Emily's done nothing for which she should be upbraided, and I beg that you not do so."

"Never liked the late countess," Uncle Ethelbert said. "Snooty duke's daughter's what she was! Thought she was too good for a mere earl, if you ask me."

"No one asked," Aynsley shouted. "That will be enough talk of the late countess."

He wanted to extricate himself from the game without offending his daughter or nephew, without declaring he was ready for bed, either. He and Rebecca had won the first rubber, and they were now on the second, which looked as if their opponents would win. "I believe this will be the last rubber," he finally said.

Peter eyed him. "You must be tired to death after riding all day."

"That I am, but I also have much to impart to my wife before we go to bed."

"I daresay my sister has tasked you with volumes to report to me."

Thank God for Rebecca's quick thinking. "Indeed, she did."

Peter took the last trump, and they called the evening an even match.

"I should like a chance to annihilate you at a later date," Peter said, peering at his uncle.

"There will be a rematch, but you mistake the victors," Aynsley said, smiling at his nephew and daughter.

Once he was alone with Rebecca, he suggested they move to the sofa in front of the fire. He sat next to her and drew her hand within his. Contentment reached deep within him like the warmth of the fire.

"You must tell me all about the passage of the tax bill," she said.

"A lot of my success came at your sister's. She had assembled a great many Members of Parliament."

"Were you the one who introduced the topic at her table?"

He nodded. "As a matter of fact, I was."

"Pray, how did you begin?"

"I prefaced my remarks by telling them I had never once supported a tax increase, and I've been in Parliament half my life—in Commons before I succeeded my father."

"A very good way to begin."

"Then I proceeded to tell them why we need the additional taxes."

"I would imagine the most persuasive argument was the war. If we can't arm forces to beat Napoleon, there's no telling how much more men of property—men like those dining at my sister's—would stand to lose if the French win this wretched war."

That Rebecca's thoughts so closely mirrored his own never failed to amaze him. He was prodigiously glad she was possessed of intelligence, too. "I believe you're right."

"I'm so very proud of you, John. And I think I may not dislike Lord Sethbridge as much as I once did, owing to the fact he values you as you should be valued."

She called me John. Upon her lips his Christian name was to his ears the sweetest endearment. "Spoken like a prejudiced wife." His eyes softened as he stroked her cheek with a knuckle.

She favored him with a smile. "I am so very happy to be your wife."

"And I am happy that I've found you."

"Pray, don't leave me again."

"I assure you I don't want to. Dunton's the place I love best." He loved her, too, but he wouldn't tell her just yet. She likely was experiencing too many new, unfamiliar feelings to comprehend them all. He stifled a yawn.

"Peter is right," she said. "You must be whipped after riding all day. Why do you not go to bed early and promise to take me riding with you in the morning? Seeing Dunton as the green is being restored to the trees and lawns will do your heart good."

"Springtime at Dunton is wonderful. I do look forward to seeing it with you after breakfast." He rose, then offered her his hand.

They climbed the stairs and came to her bedchamber. Leaving her there at the door was going to be one of the hardest things he had ever done. He did not want to leave her ever again. He wanted to let her know how much he had come to love her.

She stopped and faced him, one hand on the ornate doorknob.

He moved closer and lowered his head to her for just a taste of her sweet lips, then he forced himself to pull away. "Good night, my love."

He could tell she watched him as he strode down the corridor to his own chambers.

Rebecca fairly danced into her chamber. *John is home! My husband is home!*

What in heaven's name had gotten into her? She had launched herself into her husband's arms that afternoon, and if that weren't bold enough, she had most willingly lifted her face to his for a kiss right there on the steps to Dunton Hall!

While that had not been the first time her husband had kissed her, that had been the first time in her eight and twenty years a kiss had affected her so profoundly. Maggie had told her. Verity had told her. But Rebecca never had believed them when they told her she would enjoy being kissed by a husband with whom she was in love.

She stopped in her stride midway between the door and window where she had placed her new desk. *In love?* Frozen to the broadloom carpet, she was completely, utterly, devastatingly dazed.

How could she have been so foolish not to have understood this wondrous transformation that had come over her these past several weeks? She was in love with her husband. That explained why she had been so forlorn during his absence. That explained the gladness that filled her soul when she beheld him standing in front of Dunton that afternoon. That explained why she wanted to be with him, to speak to him, to touch him, every day of her life.

She loved him. She loved every single thing about this noble man she had married. At the dinner table that night she realized she loved to look at him, at that face that was still boyish despite his maturity. She loved that he was possessed of a fine mind and keen sense of intelligence. She loved that he was an honorable man who could never neglect his duties. She loved that he was a good man and a fine father. She could have looked over the entire earth and never found a man so well suited to her.

The revelation that she had fallen in love with her husband lifted a heavy burden from her. Since the day she had spoken her wedding vows, she had felt a fraud. She had been ashamed to have pledged herself only halfheartedly during that somber, religious ceremony.

She had known the Lord had guided her to John. She should have known that the Lord would see her to the natural completion of this most sacred sacrament.

She collapsed onto the sofa in front of the fire. What if John did not feel the same? Her thoughts flitted back over the evening's proceedings. Hadn't he said, "I am happy to have found you"? Hadn't he called her *my love* just minutes ago? Hadn't he tenderly kissed her?

Perhaps he did not yet realize he was falling in love with her. *Please, God, let him love me, too. Let us fulfill our wedding vows.*

What was she to do now? The former Rebecca Peabody was a fish out of water when it came to matters of the heart.

If John did not return her love, she would just die. Such sentiment seemed like something a pretty young thing—not the mature married woman she had become—would think. Even if he could never love her, she would be grateful just to spend her life with him.

She watched the flames until her fire went cold, then she undressed and went to bed, but she could not sleep. Every thought centered upon the wondrous discovery that she was in love with her husband.

Her last thought before finally falling asleep just before dawn was that rain was softly drumming against her windows. Now she wouldn't be able to ride with him. How would she contrive to be alone with him? How would she be able to tell him her wondrous news?

Chapter Fifteen

Neither the gray skies nor the soft patter of rain against her windows the following morning was going to dampen Rebecca's spirits. She sat in front of her looking glass, put on her spectacles so she could see, then instructed Pru to make her pretty.

She stared into the glass, profoundly disappointed in what she saw. How could she look so much like Maggie, yet lack her sister's beauty?

It was the spectacles. Uncle Ethelbert was right. No woman wearing them could ever aspire to true beauty.

Sweet heavens! Why was she—a woman who'd always fancied herself a bluestocking—contemplating her own nonexistent beauty?

Because she did so want John to think her lovely.

"Yer always pretty, milady."

Rebecca frowned. "Pray, don't address me in that way."

Pru brushed out her mistress's lustrous locks, then began to pin the thick dark hair away from Rebecca's face. "Yer husband must be the most tolerant man in the kingdom to put up with yer stubborn ways. Any other man would be wounded that his wife did not want to share his title."

Could John possibly be wounded—or even angry—over her refusal to be known as his countess? He had told her he was proud of his family, proud of being the Earl of Aynsley. Was it possible he found her aversion to titles a slap in his face? The very notion of offending him upset her. She was proud of her husband. She was proud to be married to him. She *was* the Countess of Aynsley, and she should be proud to be known as John's wife.

The use of his title had been one of those marital compromises they had agreed upon at the start of this marriage. What a different person she had been then than she was now.

"Do you really think it bothers my husband that I don't wish to be known as his *lady?*"

"I couldn't say, but I know it bothers the servants that you're not proud of their master. He's much beloved."

Especially by me. Rebecca had never done a rash thing in her life. She never made a decision without analyzing it for a considerable period of time. But in the past few seconds she had been conversing with her maid, she came to the decision that she had been wrong to eschew her husband's title as well as her own. "Perhaps I should reconsider my abhorrence of titles."

"Does that mean I can call you milady?" Pru stood back and examined Rebecca's hair.

"I suppose it does."

"Milady looks very lovely today."

"I will need a dress with pockets."

"Why do you need pockets?"

Rebecca shrugged. "I may wish to slip my spectacles in them from time to time."

"Yer acting like a debutante in love."

"Just a countess in love." That was the first time Rebecca had ever referred to herself as a countess, and she suddenly felt as if she were wrapped within her husband's protective arms. It was also the first time in her eight and twenty years she had admitted to being in love. "What a pity the rain will keep me from riding with my husband this morning."

"Oh, I almost forgot. I've got a letter for you from his lordship."

Even before she opened the missive, Rebecca knew that she would not get to spend the morning with John. She unfolded the letter and began to read.

> My Dearest Rebecca,
> I'm disappointed the rain will prevent us from riding together this morning. I have donned my great coat and oilskins and will meet with my steward, as there are a great many things we need to go over after my long absence. Unless the weather turns much worse than it is this morning, I will likely be with him most of the day. I'm looking forward to seeing the children's production tonight.
> A.

What did it matter now if she contrived to look pretty? John would not see her. She felt worse than a child whose plum pudding had been snatched away.

Peter was in the morning room when she arrived. It was the first morning she had seen him since he had accepted her proposition. "You're just the lady I wanted to see."

Rebecca poured herself tea, took a slice of toast and came to sit next to him. "I confess I've been anxious to speak privately with you to see how the farm goes, but you're never here."

"Farming is arduous work."

"Indeed it is."

Emily entered the chamber. "I declare, Peter, this is the first time I've seen you in the morning in weeks!"

He shrugged. "The rain forces me to stay indoors."

Emily's face brightened. "Perhaps we could all play whist?"

"Alas, your papa could not be dissuaded from meeting with Mr. Stanley," Rebecca said.

As Emily filled a plate and came to sit across the small table from her, Rebecca offered her the marmalade. "Will there be a dress rehearsal?" Rebecca asked.

"Yes, this afternoon."

"Your father and I are very much looking forward to seeing the production. It seems an awful lot of effort for just the two of us to see. Would you mind if I invited Mrs. Cotton and Miss Seton?"

Emily gave her a rare smile. "That would be a splendid idea. I'm sure the lads will enjoy the opportunity to perform in front of a larger audience."

Peter and Rebecca finished their toast before Emily. "Pray, Rebecca, there are a few matters I wished to discuss with you," he said. "Would you be kind enough to stroll with me in the gallery?"

Oh, dear, she hated anything that would exclude—and possibly alienate—Emily, but she knew Peter would want to keep her informed about the farm. "If you can be quick about it. I have other pressing matters." Not that writing to Maggie was particularly pressing, but she did not want to keep Peter from being with Emily. "What a fine day it is for you and Emily to set up the chessboard in front of the fire."

Despite her efforts to placate her stepdaughter, Emily glared at Rebecca as she left the room with Peter.

When she reached the doorway, Rebecca turned back to Emily, desperate to say something to cull her favor. "By the way, I have decided I no longer have an aversion to titles, Lady Emily."

"Does that mean that you dislike me addressing you as Rebecca?" There was malice on Emily's tongue when her stepmother's name rolled off it.

"I have no preferences. I should like you to feel free to call me whatever you like."

In the gallery, she and Peter strolled its one-hundred-foot length to the accompaniment of the pattering of rain upon the chamber's wall of windows.

"How goes our project?" she asked.

"It's been very hard work. I've been preparing the soil for planting."

She was remarkably ignorant about farming. "And how does one do that?"

"By tilling and amending the soil."

"Oh, dear, did you even have any equipment?"

He nodded. "There was some, antiquated though it might be."

"When will you be ready to plant?"

"That's why I needed to speak to you. I need to buy seed..."

"And of course you shall need money. How much?"

"Fifty guineas should cover it since the farm's not that large."

Fifty guineas was all she had for the entire quarter. "I will go and get it now."

"Then I can take the wagon to Birmingham to procure it today."

"You're sure you want to go in this weather?"

He shrugged. "A little wet never hurt a man. Look at Uncle."

Like an idiot, her glance flicked to the window, where she hoped to see John riding home. She was disappointed.

"I didn't mean that literally," he said with a laugh.

They had returned to where they had started. "Allow me to look at your hands," she said.

"Why?"

"Because I wish to determine if your hands look like a gentleman's."

He held them out to her. "I assure you they don't."

As she stood there looking at his outstretched, calloused hand, Emily strode into the chamber but came to an abrupt halt when she saw their hands touching. "Don't let me disturb anything," she hissed.

Rebecca looked up. "You're not. I was just leaving."

Anger flashed across Emily's face. "As am I!" Then she began to run away, Rebecca on her heels.

"Pray, Lady Emily, don't be angry," Rebecca said.

Now crying, Emily stopped. "You've destroyed my happiness since the day you came here."

"I am so sorry if you feel that way. I know I cannot change the way you feel about me, but I assure you no matter how deeply you might dislike me, I still love you. You are the beloved daughter of the man who is beloved by me."

"How can you say that when it's Peter you love?"

"Peter? That's the most ridiculous thing I've ever heard! The only man I could ever love is the wonderful man I married, and I assure you, Peter loves you with all his heart. Pray, go to him now. Ask him if that is not so."

Emily shook her head and continued on down the corridor.

That evening Lord and Lady Aynsley, along with Mrs. Cotton and Miss Seton, sat in chairs near the nursery's stage to view the play. Once the audience was seated, Emily, dressed in fashions like those his mother might have worn when she was a young woman, slipped onto the stage through a narrow opening in the curtains.

Unlike the current fashions, which rather hugged the feminine body, the dress Em wore had a voluminous skirt that accentuated her tiny waist. She had piles of powdered hair weighing down her head and wore a patch, bringing to mind Marie Antoinette. "Good evening, ladies and gentlemen," she began. "I would like to welcome you to a production of *The Prodigal Son,* written by Lady Emily Compton and set in England a half century ago."

The curtains opened to reveal a set the children had painted to look like a castle. Emily took her place seated in a thronelike armchair with Uncle Ethelbert seated beside her. She once again addressed the audience. "I am Lady Windsor, and the aristocratic man you see beside me is Lord Windsor. We have four sons." She then proceeded to introduce her three brothers and Peter—using their fictional names.

As the story transpired, the three youngest sons were most obedient and industrious. The oldest son, played by Peter, however, never wanted to do his share of the work, and he eventually took his share of the family fortune and left.

There followed a scene in which he gambled away his money and lived in a disreputable manner, drinking wildly.

During his absence, his brothers worked very hard tilling the soil, with an actual hand plow guided by Spencer, Alex counting sacks of grain, and taking care of the animals, acted out by Chuckie giving food and water to a dog.

The curtains closed, and Chuckie carried a sign across the stage that read, Time Passed.

The next scene saw Peter scrubbing floors and wiping away sweat while holding his stomach. "I'm so hungry," he said. "The servants in my parents' house eat much better than me." He got up and tossed away his dirty cloth. "I'm going back to my parents' house and beg to become one of their servants." He hung his head. "I don't deserve anything more the way I have acted."

After the passage of many years, Emily's hair (actually a wig) had become whiter. The family was together one day when the long-lost son returned. Each of his brothers criticized him. Chuckie delighted in saying, "You've been very bad!"

"We will not share our hard-earned money with you," Alex said.

Spencer frowned. "Nor do you deserve any of our land."

Then Emily, as the mother, held up her hand. "Pray, boys! All of you are my children. I love all of you equally." She held out her arms, and Peter rushed into them. "Welcome home, my much-beloved son."

The brothers shouted that he didn't deserve such a reception, but she said, "Your brother's return calls for a celebration. My son was lost, but now he is found. Pray, lads, bring him fine clothing."

As the curtains closed, Spencer stepped out onto the stage and said, "Jesus used the story of the prodigal son to demonstrate that no matter how far His children stray and how bad they have been, the Heavenly Father will always have it in His heart to forgive them."

At the completion of the play, the adults gave them a standing ovation. "Bravo!" said Aynsley as he stood, clapping enthusiastically as his eyes moistened.

Then he looked down at Rebecca, who also had stood, along with Miss Seton and Mrs. Cotton. "Thank you," he mouthed before climbing the stage steps to shake the actors' hands and compliment them on a job well done. When he came to Emily, his eyes watered again, and he held out his arms. "I assure you, tonight's production is much finer than anything that has ever before been performed in this nursery. I'm so proud of you."

Emily's eyes misted, too. "I must thank her ladyship for suggesting it in the first place. It's been ever so fun for all of us."

He had known his daughter would come around. It wasn't her nature to be vindictive. "I'm very pleased to hear you say that, love."

As Emily approached Rebecca, he hoped she wouldn't address her as she'd just done. To his chagrin, his wife abhorred being addressed by her title.

"Oh, Lady Emily! I never dreamed we would be

treated to such a totally delightful presentation. Costumes! And sets! And very fine acting, I might add," Rebecca said. "I don't know when I've had such an entertaining evening."

"Thank you, my lady. I am grateful to you for suggesting it."

"Pray, may we hope there will be more productions in the future? We all enjoyed it ever so much."

By now her brothers had gathered around Emily. "What do you think, lads?" Emily asked.

"Oh, please!" Alex said.

"I think it should be a monthly occurrence," Spencer added.

"What do you think, Uncle Ethelbert?" Emily asked.

"What do I think about what?"

"Would you be willing to come up to the big house and perform again?" Peter shouted.

"Could I be a swordfighter next time?"

All eyes turned to Emily.

"Well, authoress, what do you think?" Peter asked.

"We shall have to see."

They all laughed.

His wife's hand in his, Aynsley began to walk her to the library. "What is going on with you and Emily lady-ing each other?"

"I have decided that I'm proud to be your wife, and I will be proud to be addressed as Lady Aynsley."

He stopped in the middle of the corridor, facing her. "That makes me very happy."

She had not seen such a look of pleasure on his face in a very long time. "Then my previous abhorrence to nobility displeased you?"

"I was not happy about it, but it was one of those compromises that are part of any successful marriage." He continued on toward the library.

Only the fire and a single wall sconce lit the cool chamber when they entered it. "I should like for us to go stand by the fire," she said.

Near the fire the temperature was comfortable, the fire's warmth welcome. As the two of them stood there in the dark room, he thought of another night the two of them had stood before a fire in a dimly lit library. "Do you know what this reminds me of?" he asked.

"Of course. That's why I wanted to walk here straight away, why I didn't want you to light the lamp."

He drew closer to her and spoke in a low, husky voice. "And why would that be, my lady?"

"I don't know that I can put it into words. I believe we both discovered that night in Lord Warwick's library that there was a connection between us which could grow and flourish—under the proper set of circumstances."

"Yes, it was the same for me." He came even closer and gathered her into his arms. He liked the feel of her head nestled into his chest and her arms encircling him. "I want to thank you."

"For using your title?"

"No. Yes."

They both laughed.

"What I meant was, while I am delighted that you're no longer ashamed of my title, I wish to thank you for everything you've done to make tonight one of the best nights of my life. I cannot remember when I've enjoyed anything as much as the play."

"It was wonderful, but Emily deserves all the credit. She has such amazing vision and tenacity."

"I was proud of her." He dropped soft kisses into her hair, which smelled of rose water.

"Weren't the lads adorable?"

"Yes, and despite the costumes I had no difficulty recognizing them."

She pulled away and looked into his face, grinning. "Where are your spectacles? I know you were wearing them during the play."

"They're in my pocket."

"And what, may I ask, are they doing in your pocket?"

"I hardly need them to stand here with you in this darkened chamber."

"Why did you remove them?"

She shrugged.

"Come now, Rebecca. I know you don't do anything unless you have a good reason."

"If you must know, I wished to look pretty."

His pulse accelerated. She wished to look pretty for him. She had circled her arms around him. She must be falling in love with him, but he would not press her. She would reveal her feelings in her own time. He lifted her chin and kissed the top of her nose. "You're always pretty to me. With or without your spectacles. Now, pray love, put on your spectacles. I've become accustomed to seeing you in them, and I find the image much to my liking."

She shook her head. "Not tonight. There's something magical about tonight, and I want to believe…"

"That you're beautiful," he murmured, "because you are." His head lowered to brush his lips across hers for a sweet kiss. "In fact, my lady, I find you are much to my liking."

It was one of the disappointments in his life that he'd never told a woman he loved her. Neither he nor Dorothy ever pretended that theirs was a love match. After four decades of life, he'd come to believe there would never be a love match for him. Dorothy had told him he was a bore, yet Rebecca truly enjoyed being with him. She did not seem to find him dull. Why could he not bring himself to utter the words *I love you?*

"I did not realize how much I liked you until that morning you told me you had to leave. I felt as if I were losing my best friend."

"That's because we have become best friends." Why, then, would she not share with him her P. Corpus identity? Now that she had no aversion to his title, her concealment was the only obstacle to this becoming a blissful marriage.

But it was a formidable obstacle. He had learned with Dorothy that if truth wasn't the cornerstone of a marriage, its very foundation would crumble. His chest tightened. He didn't want this marriage to crumble.

"Yes, I discovered that when you left."

He took her hand and kissed the back of it. "Me, too."

"I am very happy to hear that. When you did not even ask if I wished to join you in London, I thought perhaps that...you might be tired of me."

He broke out laughing.

"I fail to see what's so funny."

"You, my dearest. How can one get tired of one who shares one's thoughts?"

The door to the library banged open, and Chuckie came strolling in, rubbing his eyes.

"Why are you not helping your brothers take down the sets?" Aynsley asked. As soon as the words were out of his mouth, he realized something was wrong.

Rebecca moved to the child. "What's the matter, love?"

"My ear hurts."

She glanced from Chuckie to him. "Has he had this problem before?"

He frowned. "He gets beastly sick when it happens."

Tears began to roll down Chuckie's chubby cheeks. "Mawk said when he was little one time when he was sick he got to sleep in the big bed in the countess's room with our other mother."

Her voice softened. "Did you want to come sleep with me tonight?"

Nodding, he burst into sobs and fell into her arms.

Aynsley's heart swelled as he watched them together.

And he knew he loved his wife deeply.

Chapter Sixteen

The gusty winds whistling relentlessly outside her bedchamber that night reinforced her deep sense of contentment as she lay warmly snuggled in the darkness with Chuckie beside her and the velvet curtains enclosing their bed. He had gone to sleep soon after his head hit the pillow. She prayed her thanks to God for sending her to John and his family.

As she did every night, she continued to pray the Bible verse from Matthew that had guided her relations with Emily during these past several weeks. *Bless them that curse you, do good to them that hate you, and pray for them which despitefully use you and persecute you.* Not that Emily hated her. Rebecca knew there was much good in her stepdaughter. She could well understand how difficult it must be for Emily not only to have a complete stranger supplant her as mistress at Dunton but also to steal away some of her father's affections. In time, Emily would come to understand Rebecca would be her champion, never her enemy. *Please let it be so.*

Before she dropped off into sleep, she decided that the next day she would find a way to tell John she had fallen in love with him. She was quite certain she was smiling when the blanket of sleep rolled over her.

Her sleep, though, was short-lived. Chuckie awakened, crying from the pain of his earache. How she wished it could have been she and not this sweet child who had to endure the pain, and how she wished she had an inkling of what could be done to relieve his pain. It was times like this she felt totally inadequate to be a mother.

She fleetingly thought of how miraculously laudanum relieved pain, but she remembered a horror story back in Virginia of a two-year-old girl who died after her mother gave her laudanum when she was sick. Though the mother had blamed her child's death on the sickness, Rebecca's papa insisted that no child should ever take laudanum, that it was too potent. The very notion of losing Chuckie caused Rebecca's heartbeat to quicken, her stomach to clench.

Why did he have to get sick late at night? Were it daytime, she could have sent for a physician. Was there even a physician near Wey? She would find out first thing in the morning. If there wasn't, she would send someone to an apothecary in Birmingham.

But what to do now? She drew him into her arms and was terrified to discover he had fever.

While Rebecca was only too aware of her own limitations, she realized the nurse had more experience than she at such matters. "Come, my love, we'll go see what Beaver thinks. She'll know how to make you feel better." Carrying him in her arms, she went to his bedchamber and tapped at the door. A moment later, Beaver opened the door. She stood there in her nightcap while tying a wrapper around her ample waist.

"I'm beastly sorry for disturbing you," Rebecca began, "but I thought you might know some way of relieving Chuckie's ear pain."

The old woman nodded. "Indeed I do. All the Compton children 'ave suffered with ear complaints. Just you wait 'ere. Beaver will be right back with some warm mint oil to put in me laddie's ear."

Rebecca went to the rocking chair and began to rock the whimpering child. "I'm so sorry, my love. We'll help make you feel better."

"Then can I come back to the big bed with you?"

She held him a bit closer while thanking the Lord for the gift of this child. She thought at a time like this Chuckie would naturally prefer the nurse who had been with him all his life over the stepmother he had known but for a few weeks. How very blessed she was to have earned his affection. "Of course you can, my little love, if that's what you want."

Minutes later Beaver returned and administered the drops into his sore ear. When she finished she asked if he wanted warm milk.

He shook his head, tears trickling down his cheek. "Me hot."

Rebecca gave the old nurse an imploring look. "Any advice for combating fever?"

"I hates for your ladyship to have to worry with this. It's me job to take care of me laddie."

"No matter which of us he's with, I would still worry about our lad. I rather fancy looking after him when he's sick, but I will need guidance from you, my dear Beaver." She truly did not want to offend the poor nurse, whose feelings were already bound to be bruised because Chuckie had chosen Rebecca over her.

"Mostly what I know about fevers is they always just have to run their course. They say the fever's what gets the bad stuff out of the body. The pity of it is, they always seem to come at night."

"Is it best to cover him—or not to cover him?" Rebecca asked.

"Let him be your guide, milady. When the chills come, pile on the blankets. When the heat sends the vapors flowing from the body, allow the coverings to come off."

Rebecca stood, with a limp Chuckie still in her arms. "Thank you. I sincerely hope I won't have to awaken you again."

"Don't you worry none about that."

The mint oil did seem to relieve his suffering, and not long after they returned to the big bed he went back to sleep—as did she.

When she awakened and parted the bed curtains, she was surprised that Chuckie had slept through the night. Surprised and thankful. Curious to determine if his fever had passed, she set a gentle hand to his forehead and was relieved to discover it felt normal.

His blond lashes fluttered, then his big blue eyes opened, and a smile transformed his face when he saw her.

"Good morning, love. How do you feel?"

He bolted up in the bed. "Good."

She fully opened the bed curtains. "Shall we go see if your papa's awake?"

"Will you carry me like you did last night?"

"You little goose! All right, if you'd like."

As soon as she got to her husband's chamber door, she paused. She had to prepare herself for the fact he would probably be in his nightshirt. Having Chuckie with her would lessen any embarrassment and would make them seem more like a family. If she was ready to be a true wife to him, she should not be embarrassed over the sight of her own husband in his nightshirt.

She drew in her breath and rapped at the door.

Aynsley came awake, suddenly realizing that Rebecca stood on the other side of his chamber door. He sat up. "Come in."

Seeing her with Chuckie in her arms nearly took his breath away. Rebecca had never looked so lovely. She wore a thick, snow-white night shift, no spectacles, and for a moment did not look old enough to be Chuckie's mother. Not that she was, actually. "I must say Chuckie looks vastly improved from last night. How do you feel, lad?"

"Good. Can I get in your bed? I slept in Mother's last night."

His son was sure to have his stepmother twisted about his baby finger. "Get over here, you little scamp."

The child scurried over and climbed upon his bed. Aynsley pulled him onto his lap and smacked a kiss on top his fair head.

"Chuckie was in much pain last night, and was feverish. I was a bit bewildered as to what to do so I was obliged to awaken Beaver."

"She's had enough experience with such matters. Did she help?"

"Yes. She warmed some mint oil and put a few drops in his ear. That seemed to ease his discomfort."

He felt guilty that she'd had to face what must have

been a fearsome situation alone. "You could have awakened me, you know."

Amusement on her face, she cocked a brow. "Would you have known what to do?"

He shrugged. "Probably not, but I would like to have lent you support."

She favored him with a smile. "Tell me, my lord, is there a physician hereabouts?"

"As a matter of fact, we've got one in Wey."

"Should we not have him take a look at Chuckie today?"

"If he were still feverish, I'd send for him, but look at the boy! Who would believe him sick? He seems to be well on the road to recovery."

"Beaver said these fevers always come at night. If it should return tonight, should we summon the physician at that time?"

"I'd rather not call him out in the middle of the night for what is likely a routine childhood fever."

Her face grim, she nodded.

"Can we play the tickling game, Papa?"

"In a minute."

"After you play the tickling game, my lord, would you like to join me in the morning room?" his wife asked.

"Indeed I would."

"I should be dressed and there in twenty minutes." She started for her own chamber.

"Then that gives me five minutes for the tickling game."

On the way to the morning room Aynsley picked up the post, which had been stacked upon his desk in the library. He would bring along yesterday's *Morning Chronicle*—just arrived from London—to read over while he took his tea and toast. He liked to stay abreast of parliamentary occurrences.

He had not made it out of the library when a headline arrested his attention. And made him feel as if he had been kicked in the gut. Lords Sethbridge and Aynsley Form Pact to Extend Franchise Next Year.

Anger as corrosive as acid slammed through him as he began to read the article.

> The Earl of Aynsley has been credited with successfully championing Lord Sethbridge's bill to raise taxes, the passage of which was secured early this week, despite initial resistance from members of the venerable House of Lords. *The Chronicle* has learned that the two members of the House of Lords have formed a pact. Lord Sethbridge, who has always opposed any new law that would give the right to vote to the masses, has now changed his mind. In exchange for Lord Aynsley's help in passing the tax increase, Lord Sethbridge has pledged to help Lord Aynsley get votes for a franchise-expansion bill next year.
>
> It has been reported that Lord Aynsley plans to spend the next year gathering votes for a bill to give the right to vote to more men.

How could the newspaper have gotten hold of such information? Only three people knew. He was certain Lord Sethbridge, who was only focused on the current session right now and who was only reluctantly planning to endorse Aynsley's voting-expansion bill next year, would never have let the cat out of the bag.

Rebecca!

What a fool he'd been to trust her! She was just as deceitful as Dorothy had been. He still stung from Dorothy's deceit. She, too, had gone behind his back. The duke's daughter whom he had married had lied to his colleagues in Parliament, telling them he endorsed her father's bill. His wife's painful betrayal had authored an estrangement that had not been repaired until she'd drawn her final breath.

He should have known when Rebecca refused to reveal her P. Corpus identity that she did not really look upon this marriage as a true partnership, that she was unwilling to be truthful with him.

He had thought her different from others of her gender. He had thought their marriage united two like-minded souls for the rest of their days. He had come to believe that she cared about him. Romantically.

Had he so thoroughly longed for a woman to love and share his life with that he'd been duped by a conniving female?

Even knowing that Rebecca had to be the one who had betrayed him, it was hard to credit her with such deception. He thought he had come to know her. Had he imbued his wife with worthy qualities she did not possess? Had he been blinded by what he thought was her sweetness and intelligence? How could she have played him for such a fool?

A blistering anger strummed through him. Even more than the fury, he felt a deep sense of loss. Almost as if a loved one had died.

He supposed the Rebecca he had grown to love *had*

died. Because she had never existed. His neediness had conjured up a perfect wife, and he had credited his bride with all the qualities he sought in a life's mate.

At his age, he should have known better.

He stormed to the morning room and stood in its doorway, glaring at her. He had no desire to even be in the same room with the woman who had betrayed him almost as surely as an adulteress.

She spun around to face him, her face lifted into a bright smile, her spectacles absent. For a second he could not believe her betrayal. She looked so very sweet, so sincere. "What is the matter, my dearest?"

He clutched the newspaper in his hand so hard, his knuckles turned white. "This!"

The smile on her face crashed as she leaped to her feet and came to pry the *Morning Chronicle* from his hand. After she read it, she looked up at him with an expression every bit as angry as his own. "Who could have betrayed us like this?"

He gave a bitter laugh. "*Us,* indeed! You have played your charade long enough."

"Whatever can you mean?"

"I will never believe that Lord Sethbridge would even consider addressing such a topic until the end of the current parliamentary session."

"Then who?" Her hand came to cover her mouth. "Surely you cannot believe it was I!"

He studied that pretty face of hers. How innocent she looked. He harrumphed. "Can you look me in the eye and claim that you've always been completely honest with me since the day we married? Have you ever perhaps omitted to tell me something?"

"I have never lied—" The words froze on her lips,

and a wild, frightened look leaped to her eyes. "I may have omitted to tell you something. What is it you wish to know?"

"What things have you concealed from me, Rebecca?"

"Please, my lord, I beg that we go to your library for this discussion."

He was so angry with her, he did not want to be in the same chamber with her, but he had no desire for the servants or his children to hear them arguing.

"Very well." He stormed off to the library.

Slamming the library door behind them, he faced her. "Explain yourself."

"Please, my lord, let's sit and discuss this like rational adults."

His body rigid, he went to his desk and sat, his fiery eyes never leaving hers as she went to the sofa and sat down facing him. He folded his arms across his chest. "I'm waiting."

"I confess I've felt wretched for withholding information from you."

"And what information would that be?"

A grave look on her face, she met his gaze. "I am the essayist P. Corpus."

"Why have you not told me this before?"

"Before I married, I thought my writing was the most important thing in my life. I was afraid if you found out about it, you might forbid me to continue and I would have been obliged to obey you."

"Why would you think I would prohibit you from your clandestine writing?"

"I didn't know you well enough to know how you would address such a situation."

"You must believe me an ogre."

She stared defiantly at him. "Actually, not until the last five minutes."

"You said before you married, your writing was the most important thing in your life. What has changed?"

Her eyes filled with tears. Had it been a day earlier, such a sight would have fairly broken his heart, but not now. Now his sense of betrayal was so strong and his anger so potent, he could hardly stand to look at her.

"Now..." She started to sob and buried her face into her hands and finished her sentence between more sobbing. "Now you and your family—which I had begun to think of as *my* family—are what mean the most to me."

He shook his head. "How can you expect me to believe anything you say?"

"Because I am telling you the truth. I swear to the Lord in heaven that I am not the one who betrayed you."

He stalked off. He felt like taking a bruising ride.

The farther away he strode, the more her words intruded. *I swear to the Lord in heaven I am not the one who betrayed you.* Rebecca would never take the Lord's name for a falsehood. That much he *did* know about her.

Which made him feel even lower. Sweet heavens, had he falsely accused her? Was it possible someone else had betrayed him?

Chapter Seventeen

Her body racked with tears, Rebecca raced up the stairs. She prayed she would make it to her chamber before one of the children saw her, but at the landing she nearly collided with Emily.

"Whatever is the matter?" Emily asked, her eyes wide with surprise as they followed Rebecca.

Incapable of responding, her stepmother merely shook her head and quickened her pace until she reached her bedchamber. There, she locked the door behind her and flung herself upon her bed for a good cry.

She had never experienced such a mixture of emotions in her entire eight and twenty years. Her initial boiling anger simmered into a numbing sorrow. How could she be mad at John when she had deceived him through omission since the day they had married? She should have been completely honest with him. Now she was paying for her deception with a heart that felt as if it were surely being strangled of its budding life.

That he was so quick to blame her for betraying him wounded her excessively. How could he not understand that she would never do anything to hurt him? Could he not see that she was in love with him?

Love. Poets and philosophers had dipped their pens in the blood wrung from wounded hearts for centuries. It had taken her almost three decades to understand that kind of love. Now she felt the gnawing loss and aching love for John Compton, the Earl of Aynsley.

For just a moment the night before, she had thought John looked at her with love shining in his eyes. For those fleeting seconds she had felt that deep connection that had always bound her to him; she had felt that he returned her love in full measure.

But had he loved her, he would not have been so quick to condemn her. She did not know which hurt the most—the loss of his love or never having possessed it in the first place. She did know she had never felt more wretched in her life.

She lay there on her bed, thinking about the disclosure to the *Morning Chronicle.* Lord Sethbridge must have done so in order to undermine John's efforts on behalf of franchise expansion during the next year. The peer had always been opposed to granting the vote to the lower classes. By releasing terms of his agreement with John, he was sure to rally most of the other peers to act against her husband.

Had John been able to approach them in his own way and in his own time, he would have had a good likelihood of changing their positions on the matter.

But now all was lost.

And he blamed her.

Her tears gave way to anger. After she dried her tears, she left her bed and went to her basin to splash cool water over her eyelids.

He may not want her for his wife. His children might not want her for their mother. But, whether they liked it or not, she was the Countess Aynsley, legally wed in a Christian ceremony in which she recited vows she intended to keep.

She was meeting with Mrs. Cotton this morning to go over the account books, and she had made plans to take Uncle Ethelbert for a walk this afternoon. She had no time to dwell on her pitiably bruised heart.

After she walked Uncle Ethelbert that afternoon, she went to the nursery to check on Chuckie. Beaver was sitting in a chair knitting while Chuckie was lying on the wooden floor with his tin soldiers. But he was not playing with them. He looked incredibly lethargic.

She addressed the nurse. "Chuckie doesn't look well."

"I'll grant you, this laddie with not a drop of energy is not our Chuckie. I daresay it will take a few days for his good health to return."

Chuckie sat up and offered Rebecca a smile. "Hello, Mother."

"Hello, my sweet. How do you feel?"

"I can't undersplain it."

Undersplain! Leave it to a child to be so creative with language. "I know, my lamb. Is there something you'd like to do now? Something fun, perhaps?"

Puffy pouches underscored his eyes. "I feel like being in your big bed with the curtains around it. But not alone."

"Oh, I see, you want me to stay with you."

He gave her a forlorn nod.

The little boy knew exactly how to get whatever he

wanted from her. She was powerless to resist his slightest request. "All right, you little goose. Come on."

Even his step was lethargic as he came to her. "Can you carry me?" He looked up at her with those big blue eyes, and she could not sweep him into her arms fast enough.

But as she lifted him into her arms, she became alarmed. His fever had returned. She turned to Beaver. "Did you know Chuckie's fever's come back?"

The nurse's face fell. "I did not. Why didn't you tell Beaver, laddie?"

Chuckie, his arms encircling Rebecca's neck, shrugged.

Instead of going to her bedchamber, Rebecca went to the library in the hopes her husband was there. She knew he wouldn't want to see her or talk to her, but this was not about them. This was about a sick little boy whom they both loved.

When she opened the library door and saw her husband sitting behind his desk, she did not know if she was glad to see him or not. Had he not been there she would have demanded that a groom or footman or some such servant go seek the physician. Now she would have to abide by her husband's decision.

Their eyes met and held for a moment. Until today she would not have thought him capable of so cold a look. She was totally unprepared for how hurtful it was. "Yes?" he asked, not disguising his displeasure.

"I want to send for the physician. Chuckie's fever has returned."

Her husband's gaze darted to his son. "The lad's too old to be carried around like a baby."

Now Aynsley got her anger riled! "He happens to be

our baby, and if being carried makes him feel better, then I am most happy to placate him."

"What's the matter, lad?" Her husband's voice had gentled.

Chuckie shrugged again. "I can't undersplain."

She kissed the top of his blond head. "The fever has sapped away all his energy."

"I'll send for the physician." He glared at her. "Will there be anything else?" His voice was dismissive.

"Nothing at all."

When she reached the door, he said, "By the way, I've found some of your letters in this top drawer. Should you like them?"

What letters? Then she remembered she'd put a couple of his letters there. "Yes, I should."

He brought them to her.

In her bedchamber, she tucked Chuckie into the bed and gathered the curtains around it. Bringing her lap desk, pen and paper and the letters John had just given her, she joined him. She planned to write letters while Chuckie napped.

But first she would reread the letters John had written to her when he was in London—letters written when he felt more kindly toward her.

As she unfolded the first, she wondered if he had read them over again when he'd found them in his desk drawer. One really should not leave personal letters lying about. What if he had written something intimate? Or what if…sweet heavens! What if someone read about the secret only three of them knew—the pact formed between John and Lord Sethbridge?

She quickly found the place in the letter in which he referred to the secret only three of them knew. In that fleeting second, she knew without a doubt that Emily had read the letters. The knowledge was like a blow to her windpipe. Emily wanted to do something that would reflect so badly upon Rebecca that John might banish her to another of his properties.

The very suspicion made her feel wretchedly guilty. Emily could be perfectly innocent. Lord Sethbridge could easily have alerted the *Morning Chronicle,* but the powerful peer did have his hands full with current legislation. It stretched credibility to imagine him already focusing on next year's session. And, besides, the *Morning Chronicle* was a Whig newspaper. Were Lord Sethbridge going to release information, wouldn't he have used his influence with *The Times* instead?

The more she thought about it, the more convinced she became that Emily had been the *Morning Chronicle*'s informant. How could the girl hate her so much? Rebecca had never directed a single mean-spirited word, thought or action against Emily. Yet Emily hated her so much she was willing to work against her own father in the hopes of ridding Dunton Hall of her father's wife.

Tears pricked at her eyes as she began to recite the often-recited passage from Matthew. *Bless them that curse you, do good to them that hate you, and pray for them which despitefully use you and persecute you.*

Please, God, rid me of this anger I feel toward Emily now. Help me to love her as I love Chuckie and Alex and Spencer.

And please don't let me cry in front of Chuckie!

She looked down at him. He was fast asleep, his hair moist around his temples.

She thought of telling John her suspicions about Emily, but knew she could not. She would have to confront the girl first. But would someone so poisoned even admit to such an action? And what would be accomplished if she did find out the truth? Did she really want John to transfer his wrath to his only daughter? Did she want to be the instrument that came between him and his daughter?

Sometimes truth was more damaging than silence. She came to the anguishing decision she would remain silent. If John was not inclined to trust in her, then he wasn't the husband she had fallen in love with.

Either way, she hurt like she had never hurt.

Once she finished reading over her husband's letters, she took up her pen to write to Verity. As she was completing a nice, long letter, there was a knock at her door. "Come in," she said, widening the opening in the bed curtains and beginning to climb off the bed.

John, accompanied by another man, stood in her doorway. "I've been looking everywhere for you," he snapped. "Is Chuckie still with you?"

"He's fast asleep in my bed. For some peculiar reason, he's formed a most sincere attachment to my bed."

Her husband nodded. "I've brought the physician, Mr. Mostyn."

"How do you do?" she asked, peering at the surprisingly well-dressed physician who appeared closer to her age than to John's. Because the fair-complexioned man was so gaunt and thin, it was difficult to imagine him being the vehicle to restore one to good health.

Mr. Mostyn bowed. "Let's take a look at the lad."

The child was sleeping so soundly he had slept through their conversation and had to be awakened by the physician.

Rebecca stood next to Mr. Mostyn so that Chuckie

would see her and not be frightened by awaking to a strange man standing over him.

There was a frightened look on Chuckie's face when he looked up and saw Mr. Mostyn. Rebecca offered a wan smile. "Mr. Mostyn's come to get you well, my love." It saddened her that he was so listless he had made no effort to sit.

The physician examined him and proclaimed that Chuckie had inflamed glands in his throat and that administering aqua cordials would reduce the fever and promote sleep. "I'll come back tomorrow and have another look at him."

She nodded, then met her husband's gaze. "If anyone should need me, I'll be here. Chuckie doesn't like to be alone."

"If you need someone to relieve you, you can send for me."

"If you don't mind, I'll just have a tray sent up at dinner." She glanced toward the bed. "Make that two. I hope I can get him to eat."

Aynsley saw the doctor to the door, making small talk with him while all the time his thoughts were on Rebecca. No matter how cruelly she had betrayed him, he felt ashamed of himself for the beastly way he was treating her.

Now that he'd had several hours to cool his boiling blood, he began to question his initial assumptions that Rebecca had to be the one who betrayed him. Because of Dorothy, he assumed all women were liars. Even though every facet of Rebecca's life was guided by the highest principles, he'd been quick to condemn her because she'd withheld an important truth from him—even when she had sworn she'd never told him a lie.

She had also sworn to that God she held in such reverence that she had not given the information to the *Morning Chronicle.* Now he was inclined to believe her.

Because he had known Lord Sethbridge, who was an honorable man, for almost as many years as Rebecca had been alive, he felt with certainty that his colleague in Lords would never have released the information. Especially not now while he was dealing with much more urgent matters in an actual parliamentary session.

The reality was that one of those two he had trusted had betrayed him.

"Why was Mr. Mostyn here?" Emily asked, approaching her father in the entry hall.

"Chuckie's sick."

Her brows lowered. "Since when?"

"Since last night, not long after the play. He was better this morning, but his fever returned this afternoon, and Rebecca wanted Mostyn to have a look at him."

She followed him into the library. "What did Mr. Mostyn say?"

Aynsley shrugged. "His glands are swollen, and there's inflammation in his ear passages. Poor lad's feeling very low."

"I'll go and see him."

Would she still want to see him when she knew where he was? "He's in the countess's bedchamber."

She came to a sudden stop and whirled to him. "What's he doing there?"

"He's taken a fancy to big beds that have curtains around them, but he doesn't want to be there alone."

Would his daughter have the good manners to offer to relieve her stepmother?

"What will she do for dinner?"

"She's having a tray in her room." It always gave him pleasure to look at his lovely daughter. Today she looked like an angel in an ivory muslin dress sprigged with lavender roses and ribbons. The blue of her eyes almost took on a purple cast. It was a pity and a disappointment she did not act like an angel.

Emily came back into the library and dropped into the sofa. "Papa?"

"Yes, my dear?"

"Why would her ladyship be giving money to Peter?"

His heartbeat thudded. He met Emily's somber gaze. "I didn't know that she was. Have you asked Peter?"

"I'm out of charity with him, if you must know."

"Why are you out of charity with your cousin?"

"We used to have so much fun together. Before she came."

His insides jarred. His pulse accelerated. "What are you implying?" Peter was much closer to Rebecca's age than he was. Surely she… No, not Rebecca. If she gave a vow of fidelity, she would keep it. He felt certain of that.

She shrugged. "I thought Peter must have fallen in love with her, and I made similar accusations to her."

He could barely get out the words, he was holding his breath so. "What did she have to say to that?"

"She told me Peter was very much in love with me and wanted to marry me more than anything."

The air seemed to swish from his lungs. "You've only to look at him to understand that."

"I don't know what to believe anymore. He's so different."

"In what way?"

She thought about it for a moment before answering. "He's more mature, actually."

He had thought the very same thing. "It appeared you two were getting along well during the play."

"We all had great fun practicing and painting sets every evening."

"And we all had great fun watching it. I look forward to the next. Have you decided what your next project will be?"

She got to her feet. "No. I believe I shall go take a walk all by myself. That's when I think most clearly."

The dining room had never been more somber than it had been earlier that night, without Rebecca. The absence of Dorothy's portrait only served to remind all of them that Dunton Hall had a new mistress, a new mistress who took her mothering duties seriously. He felt wretched he had treated her in so vile a manner.

Emily and Peter barely spoke. Had Rebecca been present, she would have kept up a lively banter.

He had to admit it—he missed her—even if he was angry with her.

When bedtime came, he knew he would have to see her because he needed to peek in on Chuckie. He knocked on Rebecca's chamber door.

"Come in."

As he moved into the semidark chamber, she parted the bed curtains, and when she saw him, she opened them wider. She wore that snow-white nightgown, spectacles, and held a book in her hand.

"I wished to check on Chuckie," he said.

"I was obliged to send for Beaver an hour ago to administer more drops in his ear. He's been very sick. The fever hasn't abated for a single minute." She could not conceal the worry in her hoarse whisper. "He's asleep now, but the pain will awaken him anew."

He nodded and spoke in a low voice. "I've been through this with the other children. Nasty business, but he'll probably be better again in the morning." He walked to Chuckie's side of the bed and pulled back the curtain to peer at him, not without his heart swelling. Aynsley's lashes lifted, and he met Rebecca's grave expression. "I will expect you to awaken me should you need me for any reason."

A solemn nod was her only response.

She did not awaken him that night, but on the third night she did.

His son was critically ill, and his wife was just short of hysteria.

Chapter Eighteen

Neither the physician's visits nor Beaver's mint drops made any difference in Chuckie's condition. His fever continued to rage. He no longer cried out from the ear pain, though Rebecca thought she might have preferred that pitiful sound to the complete listlessness that now decimated the child. For hours he had lain in her bed, oblivious to any comment she would make.

She had asked if he would like her to read him a story, but he did not respond. That alarmed her because he was always begging her to read to him. She tried to think of all the things he liked best. What about toad-in-the-hole biscuits—which he'd always happily devoured? But he barely managed to shake his head. The thing he loved most—other than riding the pony, which was out of the question now—was to climb upon his papa's shoulders for a piggyback ride. She asked if he would like that, but he made no response, other than a halfhearted blink of his eyes.

Even Beaver, who had vast experience with sick children, was baffled and worried. "Do you mean none of the children have ever had complaints like this?" Rebecca asked.

The old nurse sadly shook her head. "Not to where they wouldn't talk no more."

The words were like the slash of a saber to Rebecca's already bruised heart. Yesterday she had thought nothing could hurt worse than losing her husband's affection; now, she dreaded something even worse. Getting Chuckie well was the most important thing in her life. The sicker he became, the more fearful she grew.

The very thought of losing him brought tears to her eyes and a physical depression like nothing she had ever experienced, nor could she *undersplain* it, she thought, a feeble smile on her lips as she watched the rising and falling of his little chest. Since she felt that as long as she was watching him closely he couldn't die, she was afraid to remove her gaze from him.

When she'd gone for two days without sleep, she knew she would have to renew herself. For his sake. That's when she and Beaver started spelling each other watching over him.

On the third day of his illness Emily came to visit her youngest brother, which Rebecca felt must have taken a great deal of condescending on the girl's part. All their estrangement was forgotten the minute Emily clapped her eyes on the pitiful sight of the dangerously ill three-year-old. Her tears came immediately, and as if to assure herself he wasn't dead, she took his listless hand.

She looked up into Rebecca's troubled face. "I had no idea he was so sick."

All Rebecca could do was nod. Her own eyes kept filling with tears.

"What does Mr. Mostyn say?"

Rebecca shrugged. "It gives me no satisfaction that he's finally agreeing with my worries."

Emily gasped.

"Does my father know?"

"Your father is out of charity with me, so he comes but once a day to check on Chuckie. He's been nothing but optimistic, assuring me that Chuckie's recovery is imminent." That was all she would say to Emily on the matter of her marital estrangement. The girl was bound to know the source of his anger with Rebecca since she had to be the perpetrator of their rift.

Late that night, after Beaver and Emily had left Rebecca's bedchamber and after the household had fallen asleep, Chuckie went into convulsions.

Rebecca screamed, hoping her husband would hear and come to her chamber.

Aynsley had been sleeping soundly when a distant frantic noise awakened him. Even though the walls of Dunton were excessively thick, and two dressing rooms separated the earl's and countess's chambers, for some unexplainable reason, he'd been able to hear Rebecca's forlorn call.

Immediately, he knew it was her voice that had severed him from sleep, knew that something dreadful had happened. He threw off his blankets and took off running to her chamber.

His first harrowing thought was that Chuckie had died. Surely only death could prompt such a woebegone wail. Unimaginably painful panic gripped him. He did not think he could bear to learn what he most feared.

Rebecca stood in the darkened room, illuminated by the bedside oil lamp as she leaned over the bed, prostrate. She was nearly senseless. "Please help. Dear Lord!" Her eyes were riveted to the bed.

Half afraid of what he might find, he approached the bed with a viciously pounding heart and whipped back the curtains.

Convulsions had seized Chuckie's small body, causing him to jerk uncontrollably. "I'll take him. Quick, go get Beaver, and send for Mostyn!"

He hauled the child's hot, wet body into his arms and held him close, his own pulse pounding prodigiously. He paced the floor, holding the child tightly and trying to speak reassuring words of comfort, even though he knew his boy was not conscious.

The time Rebecca was gone seemed interminable. Though he had not given much thought to God in the past few years, he did now. In his time of greatest need, there was only one who had the power to answer his prayer. His tears now falling, he prayed fervently to the Lord. *I beg, my Lord, You not forsake me or my poor son in our hour of need as I have forsaken You. I thought I had become a nonbeliever until I was tested, and now all my former love for You has come back tenfold. I beseech You to hear my prayer, my Lord, and I vow to abide by whatever You decide. I vow to let You be my guide in doing Christian works, not only with my family and in my village but also in Parliament. I ask this in Jesus's name. Amen.*

By the time Rebecca returned with Beaver, the intensity of Chuckie's convulsions had lessened.

Beaver nodded and winced when she saw Chuckie's severe trembling. "I've only seen this once before, and it was when the fever was so severe it made the child delirious."

Rebecca nodded. "That's how he's been the past several hours. Insensible."

"Perhaps we should try to cool him," Beaver said.

Aynsley nodded. "It's worth a try." He lay the lad back on the bed and began to undress him while Beaver went to fetch water to put in Rebecca's washbasin.

Over the next twenty minutes, they attempted to cool his fevered body. The convulsions finally ceased, but Chuckie still did not regain true consciousness. He did manage to bleat nonsensical words, which Rebecca professed to be happy to hear. "'Tis his first utterance in many hours."

"Then I daresay your prayers must be working," he said.

"How did you know I've been praying?" Rebecca asked.

"I know you."

Once Chuckie lay peacefully on top of Rebecca's bedcoverings, Aynsley sent Beaver back to her bed. "We'll send for you if you're needed."

As the door shut behind Beaver, he met Rebecca's stormy gaze and was powerless not to open his arms to her. She rushed into his embrace, weeping. The two of them stood there in her dark bedchamber holding each other tightly. The wrenching sound of her cries was oddly comforting—not because he could ever take pleasure in her suffering but because her misery perfectly mirrored that which he felt but was incapable of demonstrating.

He had thought by holding his wife in his arms he could console her. Now he understood he needed her even more than she needed him.

"I'm so worried," she managed between sobs.

"He'll be fine." He wished he could believe his own words.

"Have you prayed?"

He nodded. "It's your prayers—not those from a sinner like me—which the Lord would see fit to answer."

"You might not have worshipped God as you should have, my love, but you're a good man, a man who lends his voice to those who have none."

In the midst of the worst gloom he could ever remember, his wife had interjected a ray of shining hope. "What did you just call me?"

"What does it matter?" She shrugged. "I don't care if I embarrass myself. I don't care about anything except Chuckie getting well." She peered up at him. "You see, I've fallen in love with you." She gave a little laugh. "Just when you took me into dislike."

He lifted her chin. "I wanted to dislike you, but it's difficult to dislike one with whom you're in love."

Her eyes widened. "How can you love me if you believe I'm a liar as well as a woman who'd betray you?"

"I don't believe you're a liar, nor do I think you'd betray me." He pressed his lips to her forehead. "Can you ever forgive me those wicked accusations?"

"Of course, my dearest. I brought it upon myself by not being honest with you about P. Corpus. I swear I will never lie to you as long as I live."

He savored the feel of her as his eyes filled with tears and his voice became choked. "I know."

The physician arrived an hour later. By then it was three in the morning. He examined Chuckie and repeated the same impotent instructions, then stood there wringing his hands in much the same way she and John had. Rebecca was beginning to think he did not know any more about getting Chuckie well than she did.

"Do not be alarmed over convulsions," he told them. "I will own, they're frightful to see, but they're actually quite common in children, and I assure you most of those children fully recover."

That, at least, was reassuring.

Mr. Mostyn took his leave and told them he would be back the following day.

Rebecca would do anything in her power to send her precious stepson back on the road to recovery, but she knew such power rested solely with the Almighty. Since the first night Chuckie had felt poorly, she had not stopped imploring God to heal the child who meant so much to her. Now that John, too, had mended his breach with the Lord, she had renewed hope that their dual appeal would be heard.

Despite the heaviness in her heart, she was comforted when John climbed onto her bed. Chuckie's limp body lay in the center, with her on his left and his father on his right. Her husband's presence helped to ease the ache that gnawed her insides.

Though he was still listless the following morning, Rebecca thought Chuckie's fever was much less intense. John kissed each of them on the forehead. "I need a shave. Would you like me to have tea sent up?"

"Yes, please."

A moment later Emily was in the chamber, swiftly moving to Rebecca's bed to check the patient. She closed her eyes tightly and sighed. "I have prayed so mightily, I had hoped for improvement."

Teary eyed, Rebecca faced Emily. "We've all been praying."

Emily's gaze swept around the curtained bed. "It's so dark and dreary, why do you not open these curtains to let in the morning light?"

"Chuckie fancies this comforting, being within the enclosing curtains—as long as someone is here with him!" She tried to sound bright.

"It's a credit to you that you're the person he most wants."

Those were the nicest words Emily had ever spoken to her. "Thank you. I am honored to have won his affection, but I assure you I return it a hundred fold."

"Yes, I can see that." Emily's voice had softened. "I owe you an apology. I've behaved abominably to you."

"You've done nothing which could destroy my affection for you."

"You don't know how I've wronged you."

Rebecca peered into her eyes, eyes that were so much like Chuckie's. "I think I do."

"What do you mean?" Emily's brows lifted.

"Did you perchance look over one of the letters your father wrote to me that I carelessly left in the library's desk?"

"You know!" Emily covered her face with her hands and began to cry. "I'm so ashamed," she managed between sobs. "I'm s-s-s-so sorry."

"I forgive you. *Judge not, and ye shall not be judged; condemn not, and ye shall not be condemned; forgive, and ye shall be forgiven.*"

"Why has my father not reprimanded me because of my wicked actions?"

"Your father doesn't know."

"Surely you told him?"

Rebecca shook her head. "I confess, at first I wanted

to—to exonerate myself—but I did not want to do anything which might diminish the happiness in our family." She moved to her stepdaughter and hugged her.

Which made Emily cry even harder as her arms encircled Rebecca.

"As important as your father's duties in the House of Lords are, the most important thing in his life is his family."

"I don't see how he could possibly still love me."

"You cannot destroy the kind of love a father holds for his daughter."

"I have still another confession."

Rebecca patted her back.

"I forbade Spencer and Alex to call you Mother."

Rebecca was tremendously relieved to learn she had done nothing to destroy Spencer's affection. "There's nothing wicked in that, love. It's perfectly understandable you'd not want your mother either forgotten or replaced. Now, let's not discuss this further. All is forgiven and forgotten. From this moment, we will start anew. I beg that you dry your tears."

"I don't know how you can think of us as family when I've been so horrid."

"I never thought to have a family of my own. I confess there were at least seven reasons I wanted to marry your father—other than my affection for him."

Emily swiped at her slick cheeks and eyed Rebecca skeptically. "You truly wanted a ready-made family?"

Rebecca nodded. Had it not been for the fact that Aynsley had seven motherless children, she would never have been able to gather the courage to make the bold proposal that resulted in their marriage—and brought her to these children who had come to mean so much to her.

Thank You, God, for answering my prayers, for filling my heart with love for Emily and for allowing us to move forward with the affection of a mother and daughter. "I will confess, my very dear Emily, that I'm often guided by the Bible. 'Bless them that curse you, do good to them that hate you, and pray for them which despitefully use you and persecute you.' If you recite things often enough, I have found that the Lord makes everything right."

Then Rebecca's somber gaze swept to Chuckie lying so eerily still, and her eyes filled with tears, her heart with unspeakable dread. "I pray the Lord continues to answer my prayers, to make everything right." She looked into Emily's misting blue eyes. Rebecca was powerless to prevent her tears from spilling onto her cheeks, powerless to keep her voice from cracking when she said, "All of our prayers."

Aynsley had quietly entered Rebecca's bedchamber and was shocked to find his wife and daughter embracing. "Now this is the best sight I've seen in a long while."

They spun around to face him. To his delight, both smiled.

He came to hug each of them. "You've made me very happy."

"You're not angry with me?" Emily asked.

"I was disappointed in you, but Rebecca would not allow me to speak to you."

Emily's gaze met her stepmother's. "You wanted my affections earned, not forced?"

"Exactly. And it was well worth the wait. I cannot tell you how good this makes me feel—in spite of..." She tossed her glance to the bed.

Chuckie was stirring.

They all rushed to the bedside in time to see his eyes open. His gaze fanned over those assembled by his bed, and a smile lifted the corners of his mouth. "Papa?"

"Yes, son?"

"Mother said you would give me a piggyback ride."

Aynsley's gaze flicked to Rebecca's happy face. "Do you feel like it, lad?"

Chuckie sat up. "Can we do it now?"

Thank You, God. "Indeed we can!"

Chapter Nineteen

On Sunday the whole family went to church. They had cautiously watched Chuckie for three more days before Rebecca would permit him to go out of doors. Every hour Aynsley prayed his thanks to the Lord that his son's fever had not returned.

Chuckie appeared to have recovered fully.

As Aynsley sat there in the Lord's house surrounded by his family, he experienced a profound feeling of well-being. His gaze moved from Spencer to Alex. They were behaving admirably. Then he cast a glance at Emily, who sat next to Peter. The day before, she had tearfully confessed to him that she was the one who had written to the *Morning Chronicle.* As disappointed as he was, he told her he was proud of the courage she demonstrated by owning up to her misdeeds. As she sat in his library weeping, he came to hug her and assure her that he loved her and always would.

Just before the service started, he eyed his wife. Chuckie had climbed upon her lap. His heart expanded as he watched them. He realized he owed God thanks, too, for bringing Rebecca into his life. At the age of three and forty years, he finally knew what it was to be in love. How fortunate he was to have her for his wife.

After the service, the family chose to walk home, owing to the warm spring day. "I believe I'd like to look at your farm," he told his wife.

He glanced at Emily, who was walking beside them between him and Peter. "Did you know what I gave Rebecca as a wedding gift?"

She shook her head.

"Abington's old farm."

"Whatever are you going to do with that, my lady?" Emily asked.

Peter cleared his throat. "She has engaged the services of a hardworking man who hopes to prove he's capable of managing aristocrats' properties."

Aynsley whipped toward his wife. "How could you afford a good man? And why would a man be willing to work on so small a piece of property?"

Rebecca shrugged. "I found a man who wants to prove himself worthy of marrying a much-cherished daughter."

Emily gasped, her hand flying to her mouth. "It's Peter! Is it not?"

"Indeed," Peter answered, smiling down at Emily. "I had wanted to surprise you and Uncle after I had succeeded in transforming the barren parcel."

"He's been educating himself about farming, and he's even doing all the labor because we haven't enough to pay workers," Rebecca said.

Powerful emotions surged through Aynsley. He was so incredibly proud of his nephew, so pleased that he loved Emily enough to prove it by slaving like a common laborer even though he was the grandson of an earl.

No man could ever be a better husband to his beloved daughter. "What's your crop going to be?"

There was deep satisfaction in Peter's voice when he responded. "Barley. It's already planted."

"You planted two hectares all by yourself?"

"I did. I worked from sunup to sundown."

"Then that's where you've been going!" Emily said, admiration in her voice.

"I believe we should wait and let you surprise us," Aynsley said.

"You all are invited to the autumn harvest."

"I cannot wait," Emily said. "Pray, allow me to see what you've already done."

Aynsley thought this might be a good time to allow Peter and Emily some privacy. "You two go on and take a look at the farm. My wife and I shall wait for the autumn harvest."

He watched them as they walked away. He wanted them to be as happy in each other as he was with Rebecca. "I've decided not to put Emily through a Season."

"I'm pleased that you've come to the right decision. You'll bless her marriage to Peter?"

"If he continues the industry he's now demonstrating, then yes."

"I have seen what he's been doing on my farm. I think you'll be enormously proud of him."

"I already am. Even if his crops were to fail, he's already earned my approval."

"I thought if he could demonstrate his capabilities you might one day allow him to manage one of your properties. That would also ensure that Emily has a roof over her head."

"Brilliant idea! Just another reason for marrying a

woman capable of cataloging large, private libraries," he said with a wink.

His three youngest sons ran ahead of them. "Do you think it all right for Chuckie to be exerting so much energy?" he asked.

"I learned when he was sick he can't do what his body won't allow him to do—no matter how strongly the mind feels otherwise."

He took his wife's hand. "I daresay you're right. I am most satisfied that I married so wise a woman. You probably know my marriage to Dorothy was never a love match."

She gasped. "You mean you weren't terribly in love with her?"

"Neither of us ever pretended to be in love. I was one and twenty when we met and eager to advance my career in the House of Commons. I could do so by marrying her. Her father was a powerful duke who was a great aid to my electioneering. He was grateful to me for taking her off the shelf."

"I cannot imagine why she was on the shelf. She looks rather pretty in her portrait, and she *was* a duke's daughter."

"Her personality was…abrasive."

They walked some little distance before she continued. "So you married her to advance your career in the House of Commons, then your father had the effrontery to die unexpectedly and send you to the House of Lords?"

He nodded. "Despite the absence of love in our marriage, I have no regrets."

"Of course not! Had you not married her, we wouldn't have these wonderful children."

Far ahead of them, his boys were still running. It was difficult to imagine how sick Chuckie had been just days earlier, his recovery was so remarkable.

"My darling?" Rebecca lifted her sweet face to his.

"Yes?"

"When did you discover I was P. Corpus?"

"Shortly after the day you asked me to marry you."

Her mouth gaped open in awe. "Pray, how could you? No one knew, except for me and Lady Agar."

"Anyone with a smattering of Latin could easily work out the name. Once I hit on that—admittedly because you'd just left—it occurred to me the sentiments expounded upon by P. Corpus could very well have been composed by a woman."

"I can't believe you've known my secret all this time but didn't tell me. That's almost as wicked as me keeping my P. Corpus identity from you."

"Neither of us was very honest."

"Since you're pledging to be truthful," she said, "I must know your true feelings about P. Corpus."

"I always admired and wanted to meet the man I thought was P. Corpus."

"You really did admire me?"

"Greatly. When I deduced that you were the essayist, it suddenly became clear to me that P. Corpus had to be a female because no man could write with such passion."

"You thought me passionate? I declare, no other man would ever find me so."

"I'm not thinking of carnal passion, my sweet. I'm thinking of the way you so passionately cared for our little son when he was sick. I think of your unwavering resistance to child laborers. I think of a woman so passionate about what she's doing, she'd catalog Lord Agar's entire library in a matter of weeks."

They both laughed. "I daresay you've grown weary of hearing about my proficiency at cataloging the largest private library in Great Britain. Did I say that passionately enough?"

Chuckling, he lifted her hand to his lips. "I will never grow tired of anything about you, my dearest, dearest love."

"I am trying to compose a passionate response." She drew in her breath and let out an exaggerated sigh of contentment. "Had I the selection of any man in the universe to unite myself with, you would be my resounding choice."

The boys had run so far ahead of them, he could only barely see them. He peered down at his wife. Neither of them spoke for a moment, resting in the peace and contentment of each others' presence.

"I suppose what I just said falls rather short of being passionate," she said, lifting her face. "I don't suppose I've ever come out and actually said *I love you* so I will tell you I not only love you more than I ever thought it possible to love, but I love everything about you.

"I love the way you look when you smile—which you do uncommonly often. I love to listen to you speak of reform. I love the way our laughing eyes meet over shared amusements. I love your strength of character and the leadership you provide to all those around you. I love that you're exceedingly intelligent without being arrogant. Most of all, I especially love those children, each of whom has a little part of you in them."

Her eloquence nearly moved him to tears. "I wish

every man in the kingdom could be as happy as I am now."

She squeezed his hand. "Yes, I feel the same. Just months ago I had nothing, and now I have everything."

It was the very same with him.

They reached Dunton Hall where his boys were playing witches on the grass. With Rebecca's hand in his, he stood there for a moment, thanking God for all his blessings and vowing to work toward making happiness available to everyone in England.

Epilogue

Six months later

"I am perfectly capable of walking to my farm," an exasperated Rebecca said to her husband. John was entirely too protective of her—and the babe in her womb.

"Indulge your devoted husband." He tenderly lifted her into the open barouche, where the three youngest lads had squeezed into the opposite seat. Emily and Fordyce, who was now home from Oxford, had gone ahead on their horses.

This was an exciting occasion in the Compton family. Peter was harvesting his first crop.

John came to sit beside her, taking her hand in his as their driver flicked the ribbons. "By the way, love," he said, "I have an announcement I think will please you."

She cocked a single brow as she met his eyes.

"I have established a school in Wales for the lads who previously worked in my mines."

"Previously?"

He nodded. "I have started a sewing cooperative for the widowed mothers so they won't have to send their lads to work the mines. There's a man in London who'll sell their products."

She threw her arms around his neck. "Oh, my darling! I am so very proud of you."

"Ever since Chuckie was sick, I've been more acutely aware of how precious one's children are. You've been right all along to chastise me for employing young boys in so dangerous an occupation."

Her glance whisked to the three youngest lads. Each of them was very precious to her, and now she'd learned to love Fordyce and Mark, too. She prayed every day for Geoffrey's safe return. "Does that mean we'll work toward reform of child labor in Parliament?"

Her husband nodded, a twinkle in his eyes. "Indeed *we* shall."

Their marriage was a true partnership. Her life was so full she had not written a single essay since the day she'd wed, but she had helped John draft speeches that were heartily approved when he delivered them in the House of Lords.

When they reached her farm, John was shocked over the transformation. Neat rows of flourishing barley filled every inch of the farm. Peter had borrowed John's thrasher, and an assemblage of field hands had gathered to help harvest the crop. "I cannot believe it. It was never so productive even when old Mr. Abington was alive."

His gaze flicked to Emily. Love shone in her eyes as she watched Peter directing the workers.

Dunton Hall servants were busy setting tables for a picnic where they could all gather for a midday meal. When they finished, the family members and workers assembled around the long table and bowed their heads while John led them in prayer. "We give our thanks to the Lord for all the blessings He's bestowed upon us, most especially for our family. May our Heavenly Father continue to bless this family, especially Geoff in war and Mark at school, and restore them safely to us." He looked up at Peter. "Soon Peter and my much-loved daughter will be uniting in marriage, and it's my hope they will be as happy as Rebecca and I."

Her husband looked at her, and his lazy, affectionate perusal still had the power to start a joyous fluttering in her heart. She clutched his hand and silently prayed her own thanks for her abundant blessings.

How strange it seemed that just one year earlier she'd had nothing. No home of her own. No family to call her own. And she'd thought she would never find a husband who would not only own her heart but would also come to truly be her other half.

So many times since the day she'd married John she had asked her Savior to help her honor those wedding vows she'd spoken that day at St. George's, vows which then had made her feel a fraud. During the darkest days of her marriage, she'd almost lost faith that her Savior would once more come to her aid.

Now, as she looked at John with an expanding heart, she gloried in the depth of her love for him, gloried in the knowledge that he loved her as mightily in return.

And she knew her Savior had always been present in this most satisfying of marriages. No woman in the kingdom could be as happy as she.

"I have one more announcement to make," John said. "Mr. Stanley will be retiring but not before he trains his successor as steward of Dunton. Peter and Emily will not have to leave Dunton after they marry."

A grateful Emily flew into her father's arms, expressing her gratitude, and Peter stood just behind her, his hand at her waist and a smile on his face. His gaze darted to Rebecca. "Thank you for having more faith in me than I had in myself. I owe you my happiness."

She shook her head. "It was your own hard work that has brought your success. We're all very proud of you."

"Indeed we are," John said, clapping a hand on his nephew's back. "You will make Em a fine husband."

Emily came to hug Rebecca. "I am so happy you married Papa."

Rebecca eyed her husband. "As am I. The most fortunate day of my life was the day I selected him to be my husband."

Emily looked puzzled, but John and Rebecca merely laughed and kissed one another.

* * * * *

Dear Reader,

Though I have been writing and publishing romance novels set in Regency England since 1998, this is my first one for Love Inspired Historical, and I feel I've found my home with these wholesome stories.

At the close of England's Regency period, perhaps the greatest changes ever in British government occurred. In 1832 the great Reform Bill was passed. More changes, like those limiting child labor and establishing compulsory education, came later in the century. Essentially it was a century that started with all the wealth and power resting with a few powerful families, and much of the population was illiterate and extremely poor. By the end of the century everyone possessed the right to be educated and the opportunity to improve their lot in life.

It was important to me that my hero and heroine, Rebecca and Aynsley, were working toward the reforms that were taking shape in British society. I hope I have succeeded in imbuing them with nobility of character.

For years I've been writing articles about Regency England. These can be found at my website, www.CherylBolen.com or at my blog, www.CherylsRegencyRamblings.wordpress.com. Readers can contact me through my website, too.

Blessings,
Cheryl Bolen

Questions for Discussion

1. At the beginning of the book, Rebecca risks humiliation in order to bring about the desired change in her life. What changes in your life would be important enough to risk being humiliated?

2. Though Aynsley had once preferred Rebecca's beautiful sister, he comes to judge Rebecca not on her appearance but on her ideas. How do their shared ideas bring them closer together?

3. What does Aynsley want from his marriage to Rebecca that he lacked in his first marriage?

4. How does Aynsley justify his employment of children in his mines? Does he want to help pass legislation to restrict child labor?

5. Why does Rebecca not disclose her alter ego to Aynsley? How does she justify it?

6. After her marriage, why is Rebecca unable to write her essays?

7. Rebecca insists she cannot tell a lie, but in one instance she does. When does this occur? Do you think it's permissible to compliment an undeserving person in order to avoid ill feelings?

8. Why does Emily resent her stepmother? Do these feelings make her loathsome? Can you put yourself

in her shoes and imagine what it would be like to welcome a stepmother?

9. Why would a wealthy aristocrat like Aynsley want to reduce his own power by extending the franchise so the masses would be able to vote?

10. What brings about feelings of jealousy in Rebecca? Does she act on these feelings? How does this make her feel?

11. No matter how hostile Emily is to her, Rebecca insists she loves her stepdaughter. Could you "turn the other cheek" in such a manner? Should Rebecca have returned Emily's hostility?

12. Why does Rebecca not tell Aynsley it was his daughter—not Rebecca—who betrayed him? Do you think she should have revealed the information to him? Would you have been able to conceal such a fact?

13. How did Aynsley react to Rebecca's plan to allow his uncle to participate in family dinners? Do you think Aynsley's first wife was right to exclude the uncle?

14. In what ways do you think Aynsley was a good Christian during the time he turned his back on God?

15. Do you agree with Rebecca's assessment that the Lord sent her to Aynsley and his family? Why?

16. The things that were most important to Rebecca at the beginning of the book are not what are most important at the end. What does she discover is most important?

COMING NEXT MONTH
from Love Inspired® Historical
AVAILABLE OCTOBER 30, 2012

THEIR FRONTIER FAMILY
Wilderness Brides
Lyn Cote

No one is more surprised than Sunny Licht when Noah Whitmore proposes to the unwed mother. But the chance of a fresh start makes her hope it's not too late to find happiness—and love—at last.

THE RAKE'S REDEMPTION
The Everard Legacy
Regina Scott

Recruiting Imogene Devary's assistance was just part of Vaughn Everard's quest to find his uncle's killer. Yet even as Imogene's determination to help him softens Vaughn's heart, will the truth they uncover tear them apart?

LEGACY OF LOVE
Christine Johnson

Despite her reasons for hating him, Anna Simmons needs work too badly to refuse Brandon Landers's job offer. Besides, there's rumor of hidden treasure on his land. Still, maybe the only treasure they both need is a lifetime together....

SOMEWHERE TO CALL HOME
Janet Lee Barton

Violet Burton desperately needs to pay off the mortgage on her Virginia home. Job hunting in New York leads her to childhood friend Michael Heaton...and the chance of a new, loving home for them to share.

Ellie St. James is a bodyguard on a mission to protect her newest client from dangerous threats...without letting her client's handsome grandson distract her.

Read on for a sneak peek of the exciting new Love Inspired® Suspense title,

CHRISTMAS STALKING

by Margaret Daley

Lights off, Ellie St. James scanned the mountainous terrain out her bedroom window at her new client's home in Colorado, checking the shadows for any sign of trouble. The large two-story house of redwood and glass blended in well with the rugged landscape seven thousand feet above sea level. Any other time she would appreciate the beauty, but she was here to protect Mrs. Rachel Winfield.

A faint sound punched through her musing. She whirled away from the window and snatched up her gun on the bedside table a few feet from her. Fitting the weapon into her right palm, she crept toward her door and eased it open to listen. None of the guard dogs were barking. Maybe she'd imagined the noise.

A creak, like a floorboard being stepped on, drifted up the stairs. Someone was ascending to the second floor. She and her employer were the only ones in the main house. She glanced at Mrs. Winfield's door, two down from hers, and noticed it was closed. Her client kept it that way only when she was in her bedroom.

She slipped out of her room and into the shadows in the long hallway that led to the staircase. Another sound echoed through the hall. Whoever was on the steps was at the top. She increased her speed, probing every dark recess around her for any other persons. She found the light switch, planted her bare feet a foot apart, preparing herself to confront the intruder, and flipped on the hall light.

Even though she expected the bright illumination, it took her a few seconds to adjust to it while the large man before her lifted his hand to shield the glare from his eyes. Which gave Ellie the advantage.

"Don't move," she said in her toughest voice.

The stranger dropped his hand to his side, his gray-blue eyes drilling into her, then fixing on her Wilson Combat aimed at his chest. Anger washed all surprise from his expression. "Who are you?" The question came out in a deep booming voice, all the fury in his features reflected in it.